I0645045

I was late for my appointment with my therapist. Not a good thing.

I hurried along to Dr. Ditstein's apartment. I knocked on her door, not timidly, since timid would indicate that I was reverting to a childish state and expecting punishment from a parent-figure. Nothing happened. I knocked again and bit a cuticle. Maybe she was trying to punish me. Okay, mea culpa and all that jazz, let's go, Charmaine. I called her by her first name in my mind but not to her face, unlike Ron in the group. The clock was ticking and an incarnation of my mother was snoring away on my couch.

Still nothing. This was getting silly and I was getting annoyed. I banged harder on the door and it swung open.

Definitely weird. My hand flew to my mouth. What if she'd been mugged? What if the mugger was still there? I rocked back and forth on the threshold.

Indecision, thy name is Marabella.

The apartment was silent. Taking a deep breath, I walked into the foyer and stopped when I reached the living room.

Dr. Ditstein lay face down, sprawled on the wall-to-wall, blue-and-gold Oriental. A pool of blood had spread from the back of her head.

When Marabella Vinegar finds her psychotherapist's bloody corpse, she becomes the NYPD's perp of choice. Her recently deceased mother—the bane of her existence in life—comes back as a ghost to help get her out of trouble and find the real killer. Things get even worse when, thanks to Marabella and her mother's sleuthing, someone tries to kill her. Then another body is found and Marabella is thrown in jail, awaiting trial for two murders. Can she and her mother-the-ghost-detective find the killer before Marabella becomes corpse number three?

KUDOS for *Dead Shrinks Don't Talk*

In *Dead Shrinks Don't Talk* by Sandra Gardner, Marabella Vinegar is shocked and dismayed when her mother, who has been dead for a week, shows up on Marabella's couch as a ghost, hinting that Marabella is in trouble. Marabella doesn't think she is in any trouble, and she hurries off to see her shrink, as she is late for her appointment. But when she gets there, she discovers that the shrink has been murdered, and the trouble her mother warned her of is her being the prime suspect. Since the police are convinced they have the murderer, Marabella and her mother start investigating, trying to find the real killer. But when they get too close to the truth, Marabella discovers that she is about to become a corpse herself. Well written, clever, and fun, the story combines mystery, suspense, and humor for a highly entertaining read. I thoroughly enjoyed it. ~ *Taylor Jones, The Review Team of Taylor Jones & Regan Murphy*

Dead Shrinks Don't Talk by Sandra Gardner is the story of a young woman with serious problems. Marabella Vinegar has been seeing a shrink for eight years, struggling to work out her issues with her mother. When her mother dies, Marabella is both devastated and relieved. And feeling guilty, of course. Then suddenly, a week later, her mother is back as a ghost, claiming that she has come back to help Marabella in her time of trouble. Marabella doesn't know what trouble her mother could be talking about, and she isn't sure how to deal with her mother's presence. So she heads off to her appointment with her psychiatrist, Dr. Ditstein, dying to hear her take on this latest issue with her mother. But to her dismay, Dr. Ditstein has been murdered, the police suspect Marabella, and the real killer wants her dead to keep her finding out the truth. Marabella's in trouble, all right, but how is a ghost going to help her out of this mess? *Dead Shrinks Don't Talk* is cute, clever, fast paced, and intriguing. With marvelous characters, a solid plot, and plenty of surprises, it is one you will want to keep on your shelf to read again and again, just for the sheer enjoyment. ~ *Regan Murphy, The Review Team of Taylor Jones & Regan Murphy*

ACKNOWLEDGMENTS

I would like to thank my good friends and critiquers: Susan P. Baker, Judith Lechner, and Robin Kramer. And thank you to my New England Crime Bake critiquers: Hank Phillippi Ryan, Kate Flora, and Paula Munier for their valuable suggestions. I would also like to thank Sunny Frazier for suggesting that I send the manuscript to Black Opal Books.

Most of all, I'm grateful to my husband, Lewis Gardner, for his patience and excellent editing advice.

Dead Shrinks Don't Talk

A Mother and Me Mystery

Sandra Gardner

A Black Opal Books Publication

Dead Shrinks Don't Talk

Chapter 1

My mother had only been dead a week when she appeared on my sofa. She shoved me off onto the floor, as a matter of fact. I had just settled down for a quick nap between my crazy-making job and a late-evening rendezvous with my shrink.

"A lady doesn't sit on the floor, Marabella," my mother scolded.

She pursed lips that still had traces of her favorite Revlon shade, Rose-of-Sharon, and peered at me from under her shaggy mud-brown hair. Her hair really needed cutting—shaping too, come to think of it.

"What are you doing here?" I tried to muster as much dignity as someone in my position could manage, plopped on the floor as I was. And being berated by a…my mother, who was dead! Wasn't she? "Aren't you…" My tongue tripped on the words, "Didn't you…"

Of all the crazy stunts my mother had ever pulled, this one took the cake. But I shouldn't be all that surprised, since she'd always been capable of just about anything. So why not this?

"Yes, and no." She leaned back against the sofa pillows, smoothing down the bottom of her dress, the white satin-and-lace number she'd been buried in. "You think it's that easy? Has anything in my life…"

Oh, no, I thought, *I have to keep listening to this stuff even after she's dead?*

She clapped a hand over her mouth. "No, nope, I'm not going to do it, I promised." She glared at the ceiling. "And I couldn't help it about the sofa, either. I haven't sat down in a week."

I got up off the floor, dusting off my behind. "Why are you here?"

"Why am I here? Very shortly, you're going to need me, sweetheart," she said, with a self-satisfied smile.

This was more than I could take, her thinking that I should need her help from beyond the grave. "They sent you back here? Like, on an assignment?" Like I still needed a mother's watchful eye, at the age of (gulp) thirty-nine? Granted, I occasionally had a little difficulty making decisions—okay, a lot of difficulty. And I knew I was too dependent on my therapist, Dr. Ditstein. We'd spent many cathartic hours together, much of it dealing with my relationship with my mother. And now here she was, again.

"I put in a special request," my mother said. "Because where else should a mother be when her daughter's going to be in trouble?"

"What kind of trouble?"

"You'll see," she said.

Okay, whatever it was, she wasn't going to tell me. See if I cared. I took a new tack. "How did you get here? Did you fly or what? Considering that you've always hated airplanes—were even afraid of high buildings—how the heck did you learn to fly at the age of seventy?"

"It's just something that comes naturally, sweetheart," she said. "You don't even have to think about it."

She yawned. "I'm a little tired out right now."

"Tired? You sleep? You need sleep?" I was beginning to feel dizzy.

She gave me a baleful look. "You'd be tired, too, if you'd traveled as far as I did. Remember, I volunteered for this job. For you." And she closed her eyes and stretched out full-length on the sofa.

I studied her. Something was different. She was thinner. No, not exactly thinner. There seemed to be less of her. And she was so pale.

Okay, maybe being under the ground, in the casket? I shivered, not exactly wanting to relive that scene.

The funeral had been pretty traumatic, because my mother's family's behavior at anyone's funeral was to screech, sob, and tear at their bosoms, and since bosoms in my family generally came in the large-economy size, that made for quite a bit of tearing.

Biting my cuticles—a habit I'd been trying to break ever since I had cuticles—I stared at her. What was I going to do now? Thank goodness, I had an appointment with Dr. Ditstein tonight.

I had to think. I tiptoed to my bedroom, so as not to wake her up, popped a Xanax, and crawled into my four-poster bed. It barely fit in the room, but it was heavenly to sleep in.

I pulled one of the lumpy afghans my mother had made over my head. She'd crocheted these for me so I'd have lovely hand-made keepsakes to remember her by, she told me.

The question was: Why had I kept them? According to Dr. Ditstein, it was because of my ambivalent relationship with my mother. Which, in turn, seemed to be part of the reason why I had trouble making decisions and moving on with my life?

Maybe I've finally gone over the edge, I thought,

which my best friend Toniann Di Lorenzo warns me will be my fate if I keep working at Chelsea College. Maybe I'm dreaming this—I mean, I've been working really hard—so, okay, let's say I kind of went into some kind of dream-state and conjured my mother up.

But why would I do that to myself? That much of a masochist I didn't think I was, especially now that I'd just completed my eighth year of therapy, including two years in group.

I had to hurry to get to my appointment. But before I left, I was going to find out whether or not I had hallucinated my mother.

Jumping off the bed, I went into the bathroom and splashed cold water on my face, ran a comb through my tangled hair, and shoved my bangs out of my eyes.

Now I was ready to confront my resident…whatever.

I marched back into the living room. There she was. Sound asleep. Snoring loudly. *They actually snore?* She was obviously in a state of complete exhaustion.

Didn't I realize the poor thing needed her rest, especially after what she'd just gone through? She also needed some new clothes, which I'd have to lend her, since that dress wasn't exactly meant for lounging around in. I went to the closet to retrieve another afghan.

I crept over to the sofa and covered her. A delicious smile appeared on her face—sort of beatific, come to think of it—and she snuggled down into the afghan, mumbling, "There's a good girl."

I beamed. Then I gasped. What was I doing? What was *she* doing?

I grabbed my denim jacket and oversized leather pocketbook and headed out the door.

I hoped Dr. Ditstein might have some answers. But this could be too much for even her magical talents.

Since Dr. Ditstein's place was on the East Side of

Manhattan and mine was on the West Side, I was afraid I might be late. I figured a cab would be faster than the subway. I was wrong. By the time we pulled up to Dr. Ditstein's, I was definitely late.

There were at least forty-five apartments-cum-offices in her building. It was overrun with shrinks for all disorders: sex, animals, eating, phobic, as well as those like Dr. Ditstein, who serviced run-of-the-mill neurotics. So you could usually find representatives of any type of weirdness roaming the corridors. But the building was quiet. Everyone was already fifteen minutes into their fifty-minute hours. I caught the next up elevator and pushed the button for the sixth floor.

When I got out, I heard a click from the apartment across from the elevator bay and felt eyes peering at me through the oversized peephole. *Dr. Shokum, I presume?* I had to stifle the urge to press myself up against his door and go eyeball-to-eyeball with him through the peephole. Somebody told me that Dr. Shokum was so terrified of people, he only did telephone therapy. All I ever saw was his eye. I wondered if his patients would stop going to him if they knew about his phobia. Probably not. I also heard that he gave great phone.

Other than Dr. Shokum's breathing, not a creature was stirring. I hurried along to Dr. Ditstein's apartment, knocked on her door, not timidly, since timid would indicate that I was reverting to a childish state and expecting punishment from a parent-figure. Nothing happened. I knocked again and bit a cuticle. Maybe she was trying to punish me. *Okay, mea culpa and all that jazz, let's go, Charmaine.* I called her by her first name in my mind but not to her face, unlike Ron in group. The clock was ticking, and an incarnation of my mother was snoring away on my couch.

Still nothing. This was getting silly, and I was getting

annoyed. I banged harder on the door, and it swung open.

Definitely weird. My hand flew to my mouth. What if she'd been mugged? What if the mugger was still there? I rocked back and forth on the threshold.

Indecision, thy name is Marabella.

The apartment was silent. Taking a deep breath, I walked into the foyer and stopped when I reached the living room.

Dr. Ditstein lay face down, sprawled on the wall-to-wall blue-and-gold Oriental. A pool of blood had spread from the back of her head.

Oh, my God, oh, my God! My breath was coming in gasps, and I was shaking all over. Was she shot? Stabbed? Did she fall and hit her head?

What was I going to do without Dr. Ditstein? Why did this have to happen? What kind of person would do this? Oh, God, oh, God. Maybe the person was still there. Maybe if I pretended to faint, they wouldn't think I saw anything. I made myself fall on the floor in a heap. And landed next to the body. Aarrggh.

I jumped up. This wasn't going to fool anybody, especially a killer. *A killer.* Just saying the word in my head made me shudder. Poor Dr. Ditstein. Poor me, with no Dr. Ditstein.

Should I call an ambulance? No, I better call the cops. I picked up my Droid, but my hands were shaking so hard, I dropped it on the floor. *Breathe, Marabella. In and out. The way Dr. Ditstein taught us. Breathe. Okay, now try again.* This time, I was able to make the call.

"I don't know what to do. I think there's a—dead—woman on the floor of her apartment," I stuttered, and gave them the address.

Then I bent down and made myself lift her wrist and take her pulse, just in case, even though I knew she was probably dead. Her wrist was still warm. It occurred to me that meant the murderer must have just left. And I may have just missed being his second victim. A tiny key fell out of her hand. I picked it up without thinking and shoved it into my jacket pocket.

I probably wouldn't have noticed if there was anything out of place, since I was not exactly the noticing type. I was more like the type who walked into walls. And the only thing I could focus on was all that blood, so much blood.

I didn't want to believe she was dead, my poor harmless holistic shrink, who didn't have an enemy in the world! Correction: she seemed to have had at least one. Who'd just killed the most important person in my life.

Chapter 2

I didn't want to leave poor Dr. Ditstein alone, so I sat down in the nearest chair and waited for the cops. And tried not to look at the second dead person in my life in a week.

The guilt wheels began whirring in my brain. If I hadn't been late for my appointment, my shrink might not be dead.

Or we could both be dead.

I heard footsteps, and the door flew open. Several beefy, blue-coated men stood in the entrance. Another one, tall and lean, with a sour expression, was wearing a beat-up blue jacket and brown pants.

"Detective Eddie Rivera," the wardrobe-challenged cop said, walking over to me. "Who are you? What are you doing in this apartment?"

I pulled out my driver's license with the candid shot of a Bedlam-inmate that the DMV had substituted for the real me.

He squinted at the picture and handed it back with a yawn. "I asked you what you were doing in the apartment."

I told him about being late for my appointment with Dr. Ditstein. And what I found when I got there. "Since I was the one who called you, you know I didn't do anything. Can I leave now, please?" I said.

Ignoring my request, he asked, "Did you see anything? Hear anything?" When I shook my head, he said, "How about outside, on your way in, on the elevator, on the stairs?"

"No, nothing."

"Did you touch anything in the apartment?"

"Um, I touched her wrist. When I took her pulse. She didn't have one. A pulse, I mean," I babbled. I decided not to tell him about the key. "And, um, I touched my phone when I called the police station. Of course."

He looked at me strangely, maybe because I was acting like a gibbering idiot. "Okay, is that it? That's all?" he asked. When I nodded, he said, "One of my men will take you home. But since you're a witness, I'll need to talk to you again soon." He asked for my address and phone number and ushered me out of the apartment. One of the blue-coated gentlemen escorted me into the elevator, down to the lobby, and outside into a police car.

On the way home, I began to shake in earnest. What was I going to do without Dr. Ditstein? Who could I depend on? Who could help me make decisions, now that my go-to person was dead?

Chapter 3

I dragged myself into the lobby of my building and into the elevator. When I got out, my neighbor Sam was there, bringing his trash to the trash room.

Sam shook his head. "You look terrible. Oh," he said, looking apologetic, "how could I be so thoughtless? You're upset about your mother, of course."

I leaned against the wall. "Sam, I couldn't begin to tell you. It would take all night."

"So? I'm an old man, what else have I got but time? Come in, I'll make you some tea."

I couldn't help smiling. "Sam, you're a sweetheart, but I'm pooped. I'll tell you about it as soon as I can. And by the way, I've got some audio books for you."

"I'm more worried about you than the books." He ran his hand through his thinning white hair. "But knock anytime, I'm always up." He waved goodbye and opened his apartment door.

Sam was in his late-seventies. A self-educated man who loved books, he got really depressed when he began losing his sight. So I picked up audio books for him whenever I could get to the library. He'd been a traveling salesman who'd never married because his lifestyle wouldn't have been fair to a wife, he said. But he hadn't lacked for female companionship. I'd even introduced him to my mother before she became really ill, and they'd enjoyed each other's company. In fact, I secretly got downright jealous. Dr. Ditstein's take on it was that Sam was a father-substitute for me.

My father died of a stroke when I was twelve. He was a quiet man who'd worked his behind off in his pharmacy, six days a week. When he was home, he was so dog-tired he frequently fell asleep in the TV chair right after dinner, to the tune of my mother's comment, "God forbid, but he looks like a corpse."

I grew up thinking that all men must be like my father: the man who wasn't there. According to Dr. Ditstein, this was the key to my lousy relationships with men. I couldn't bring myself to trust them. So I'd pick the wrong ones. With the good ones, things would start off okay, but then I'd do something to screw things up before they could reject me.

When I got inside my apartment, my mother was still asleep. I foraged for an extra robe and a couple of nighties plus underwear for my mother and laid them out on the chair next to the sofa. I knew she'd complain mightily about the fit.

I really loved—had really loved—my mother. I'd also heartily hated her. After all, how could you not love—and hate—a smart, funny woman who thought you were the most wonderful being on earth as long as you did what she told you to do? And I wouldn't exactly say I missed her, not that I didn't think about her a lot. She'd been a smother-loving parent, who loudly sacrificed her life for me. Breaking away would have taken independence, a quality that didn't stand a fighting chance around my mother.

I fell into bed without even attacking my new cross-word puzzle book, one of my all-purpose remedies for unwinding. Another one was my aerobics class, which I only managed to get to on a highly irregular basis—depending on how hungry I was, since I couldn't eat between work and class.

The major one—more of a lifesaver, actually—was my bedtime dose of Xanax. It helped me focus and made me believe I could cope with whatever craziness came my way—one more thing I was dependent on, besides my therapist. While I was brushing my teeth, I thought about my mother and Dr. Ditstein and took a double dose.

During the night, I felt a light touch on my cheek and the covers being pulled up around me. If this was what having my mother back again meant, maybe it wasn't so terrible.

But I didn't sleep well. A blood-drenched Dr. Ditstein was chasing me in my dreams. Though she didn't seem to want to harm me. She seemed to be trying to tell me something.

I woke up to the smell of something familiar and burning. I staggered out of bed into the kitchen. My mother was wearing my bathrobe barely tied.

"This robe doesn't exactly fit in the bust, but who's looking? Humph. Your bust, it's respectable, but it can't stack up to mine," she muttered.

She was overcooking French toast at the stove. A smoke haze curled around her. She gave me a concerned look. "Breakfast in a jiffy."

I sank into a chair at the table and choked. "There's an exhaust fan," I said.

"A little griddle smoke is nothing. I read in a column it has vitamins or minerals in it. And that exhaust fans only blow the air around."

I could have used a little of that blown air right now.

Considering last night's events, I didn't have much appetite. And her terrible cooking wouldn't help.

She looked down at the bathrobe, overflowing with its unaccustomed contents. "Maybe I could open up the seams," she said, sliding a plate of charred lumps in front of me. "Your favorite. And boy, do you need to keep up your strength with what you're going through."

I shot her a glance, but she was back at the mess on the stove again. Did they have ESP?

"It's not exactly ESP, sweetheart. But up there—" She pointed to the ceiling. "—we acquire special abilities, you might say."

"Besides the transportation issue?"

She chuckled. "In some cases, we can tell what's going to happen and who it's going to happen to. And also, I might add, read somebody's mind."

Aarggh. That had been a real problem when I was growing up, especially when I started going out with boys. And now she'd fine-tuned it?

She nodded. "But it doesn't always work right. Sometimes the system gets jammed. Or goes down. Or gets screwed up from whatever gadgets they use nowadays."

I was speechless for a moment.

"And there's more—"

I closed my eyes.

"—there's the appearing. And the disappearing. Or dematerializing, I guess it's called. That's sort of an automatic safety device. Because, otherwise, it could get a little confusing. The same with who can see and hear you."

Were we really having this conversation? About what people could and couldn't do after they—

I shook my head. This was crazy talk. Somebody must have told her about what happened. "Ma, you weren't on the phone yesterday, were you? I mean, no-body called, did they?"

I poured a ton of maple syrup over the stuff on my plastic plate. Since I tended to drop china like anorexics dropped weight, I'd finally given up and bought plastic.

She looked insulted and drew herself up to her full height. "And who would I want to talk to on the phone? My no-good relatives or so-called friends, for examp—"

"Don't start," I said.

Everyone and everything offended her. If the weather turned bad, she took it as a personal affront.

She looked at the ceiling with a worried expression. "All right, all right," she whispered. Then she said, "But I have to know, darling, why wasn't Cousin Sylvia at the funeral? A first cousin, she couldn't be there, she had someplace else better to be, like her hairdresser?"

I thought her question about attendance at her funeral to be in poor taste. "Sylvia broke her leg getting off her exercise bike," I explained.

My mother chortled. "Serves her right, the klutz. And Marty was late, so he comes just in time for the food at the *shiva*, as per usual." She shrugged. "Well, he's just a brother-in-law, so it doesn't really matter."

Marty was my Aunt Evelyn's husband, skinny as a ferret, who ate his way through any affair.

"But Evelyn—" Her eyes narrowed. "How could she wear that horrible purple thing? I happen to know that she owns a little black suit, a Chanel knock-off, she bought on sale. *This* she saves for important occasions? Not like her sister's funeral, of course."

My aunt Evelyn probably figured, why waste the Chanel knock-off on a dead person? Evelyn would have had no idea that her purple dress would come back to haunt her, so to speak.

"Eat your breakfast, it's getting cold. And we've got a murder to solve," she said.

"How did you—" I started to say, but she waved my question away. "Ma, I don't have time, and I never eat breakfast," I said, as gently as possible, given her condition.

She not only looked hurt but also seemed to be a bit paler today than last night.

"A cup of coffee will be great." I gulped it down with a handful of vitamins and patted her shoulder. "Take it easy, Ma, I've got to get ready for work now. We'll talk when I get home."

She pointed at me, wielding the pancake turner like a sword. "Take it easy?" Slicing the air with it, she added, "And are you still working at that terrible place? Where they treat you like an indentured servant?"

"Ma, you've only been gone a week." Horrified at what I said, I mumbled, "We'll talk later, okay? And don't...go out. Or answer the phone or the door, okay? I'll be in the shower."

After toweling off, I rooted in my closet for something clean and unwrinkled. I finally found a dark green blazer to go with a black watch plaid pleated skirt and a Kelly green blouse. I pulled on my sneakers and tossed my pumps in my tote bag.

Leaving the apartment, I prayed nobody would call the fire department until I got out of the building. If they did, I thought, what would they think about my mother, the apparition? As the elevator made its way down to the lobby, I realized they would probably just worry that I might be, God forbid, subletting or sharing my Upper West Side rent-stabilized digs. Never mind with whom— or what.

Chapter 4

I walked out into the street. Lucy was at her usual corner. "Hey, how's it going?" I asked.

She looked bone-tired and was coughing. But she gave me her usual toothless grin. "I bet it's going to be a good day, hon, just you wait and see. He told me so this morning," she said, pointing to the sky.

She spat into a handkerchief that looked spanking clean, like the rest of her raggedy attire. Lucy had to be the cleanest homeless person in New York.

I dropped a dollar into the Yankees cap she had at her feet. I hoped the nasty kids across the street wouldn't grab the cap again and toss it in the gutter. "Hey, take care of that cough, will you? You should get somebody over at the clinic to look at you."

She waved away my concern. "The Lord will bless you for helping old Lucy, wait and see."

I knew she wouldn't go to the free clinic unless she was at death's door. And maybe not even then. She figured the Lord would protect her.

I decided to walk the twelve blocks to the Chelsea College campus. Maybe navigating the crowded sidewalks and avoiding the maniac drivers would keep me from brooding on the scene at Dr. Ditstein's. I also thought it would make up for my no-show at aerobics lately.

My virtue was rewarded by witnessing a woman dressed to the nines, looking nonchalant while her dog crapped all over the sidewalk. She, and it, left a huge steaming pile. What class.

When I got to my building, the usual group of protesters was stationed in front of the door. They looked about the same as the ones I'd seen every one of the nineteen years I'd been in the public relations department. Wearing tee-shirts with slogans, they carried placards and were very earnest. At least they cared enough to protest. I smiled at them, wished them a nice day, and went inside.

Donna Tomiello, my boss, and Twinkie, her vicious little dog, weren't in evidence. A note taped to Donna's door said: *Emergency meeting with Board of Trustees. Lionel in the hospital getting ear spliced together after his iguana tried to bite it off. Maybe he should feed it more often, ha, ha. Interview with Dr. Adriance, the vet, scheduled for 9:30 in the cafeteria. Get Lionel's notes.*

Lionel Yung was a cute child science prodigy who'd graduated high school at fifteen. He was sent to Chelsea College because the trustees had pumped a lot of money into hiring top-notch science faculty. And his mother thought that starting at a community college would be better for him socially, since he was so young. The course-work wasn't enough to keep Lionel occupied. So he was getting work experience in our office writing science news and articles.

I occasionally reproached him for not being more interested in his Asian heritage. When I'd asked him where his family was from, he said, "The Bronx. I'm American, same as you."

His grandparents had emigrated from China, and by the time he was born, the family had been thoroughly Americanized. He got his name because his mother, Mei Lee Yung, thought it sounded American.

I spent many hours advising him about acne and girl problems. In return, I got to avoid all the science news from CC that was fit to print. I was a grade-A science-and-technophobe.

However, I was an excellent writer and editor and could spot a typo at twenty paces. This came in handy in my job as editor of the in-house newsletter. I also did the humanities and social science public relations writing. That meant a lot of ink promoting our English, soc, and psych courses. Not to mention boasting about our community involvement in substance abuse education and early childhood programs.

I was starting to hyperventilate and popped a Xanax. Lionel had scheduled some new muckity-muck scientist for a welcome-aboard interview today. This stress-maker I did not need. A ghost and a corpse and the cops were quite enough, thank you.

Standing in front of Lionel's desk, I tried to think for a moment, something I didn't do too clearly in the morning. Unfortunately, my immediate thoughts were of the dream I had last night. What was Dr. Ditstein trying to tell me? She was pointing to something in her hand. A book...or maybe a ledger. Then my mind went to the murder scene, and I shuddered. *Stop it*, I told myself.

I took a deep breath and got back to the present. If I were Lionel, where would I put a veterinarian? Under medicine? Biology? Zoology? I peered into the folders: bioengineering, quantum physics, plant chemistry—aha, there it was, under veterinary medicine. Scooping up the file, I sat down at the desk. Thank God, the physics professor, who'd graced us with his deodorant-challenged presence last semester, wasn't back again. Though since this new guy probably lived and breathed horses, who'd want to be around him?

I leafed through the file on John Adriance, DVM. Taught veterinary medicine for ten years before making full professor at Jeremiah Veterinary College in Pucksville, Pennsylvania. Hmm. Sounded like Podunk University to me. PU. Ha, ha. I'd have to remember to stifle the urge to giggle.

Besides Jeremiah, his CV said he had a large animal practice. Did that mean a large practice of nice little animals? Or a small practice of the other kind? Or both?

I should probably mention that I was generally terrified of any creature much bigger than a breadbox or that didn't have any legs or that had too many of them. That eliminated everything, I think, except cats, rabbits, gerbils, and goldfish.

I figured I was safe because it wasn't likely that Dr. Adriance traveled with his patients. *Let's see, what else?* I rifled through the folder. Oh, yeah, he was coming to Chelsea College to train veterinarians' technicians. Kind of like medical assistants. Or dental hygienists, I guess. Only they didn't have to deal with brushing or flossing. Or maybe they did. This thought made me a bit queasy on my empty stomach. I closed the file and geared myself up for the interview, stopping by my office to grab a notebook and a couple of pens. And headed to the cafeteria for the nine-thirty meeting

The early meeting was because Lionel was a morning person, a very annoying quality of his. Here I was, barely awake, heading to a rendezvous with someone who spoke a language I wouldn't understand, namely horse or dog, and whose profession I wanted nothing to do with.

I took the elevator to the basement. It was dimly lit

and dank from the water that was always dripping from somewhere. I followed the corridors to the cafeteria, peering over my shoulder. In the past couple of years, we'd had six assorted lurkers: two peeping Toms, three flashers, and one guy who just stared. I comforted myself with the fact that lurkers didn't usually kill people—like whatever scum killed poor Dr. Ditstein.

I peeked into the cafeteria to see if he was there yet. A guy in a tweedy sports jacket was sitting by himself with papers spread all over the table. Everybody else was clumped in twos and threes, so it had to be him. I waved to the people I liked, ignored the ones I didn't, and made my way to his table.

The closer I got, the more I liked what I saw. Tanned face. I know, bad for the skin, causes premature aging, possible early death—but this was worth it. Crinkles— okay, wrinkles—around deep-set brown eyes. Lots of curly dark hair, cute ears—kind of pointed around the edges—and a spectacular set of dimples, which I got to view up close as I introduced myself. Not to mention a great pair of shoulders. I couldn't see his arms and chest as to whether they were particularly furry. That would have to wait. Hopefully, not for long.

He stood up and flashed a smile. He had to be at least six feet tall.

"Sorry," I mumbled, walking up to him and shaking his hand. A quick glance at his left hand told me it was naked, thank goodness. No wedding ring. "I know you were expecting Lionel West, but he…uh…had a little accident. I'm Marabella Vinegar."

The family name, by the way, was courtesy of the kind folks at Ellis Island. We were respectable Vinnaucyurs back in south-middle Poland. My strange first name came from my grandparents on my mother's side: Marvin and Bella.

John Adriance, DVM, smiled. "My luck." Then he said hastily, "I mean, it's too bad about Lionel, of course, but I'm sure you and I will do just fine."

As he sat down, he pushed his papers into a pile next to him. With a sinking feeling, I saw they were full of statistical graphs. Not an auspicious beginning for a mathematically challenged writer.

I slid into a chair opposite him and noticed that his jacket was covered with some sort of animal hair. My hands were itching to run over his body with a dust buster.

His brown eyes gazed penetratingly at my teeth, checking me out as if I were a horse.

"I still have all thirty-two of them, no caps, and very few cavities," I said proudly, and opened wide for him to get a better view. With his looks, I didn't care if he loved me for my teeth, my hair, my firm limbs, my anything.

"Charming," he said and laughed.

I was thinking, *Whatever we do is fine with me: dinner, dancing, a quick trot around the block, a nightcap back at my place.* Then I flashed on my roommate. And the murder. I couldn't let romantic, sexy thoughts distract me, right?

I shoved my hair out of my face, took a deep breath, and tried to look businesslike. "Okay, let's get started," I said, trying not to drown in his eyes. "Um," I said, opening Lionel's folder. "I should ask you…"

He leaned back in his chair. "Ask away, I'm all yours." He grinned. This showed off his dimples even more.

Was that a promise? *Stop that*, I thought. This was supposed to be a business meeting. "I read in your file that you were at Jeremiah College in Pucksville, Pennsylvania. Doesn't sound like a real big place, Pucksville," I said, trying to bite back a giggle.

"Last census, the goats had the majority, four to one," he said.

"And Jeremiah must be very different from Chelsea College," I said.

"About as different as sheep dip and cow pies," he said with a wicked grin.

Sexy, good-looking, intelligent, and a sense of humor. *Be still, my heart.* My eyes roamed the parts of his body that were visible and finally lit on his tie, a blue-green paisley print.

"Lovely tie," I said. "Did you buy it around here?" *Oh, great. Real businesslike.*

"I haven't had much of a chance to go shopping or see anything, yet," he said. "Been too busy getting me and the boys settled in my house and preparing for this program. I really could use a friendly guide to show me around." He smiled. "How long have you lived here, anyway?"

"Oh, just all my life," I said. *The boys? His children?* "How many children do you have?" I asked, with what I hoped was studied casualness.

"None," he said, looking puzzled for a moment. "Oh, the boys." He laughed. "They're my dogs. St. Bernards."

I didn't know whether to be relieved or not, given my large animal phobia. But I tried to smile. "How did you decide to become a vet?"

"I'll tell you. But first, I want to ask if you'd be willing to help a stranger find his way around the city. I hear New Yorkers are supposed to be very savvy people."

Talk about an offer I couldn't refuse. "I'd be happy to."

"I love your chestnut mane," John Adriance said.

Another minute, I'd be Jell-O. If I were going to come up with a half-decent article—okay, any article—I'd have to steel myself to think unsexy thoughts. Animal thoughts. *No, not that kind of animal, Marabella. Horses. Cows. Sheep. Think sheep.* But sheep made me think of curly hair, my fingers running through dark curly hair.

Our eyes locked. I took a few deep breaths and remembered I was supposed to be conducting an interview. "About your plans," I said, more firmly in command, at least for the moment. "Tell me what you're going to do and how you're going to do it." Somehow, that wasn't exactly coming out right.

"You know," he said pleasantly, "maybe this isn't the right atmosphere. Is there a park or some grass around here? I'm always much more at home outdoors."

He gathered up his papers and me. Then he led me outside, kind of like he was taking me for my walk, except without a leash. And I didn't even care.

Chapter 5

I made a lunch date with Toniann, figuring this would do double-duty: allow me to do some serious venting and, hopefully, help me try to sort things out.

A couple of hours later, Toniann and I were sitting in our usual Italian restaurant, halfway between my office and hers. She was dressed in an off-white suit. It showed off her legs that wouldn't stop, and I knew she would walk away from lunch with nary a spot on it. Whereas my lunch always stuck to my clothes like Velcro.

Toniann could put away enough food at a meal to sustain a steelworker for a week and never gain a pound. She was also blessed with huge blue eyes fringed with thick dark lashes, nicely shaped lips, and a perfect oval face. The only thing she lacked in the looks department was a chest. Hers was virtually nonexistent. I must confess that her envy of my generous bosom gave me the tiniest bit of satisfaction. Okay, a lot of satisfaction.

We became instant buddies when we were both in the public relations office at Chelsea College. Toniann was the kindest person I'd ever met, generous to a fault, and utterly loyal to her friends. I knew she'd go out on a limb for me without batting one of those luscious lashes. Of course, I'd do the same for her.

Now she worked for Otis Pinckney, a lawyer and would-be politician, which meant she was paid real money, not the college's slave wages. We tried to meet for lunch or at the health club whenever we could mesh our schedules.

Right now, she was chomping away on her calzone and fries slathered with ketchup. If I didn't like her so much, I'd hate her, which I sometimes did anyway. Especially when I was sitting across from her, nudging my fork around my small, limp-leaved salad, which had already dripped a couple of oily spots on my blouse. There wasn't anything worse than usual about the salad, but I was actually in too much of a state to eat. A chorus of horrors kept wailing in my head: the murder, my mother. Well, at least it might help stave off the horrors of my hips.

"How are you holding up?" Toniann asked, reaching across the table to pat my arm.

She'd been to the funeral and had stayed with me afterward. She brought me gourmet food and tried to get me to eat, even though that was the last thing I'd felt like doing. Was that only a week ago? It felt like a year, at least. "All right, I guess."

She shook her head. "It must be such a hard thing, losing your mom."

I just nodded, not trusting myself to say anything. I realized I was going to have to tell her about my roommate and about my shrink, even though Toniann already thought I was seriously neurotic and would probably decide that I was hallucinating my mother. Maybe from all the vitamins I've been taking, like a vitamin B-12 illusion, or something.

Deciding to start with the easy part, John Adriance, I

launched into a full, spare-no-details description of our encounter.

After reaming me out for missing aerobics and my promise to get there this week, cross-my-heart-and-hope-to-die, she said, between bites, "Whaddaya gonna do about this hunk?"

"Well, I'm not taking him home with me yet." I started telling her the story about my shrink, in phases, to make it go down easier. First, the murder. Then my worries about a future interrogation from the detective.

"Geez Louise, what a bummer." She pushed her brown curls away from her face. "Maybe the cops will find the person who did it." She tilted her head to one side, something she did when she was thinking. "Well…"

"Well, what?" I asked.

"Uh, just in case…"

"Just in case?"

"Uh…" She looked down at her plate, which was pretty empty. She'd practically licked it clean, all 10,000 yummy calories of it. "…just in case this detective decides to go after you, maybe I should talk to Otis."

I choked on a lettuce leaf. "Your blowhard, toadying boss? The same Otis who you refer to in private as the ass-kisser? And why would the detective go after me, anyway? Just because I—"

"Found the body," she said, nodding. "That happens all the time, you know."

"What happens?" I was getting nervous.

"That people who find bodies get to be suspects," she said ominously.

"Gee, thanks," I said drily.

"And," she said, ignoring me, "Otis is still a practicing lawyer, even though he wants to run for city council. Besides, who else do we know that wouldn't cost a fortune?"

"Maria Perez," I said. "I heard she won the case for a woman who'd fractured her leg falling off a broken step in one of the dilapidated brownstones next to my building."

"Didn't you tell me she went back to Puerto Rico after she got married?"

I nodded. "I forgot. Well, how about your cousin Jerry? He's a lawyer, right?"

Toniann raised her eyebrows. "Oh, my god, he's a tax lawyer, and not even a good one. His clients are always getting audited."

There had to be somebody, anybody, other than Otis. "Wait, I know. Your old boyfriend, what was his name, George…"

"Grayson. He was disbarred for stealing his elderly clients' money. What a loss. He may have been a crook, but boy, was he ever good in bed." She licked her lips.

"Don't let Peter hear you say that." Peter was her current boyfriend, a struggling law student, and a really nice guy.

She sighed. "I might as well be in a convent. He falls asleep as soon as he comes back from the library."

"Once finals are over, things will be hopping again," I soothed.

"I've got the days marked off on a calendar and a new sheer black number from Victoria's Secret in my undie drawer," she said with a wicked grin. "Anyway, to get back to the subject of lawyers—I guess that leaves Otis."

I sighed.

"And—" She threw in the sweetener with a smirk. "—he'll be cheap."

"Economics aside," I said, knowing I couldn't put them aside, since I had exactly $200 in my savings account, "when's the last time he handled a criminal case?"

She wrinkled her forehead. "Lessee, there was that guy making porno movies in the nursing home. And the woman who set fire to her sister. Kind of like, remember the movie, *Whatever Happened to Baby Jane?* The woman took her sister back home after they both got out of the hospital, as I recall."

"Very admirable causes, I'm sure, but neither of them was a murder case. Which, of course, they haven't charged me with. Yet."

"Murder, shmurder," Toniann said. "People get off all the time. Or at least, they don't get the gas chamber anymore, do they?"

This was supposed to make me feel better? "As a matter of fact, New York State doesn't have a death penalty. At this point, anyway. But many thanks for bringing it to my attention." I glared at her. But she was oblivious, as usual.

"Don't worry." She patted my arm again. "You'll be in good hands with Otis. You know, just in case."

Somehow, the thought of my life being in the hands of Otis Pinckney, attorney-at-law and city council hopeful, did not make me rest easier. But I thanked her anyway, since I could end up needing a lawyer, and Otis was probably more or less affordable, if not a particularly admirable human being. Though I'd still have to take out a loan that I'd be paying off for eternity.

We signaled the waitperson—which in this place, meant standing up and walking toward the door, the only way they ever noticed you—when I realized I hadn't told her about my mother yet. But this was not something you could blurt out on the run.

"Don't worry," Toniann said, giving me a quick hug as we left the restaurant for our separate jobs.

She was working downtown, creating fictions for the press about Otis to prepare the way for his campaign, while I worked uptown. Actually, though I missed having her around all day, I was glad I'd be alone for the walk back to the office. I had a lot to think about, none of it good, not counting a certain dog-haired person with cute pointed ears. Except that somehow, I didn't think I could tell him about being deathly afraid of horses and medium or large dogs. I'd have to try to get over it, I guess. Maybe get a book on large animal phobia. Or talk to my shrink.

Guess it hasn't really sunk in yet.

Chapter 6

When I got home that night, an unpleasant surprise was leaning against my door in a rumpled brown jacket and navy pants, looking half-asleep. Detective Rivera, in the flesh.

I did not say, "Come in." But he did anyway, walking inside in front of me.

"Well?" I asked, standing next to him with my arms folded across my chest, hoping he'd be brief if I didn't invite him to sit down in the living room.

Turning to me, he said, with a yawn, "Here to ask you some questions." He consulted his black book. "Okay, let's hear all about it. What were you doing at the apartment of the deceased? And why were you seeing… uh…Dr. Ditstein?"

Taking a few cleansing breaths, the way my shrink taught us as part of her holistic therapy, I thought, a cop's life must be so boring, feeling a moment's sympathy for him having to listen to all these details, hoping to find some tiny shred of guilt. No wonder he looked so tired. *Jerk*, I thought, *he's trying to find YOU guilty. Stop feeling sorry for him.*

"You remember that I was the one who called the police first, after the murder?" I said. "So why are you interrogating me? Why aren't you out there questioning some suspects? Like the other members of the group, for instance?"

"It's been done before, you know. After you knock someone off, you call the police for cover," he informed me.

Over his shoulder, I could see my mother, dressed in one of my oversized tees and a pair of tights, signaling me from the kitchen.

"Stall, stall, and give him a nice plate of brownies. That'll soften him up. Or give him a heart attack," she said.

"Shhhhh," I whispered. "Brownies? Where would I get—"

With a flourish, she whipped out a plastic plateful, covered with a white linen napkin I'd never seen before. "Just a little something I figured you'd need when you got home. And I know how much you always loved them. But I had to use a mix. You were out of scratch ingredients."

I excused myself to the detective and went into the kitchen to fetch the brownies. My mother followed me back into the living room, settling in on the sofa.

Before I could ask her where on earth she got the napkin or the mix, since I hadn't had any ready-to-bake anything in my kitchen for the last ten pounds, I realized he was staring at me.

"How long since you've been talking to yourself? Is that why you were seeing Dr. Ditstein?" Rivera asked.

It dawned on me that my mother had decided to grace only me with the ability to see and hear her ghostly self. Oh, great, Casper the friendly mother-ghost was shy around strangers. I glared at her. She ignored me.

"Have a brownie," I said smoothly, handing him the plate. They really did look yummy. "Thanks, Ma," I signaled, this time with my eyes.

Still looking at me strangely, he turned to the brownies. I could see the internal struggle between the suspicious cop mind, especially dealing with someone he thought was probably nuts, and the heavenly chocolate smell. The chocolate won, and he scarfed three of them down in a row. He looked almost embarrassed.

"My wife, she's a nutritionist. She doesn't believe in junk food," he said with a sigh.

Then he started to sit down on my mother.

I had to get him away from the sofa before he squashed her. But how? What would make me bound up and chase after someone if I were a cop? Other than someone else with a gun?

Bolting into the bathroom, I opened the window and climbed onto the fire escape, screeching at the top of my lungs.

That got him up, gun drawn, chasing after me. "What the hell's going on?"

I crawled inside, my clothes and my hands sporting fresh rust stains, and pointed out the window. "I heard something weird out there."

He pushed past me and looked out, then back at me, and shut the window. Shaking his head, he said, "The only thing weird around here is you." Replacing the gun, he picked up the notebook, flipping the pages.

I didn't care what he thought, as long as he hadn't succeeded in turning my mother into a pancake. Trotting out to the living room, I sat down near her head at one end of the sofa and pointed to a hand-carved oak rocker across from it, one of my best flea market finds.

Rivera lowered himself into the rocker, looking wistfully at the brownies. "These are really good, you know?

Okay if I have a couple more?" he said, reaching for the plate, which I extended politely, glancing at my mother.

"Catch more flies with honey," she said.

Still chewing, he consulted his book. "Okay. Why were you seeing Dr. Ditstein?"

"I started going to Dr. Ditstein because I had…some problems…that I needed help with. I couldn't afford someone very expensive, and she was listed on the college's EAP."

"Yeah, Employee Assistance Plan." He nodded. "We got one in the Department."

"There were only a couple of names on the list. But I lucked out. She was terrific." I felt a lump growing in my throat.

"Why were you there so late at night? Don't therapists usually keep normal office hours?"

Taking a few cleansing breaths, I said, "She was trying to accommodate my schedule. I had a late appointment, my regular every-other-week appointment—"

"Why every other week?"

"Because the other week was group." I tried not to gnash my teeth. *Deep breaths, Marabella, deep cleansing breaths. Aaahhh.* "We had group therapy on alternate Thursday nights from seven to nine."

"Okay, go ahead. Then what happened?"

"I walked down the corridor, which smelled like tomato sauce, and—"

"Tomato sauce?"

"Dr. Ditstein's apartment was next to the trash room, so you'd get these strong smells. Like, if anybody stuffed a pizza box in there, there'd be tomato sauce. Or if there was Chinese take-out, probably egg roll smells and—"

His eyes were glazing over, and he yawned again. Either this was all terribly boring, or he was severely sleep deprived. Or both.

"Smells," he said. "Okay, tomato sauce. Then what?"

"What happened next was that when I knocked on the door, she didn't answer," I said. "I knocked again and didn't hear a sound. And the only sign of life was Dr. Shokum."

He sat up. "Dr. Shokum? Who's that? What was he doing there?"

"He lives across the hall from Dr. Ditstein. But he wasn't exactly *there*," I said. "I mean, he wasn't at the scene of the crime." I felt a tiny satisfaction in being able to use his language.

"So, where was Dr. Shokum?"

"Where he usually is," I said smugly. "Peeping out of his peephole."

"How do you know that?"

"Because when he opens the peephole cover to see out, it makes a snapping noise."

"Why does he do that, peeping out at people?"

"Because people say he's phobic about actually dealing with people in the flesh," I said, wondering why he needed to know all that.

"Okay," he said. "What was Dr. Ditstein like?" He yawned again. "Trying to get off caffeine," he said, making a face. He riffled through his notes. "How long were you seeing her, anyway?"

"Eight years."

He shook his head. "So, what was your feeling about her? Sometimes there's a love-hate relationship in these things. And do you know why someone would want to kill her?"

The idea of discussing my eight-year relationship with Dr. Ditstein with Detective Rivera was particularly repellent. But I didn't think I had much choice.

"Dr. Ditstein," I said, "was a kind, caring, humane person. I can't think of any reason that someone would have to hurt her." I felt tears welling up in my eyes.

"How did you get along? Ever had an argument? Ever get mad at her?"

"We got along fine. No arguments."

He yawned. "In eight years, no fights?"

The man was seriously annoying me. "Look, Detective Rivera," I said, "we might have disagreed about a few things occasionally—"

He pounced. "So, what did you *disagree* about? She say something to tick you off? Some of these therapists can be really aggressive, you know?"

Lord, give me strength. Deep breaths. "Dr. Ditstein was a very nurturing person. She was very fair about everything, in general." Except for her peculiar tolerance for Henry, which I wasn't about to tell him because Henry scared the hell out of me. "In fact, for the past couple of years, she was only seeing a few long-time patients, the members of our group, because she was so devoted to her research on mental illness in children. She wanted to try to make the world a better place." Tears stung my eyes.

"So, what did you disagree about?"

Bulldog, thy name is Rivera. I hesitated. "She and I didn't agree about one of the people in the group. I thought that person was too…uh…upset to be in group and really needed more individual therapy." This wasn't the half of it. I thought Henry was far too crazy to even be on the streets. Especially after the incidents.

Rivera was practically sniffing the air. "So what happened?"

"She didn't agree. And she was the therapist. So that was that," I said, thinking back to the times I'd pressed my case. She'd stuck to her guns, saying that she had knowledge that I didn't, that I was rushing to judgment, that I really didn't know Henry. And now she was dead.

"Who was it?"

"Henry Nusbitt!" I blurted. *Sorry, Henry, it's either you or me. And I never liked you anyway. Wait a minute! Henry will find out what I said and go after me, possibly with a blunt instrument! Calm down, Marabella. Get centered.* "Detective Rivera," I said, "I'd be extremely grateful if you didn't tell Henry who you've been talking to."

He got up. "Oh, by the way," he said, "don't leave town. I may want to question you again."

Now, where would I go with my mother on the sofa? "Okay," I said. "But what about Henry?"

"I never heard it from you." He stuffed a few more brownies into his pocket and headed for the door. "I'll tell him," he said with a laugh, "a little ghost told me."

Chapter 7

After he left, I had the horrible feeling that Rivera considered mea suspect. What could I do? *Dr. Ditstein, wherever you are, please tell me. Give me a sign. An inkling. An anything.*

Interrupting my thoughts, my mother said, "Okay, sweetheart, we've got work to do."

"What kind of work? And what about dinner?" I said, my stomach rumbling. "Don't we have to eat?"

Hoisting herself to a sitting position on the sofa, she pulled bifocals out from the bosom of the tee shirt.

"Where—" I started to ask, but thought better of it. *Let sleeping bifocals lie.*

Adjusting them on her nose, she said, "Nosh on the brownies. We'll eat later, it's in the fridge. Get me a pad of paper and a pen."

"Why?"

"You should be ashamed, something so dumb coming from your mouth, you with the one-hundred-forty IQ." She wagged a finger at me. "So we can figure this whole thing out, that's why," she said. "Or would you rather wait for that policeman to do it?"

"Detective. Are you serious? What makes you think we can do this?"

"Of course we can, why not?" She crossed her arms under her chest. "The nerve of him, asking you questions as if you were guilty of something."

I went to my bedroom to get the pad and pen from my washstand desk. Dealing with Rivera had completely unnerved me. I popped a Xanax. Then I wondered why my mother couldn't just conjure up her own writing materials, the way she did with the brownie mix and linen napkin. Maybe her conjuring abilities were rationed. Maybe she could only do so much in a day. Or maybe she was lazy. Or embarrassed to do her tricks in front of me. Or not allowed. Or maybe she didn't have magic powers at all. *Then how did she do the brownies, tell me that?* Maybe she heisted them from one of my neighbors.

I chewed a cuticle, wondering if I'd have to deal with a call about a missing box of brownie mix and a napkin: *Oh, sorry, it was my mother-the-klepto-ghost. She didn't mean to swipe your food and linen. And don't call the police, thank you. They've already been here today.*

"No, dear. It's a question of why waste these powers for something that's just as easy to get the old-fashioned way?" she called from the living room. "They're very strict about that, you know."

I slapped my forehead with my hand, feeling dizzy again. "Oh, of course, why didn't I think of that?"

"Sarcasm is not attractive." Her forehead was creased in concentration when I handed her the writing implements. "Thank you, darling. Now let's make a list."

"Of what?" I searched for any crumbs Rivera had neglected. There weren't many. "Ma, I'm starving."

"Work first, eat later." She wet the tip of the pen, a habit of hers that always drove me crazy. I was sure she'd had massive doses of felt-tip marker poisoning. Come to think of it, maybe that had finally impaired her judgment and turned her klepto. "Tell me everybody who's in your group, their names, and what they're there for. And anyone else you think might be important."

I knew this wasn't exactly easy for her, since she was convinced that I—and anyone else seeing a shrink—spent all our sessions discussing what terrible mothers we'd had. Which wasn't altogether true. I'd spent at least a few of the sessions on my father.

"I really appreciate you helping me, Ma," I said, meaning it.

She waved my thanks away. "So what's a mother for anyway? Never mind. How many?"

I thought for a minute. "Oh, I just remembered. Dr. Ditstein had a boyfriend. I saw them on the street together once. Pale, elegant, good-looking. Black hair, hanging straight down to his shoulders. Black eyes, too. Looked right through you. Had a strange accent, sounded Eastern European. At least ten years younger than her. She introduced him. Zoltan Karyoli. Not a name you'd easily forget." He'd smiled at me, revealing dazzling white teeth.

My mother was scribbling away. "The boyfriend. Okay, who else?"

"Dr. Shokum, in the apartment across from her."

"Did they get along, this Shokum, with your therapist?" she asked.

"Damned if I know."

She clucked her tongue. "Don't swear."

"Sorry."

"How many in your group?"

"Six, including me. There's Ron Dolan, Maxine Williams, Beth Hronska, Chris Ragamoni—"

"Chris man or woman?"

"Christine," I said.

"Who else?"

I sighed. "Henry Nusbitt. He's new to the group."

My mother chewed the top of her marker. "So, what's with this Henry that he gives you such heartburn?"

"It would take a lot of explaining, Ma. Henry's not…easily described."

"So, explain." She crossed her legs. "I'm listening."

Maybe the best thing would be to describe the last group session I'd been to, the one just before my mother died. The hell with the confidentiality. Dr. Ditstein was dead. And so was my mother. And I could be in serious trouble with the cops.

So I gave her a blow-by-blow account of my last group session, while she chomped away on the marker.

Chapter 8

Telling my mother really brought the whole night's events back, in living color.

We straggled in, the way we usually did, in ones and twos, more or less on time, around seven that Thursday night. Dr. Ditstein was a vision in orange: orange blouse, orange pants, orange socks, orange hair scrunchee. Since she was rather long and tall, though attractive, with frizzy red hair, this made her resemble a carrot, or maybe a scarecrow. Her hair was another subject entirely. Suffice it to say that it was unmanageable—actually, out of control was more like it. The weird thing was that Dr. Ditstein, with her bizarre appearance, was a crackerjack shrink. In fact, the stranger her attire, the better she seemed to be at her craft.

I traipsed through the foyer into the living room/cum treatment room, which I found as fascinating as her get-ups. Huge asparagus ferns on ceiling hooks quivered in the air above us, replenishing the oxygen we used up during sessions. Tie-dyed folding chairs were grouped around boxes of Kleenex and paper bags for hyperventilation emergencies. There were two armchairs, one straight-backed, one curved-backed, for Dr. Ditstein to alternate in, depending on whether or not she was in linear-thinking mode. Tonight, she dropped into the curved chair, closed her eyes, whispered her mantra three times, opened her eyes, smiled beatifically, and turned on the recorder. The usual signal to begin.

I sat next to Chris, whom I kind of related to, in terms of mother-problems, as in your usual love-and-homicidal relationship. She gave me a watery smile, and I gave her an encouraging one back. She was so used to slouching because of her height, she even did it when she sat. Though she seemed harmless enough, painfully shy, even, there was something about her that kept nagging at me, some peculiarity that I couldn't quite put my finger on. Chris was a mind/body worker, which meant, I think, that she talked to people while massaging their various body parts. Just wait till Rivera heard there was a masseuse in the group. He'd be sure she was into porn. Or was some kind of kinky sex worker.

Ron, treating us to his usual overpowering smell of *eau de cheap* aftershave, was sprawled on Chris's other side. He'd already cracked one of his sexist-pig jokes to Maxine, who hated not only his jokes but also his guts.

"Disgusting," she hissed at him, spraying spittle on his skin-tight leather pants.

A well-deserved response, I thought. Maxine was an African-American woman who'd fought her way out of the ghetto through sheer brains and street-smarts. She was also a karate expert and, one of these days, she was going to lay Ron out flat. I fervently hoped I'd be around to witness that.

Beth blew in breathless, late, as usual, her streaked-blonde hair flying. "Sorry, sorry, sorry." She flashed her capped teeth at us. "You know how it is, guys, when you're in the biz."

No, I didn't know, I wasn't in the "biz." I didn't give a rat's ass what itty bitty role her agent was supposed to have absolutely been promised, cross his heart, to his very fave star. I found Beth shallow and narcissistic. But she didn't get to me the way she got to Maxine.

Maxine shot her a filthy look. "Not all of us get to live the charmed life of a person in the *biz*."

Beth ran her fingers through her hair and gave a hearty, phony laugh. Seemed like the more she got into the biz, the more unreal she got. Maybe the bigger the rising star, the less real you were?

She gave Maxine a superior smile. "You don't know the half of it. What I went through today with my costume changes, you wouldn't believe. I guess they're just not making clothes to fit teeny waists these days."

Maxine's lips twisted, and not with a smile. "What I believe, what I believe, you bitch, is that you're a bitch," she growled.

"Stop picking on her, please," I said. "This sounds like kindergarten."

"Maxine, chill," Dr. Ditstein interjected. "You too, Marabella."

I forgot to mention that Maxine was square-shaped, with absolutely no waistline that anyone could find. Beth, on the other hand, who looked as if she had a major eating disorder, weighed in at about ninety-eight pounds soaking wet.

Beth turned to me, raising one over-plucked eyebrow, and turned up the palms of her pink jeweled fake-finger-nailed hands. "*Some* people, you know, have a pretty limited vocabulary."

"Will you please cut it out?" I said.

"Sarcasm is counterproductive, Beth," Dr. Ditstein admonished.

I figured Maxine had a problem with Beth mainly

because of Beth's looks, though our resident starlet's personality didn't exactly help matters. Beth, on the other hand, seemed to harbor a strange urge to push Maxine's buttons.

At this point, Dr. Ditstein began alternate nostril breathing, putting her thumb on one nostril, breathing in, putting her finger on the other nostril and breathing out, a sure sign of concentration. Delicately removing her fingers from her nose, she said, "Why do you suppose you have the need to make a grand entrance at group, Beth? Are you afraid we won't pay you enough attention otherwise?"

I thought she hit the nail on the head, especially after Beth began to flush, which actually seemed genuine.

"I never got any attention from my mother," Beth said. "She was too busy screwing around. And my father was God-knows-who. So I made it my business to make the other kids like me. And they sure did." A quick teeth-flash. "I was prom queen two years in a row. Guess that's what gave me a taste for the stage. That and being in the senior play. I was Juliet, of course."

"Big f-ing deal," said Maxine.

I sighed. "Please, just let her talk, okay?"

"Let's show each other a little consideration, Maxine," Dr. Ditstein said, frowning.

"The whole town turned out for the show," Beth continued, with a far-away look. "Everybody but my mother, that is. She was in some motel somewhere."

Dr. Ditstein did her yoga breathing, working her nostrils again, so I knew she wasn't through yet. With a steady gaze at Maxine, she said, "Why does Beth's choice of career upset you? Does it make your job as a comptroller less important?"

Maxine sucked in her breath. "No, I…yes, I don't know," said the person who was never at a loss for words. "I like what I do, I'm good at it."

"*Very* good, I hear," said Dr. Ditstein.

"But," Maxine said, "I'm behind the scenes all day, crunching numbers. Not out there sticking my—" She glared at Beth. "—face in front of people."

"Is that what you really want to do? Be an actress?" Dr. Ditstein asked. "You could always make a career change, you know. It's not too late."

Beth opened her mouth, obviously to say something sarcastic, but Dr. Ditstein cut her off at the pass with a forbidding look.

"Well," Maxine said, thinking. "I don't know. I never thought about doing anything else, I guess. I've always been very good at math, actually, the best in my class. *And,* by the way, the *only minority* in my class." A quick glare at Beth again. "So I just naturally went for a career in finance. And it pays *really* well." A smirk. "Plus, I have a *corner* office. With a *great* view. On the *thirty-sixth* floor. That has to count for *something.*"

Dr. Ditstein nodded. "Right."

"Hey, a gal like you—" Ron said,

Maxine gritted her teeth about the "gal" business.

"—with your corner office and big money, why would you want to give that up?"

The grit turned into a grin.

"For what? I'd love to make your kind of bread, if I could do it," he said, with a shrug. He smoothed down his hair. "I bet our *starlet* here has never even seen that kind of dough, no matter what kind of part, or should I say, body part—"

Beth turned red. "How dare you, you slimy rat!"

"Enough!" Dr. Ditstein said. "No *ad hominum* attacks from anybody."

Ron scrunched lower in his seat, assuming the male chair posture: arms folded across chest, legs spread wide open, crotch front and center. Tight pants, too, of course. Leather. To show off his…whatever, I guess. He made a career of stupid jokes, which was what he did at scuzzy nightclubs. So we had the privilege of being his practice session.

"Did you hear the one about the woman who was such a lousy cook, when the roaches came to her house, they ate first?" He laughed so hard I thought he would land on the floor.

No one else laughed.

Dr. Ditstein removed her finger from her left nostril. "Inappropriate, Ron," she said in dismissal. "Let's move on, shall we? What's on your minds tonight?"

"My mother," I began.

"Oh, I know that one," Maxine said. "Do I ever."

As per usual, nobody let me talk. Sometimes this group made me feel like Rodney Dangerfield.

"Marabella was talking," Dr. Ditstein said.

"Oops," Maxine said, with an insincere grin.

"S'okay," I mumbled, though it wasn't. "My mother is really sick. It's her heart," I said, looking down at my lap. "Serious complications from congestive heart failure." Tears welled up in my eyes.

There was a collective whoosh of breath.

"Oh, God," Beth said, "My mother had that, that's what she died from. Uh, I didn't, uh, mean that." She looked upset, for real.

"So what did you open up your big fat mouth for then?" Maxine sneered.

"Cool it, Maxine," Dr. Ditstein said.

In that whispery voice of hers that practically caused everyone to fall forward to hear her, Chris said. "At *least* Marabella has some respect for her mother. That's probably more than *most* of you could say about your own loved ones."

"Thank you for your consideration, Chris," I said, smiling at her.

Maxine and Ron both rolled their eyes.

Chris patted my arm. "I'm so sorry for your trouble. But your mother should really try to get rid of her bad energy. There's probably blockage around her heart chakra. Get rid of that with a good aura cleansing, and she'll be just fine. You'll see." She beamed a few good energy waves in my direction.

Though I knew she was trying to be helpful, it would have been a hell of a lot more helpful if they'd all let me talk. I was feeling pretty terrible.

Dr. Ditstein to the rescue. "This is Marabella's time, people," she said, giving me a kind smile.

I shot her a grateful look. "I feel guilty about my mother, because…well, I love her of course, but I still have a lot of negative feelings about her. And now, with her being so—sick." My voice cracked. Chris patted my arm again. "I can't stand the idea of losing her." I burst into tears.

Chris handed me a Kleenex. I blew my nose.

"Losing a loved one is a very heavy thing," Dr. Ditstein said. "Especially in a…should we say?…complicated relationship."

Even though I was crying, this made me laugh. "Complicated doesn't *begin* to describe me and my mother."

I had yet to mention Henry. I had been resisting this part of the story. With good reason. Henry was making disgusting snuffling sounds, as usual, ensconced in one of those leftover-from-the-sixties beanbag chairs that Dr. Ditstein had unearthed somewhere for patients who needed extra "settling," as she called it. Privately, I called it extra coddling. Anyway, Henry was nodding off, probably due to whatever anti-psychotic drugs he was on. Unfortunately, they didn't seem to do much to improve his mental state.

I'd found him pretty creepy ever since he first appeared, about two months ago, after his release from the hospital for a nervous breakdown. When he'd talk, he'd narrow his pale gray eyes and focus on each of us, in turn, as if he were measuring our response to him. And when someone else was talking, he'd stare at them.

There was the time Ron had been blathering about problems with his latest girlfriend, whom we all felt pretty sorry for. Dr. Ditstein had just asked Ron a leading question about his relationship patterns, when Henry sprang out of his chair, not an easy thing to do, planted himself in front of Ron, cursed him out, and walked back to his seat as if nothing had happened.

And during another session, one of the times when Maxine and Beth really got into it, Henry pulled out a letter opener and pretended to carve an imaginary line in between them on the rug.

Other than murmuring, "Inappropriate, Henry," Dr. Ditstein didn't even call him down about it. She went easy on him, she'd told me, because of his fragile mental health.

So, old Henry seemed to be out of it, as usual, when the conversation eventually turned from relationships with parents to childhood relationships with other kids and the special types of torture we'd had to endure during recess.

"The kids used to call me rigatoni, because my last name is Ragamoni," Chris said, looking at the floor. "Sometimes, Kraft's macaroni and cheese."

Ron snorted. Both Maxine and I glared at Ron. "Those were *little* boys who did that, right?" I said. This made no impression on Ron, of course.

"You think that's so bad?" Maxine said. "How'd you

like to be called 'Maxie Pad.' Or just 'Pad,' to my friends."

Ron was doubled over. "Hey, can I use that in my act? Of course, I'd change the name. To Mini-Pad," he hooted.

"You're a miserable person," Maxine said.

"That's inappropriate, Ron," Dr. Ditstein said. "And you know that everything here is confidential."

"I was only kidding, Charmaine, you know that," he said, giving her an oily grin.

He was the only one who called Dr. Ditstein by her first name to her face, which really annoyed me. The fact that she let him annoyed me even more. And I saw him try to put the make on her more than once. Fortunately, she had the good sense to put him in his place, actually pretty firmly, for her. He had gotten pissed about her daring to reject God's gift to women, though I suspected it was probably more of a blow to his ego than having real feelings about her.

But sometimes I did think that Dr. Ditstein was prejudiced in favor of the men in the group. At least, she never seemed to really criticize them. Though I must say that mine was a mild objection, more of an observation. Maxine, on the other hand, periodically went ballistic over what she thought was Dr. Ditstein's unfair treatment of women, by which she meant unfair treatment of Maxine. Then again, Maxine was still dealing with the detritus of leftover anger at her tall, slim, shrink sister, which she often transferred onto guess who.

Anyway, when I suggested to Dr. Ditstein in an individual session, in an objective manner, of course, about the seeming most-favored status of the males in the group, she told me to not take everything so seriously, think good thoughts, and things would work themselves out, give them time. Right. And now she was dead.

"Look at *my* name," I said, "don't you think I went through elementary school hell? I mean, the kids had so much fun with Vinegar, they didn't even bother calling me 'Hebrew National Salami' the way they did my friend, Betty Cohen."

"Funny, I never got called any names," Beth said. "I guess because the other kids all liked me."

"No accounting for tastes," Maxine muttered.

"Maxine!" Dr. Ditstein said. Then she said, gently, "Henry, what about you? Would you like to tell us how it was for you?"

He flew into a rage, if someone could be said to fly when he was all scrunched up in a beanbag chair. His face turned purple, and he let out a stream of curses. Finally, he stopped and sank back into the chair, twisting the tufts in his sweater. "You shouldn't have asked me to tell them that, Dr. Ditstein," he said. "That wasn't right. It wasn't right, at all."

Dr. Ditstein looked stricken. "I'm really sorry, Henry. I thought it would help, since we were all trying to deal with the same thing."

"No!" he yelled. "It wasn't the same! Not for me! Never!" He jumped up and slammed out the door.

"He's really rather strange," Beth said, her eyes wide.

"Rather strange?" Maxine snorted. "He's fucking nuts, that's what he is."

Chris, the sensitive soul, had tears pooling in her eyes. "I think he's very upset. And I think it's all our fault."

Dr. Ditstein looked concerned. "This is your group. What do you think happened here just now?"

"You're the one who jerked his chain," Maxine said, throwing her a dirty look. "It's your fault. Not ours. You're the professional here." Her eyes glittered.

Ron shrugged. "Hey, the guy's a wacko, so whaddya want from us?"

"You have some nerve, calling other people names," Maxine said. "How would you like it if people called *you* names?"

"Lay it on me, man," Ron snarled. "Just you try it. Then you'll see what *real* name-calling is. I'm a master."

I was afraid he was going to take a bite out of her. "Hey, it's *our group*, like Dr. Ditstein said."

Dr. Ditstein shot me a grateful look, but I could tell she was upset. "Okay, we were talking about the way peer interactions, negative peer interactions from childhood, affected us. That's pretty heavy."

"Right, hey, I didn't have it so great, either. Even the nuns in my school weren't too nice to me," Ron said, looking at the floor.

"*Big* surprise," Maxine said.

Dr. Ditstein sent her a warning look.

"But you learn to live with it, not like our friend Henry, here," Ron said. "I don't usually dwell on it, but I got the crap beaten out of me on a regular basis when I was a kid."

Maxine snickered. "Not all of it, unfortunately."

"Maxine," Dr. Ditstein said.

Beth gave a mighty groan. "What a nasty little bunch we are, aren't we?"

Just as I was collecting my thoughts, Dr. Ditstein's chimes rang. She disdained regular clocks. Too pedestrian, she said. So she used a Zen chime clock, which she set for our sessions. She closed her eyes, did her nostril thing, and then flicked off the recorder.

We left under the blazing sun of her beatific smile. The last one I ever saw.

Chapter 9

My mother looked up from the pad she'd been scribbling away on. "Not very nice people, this group of yours," she said, clucking her tongue. "You, at least, seemed to show some concern about me. Even though it was just for a little while, back there."

I rolled my eyes. "Ma—"

She waved my protest away. "Let's get going here. These people, do you know where they all live?"

I shook my head. "Not really. Except that Chris lives in the Village and Ron lives in Tribeca. And Maxine works at Stanton and Poole's. We didn't exchange addresses, because of confidentiality."

She chewed on the top of the marker.

I started to say something about chemicals and brain rot and then shrugged. She'd never listened to me when she was alive, so why would she now?

"So, the names and addresses and phone numbers must be in the doctor's files. Which, at this moment, is probably in police custody," she said, through a mouth full of toxic substances.

"Right, so that's that," I said, wondering what she was thinking.

"No, it isn't." She grinned. "I'm off to the races."

I stared, as she wafted herself up from the sofa—How did she do that?—and began to evaporate in front of my eyes. "Wait, Ma, don't go yet—" I wasn't ready to say goodbye to her again so soon, just when I'd more or less gotten used to having her back again.

"Don't worry, sweetheart, this is just a quick trip," her disembodied voice soothed. "Back in a flash."

I closed my eyes and began counting my breaths, to erase the unnerving vision of my dematerialized mother, trying to push away the question of whether my youthful quest for the perfect hallucinogen had anything to do with all this. By the time I was up to breath number eighty-nine, I felt a stirring in the air and a faint groan. I opened my eyes as she came in for a landing.

"Whew, this is hard on the arms, not to mention the rest of me," she said, dropping onto the sofa, looking exhausted. She thrust the files at me. "Here, copy these quick."

She'd really snatched the things. I guess she had turned klepto. "Ma, this is stealing!"

She looked indignant. "Number one, it is not stealing, only borrowing. Number two, I did it for you. Number three, don't talk to your mother that way."

"But—"

"And number four," she shot at me, "How else were you going to get their addresses? Tell me that, will you, oh-so-smart daughter of mine?"

She was right, of course. I sighed, picked up the files, and began flipping through them for names. First, the boyfriend. That shouldn't be too hard. How many Zoltan Karyolis could there be in a file? Oh, wait, he wouldn't be in her patient files. I'd have to try to get it from the phone book. "Okay," I said, "I'll put them in my contacts right away, and then you can, um, get these back to the cops." I didn't relish the thought of her exhausting herself again, but what were the options? I should drop off the files myself at the station? I should put them in the mail, to be traced back to me? I should throw them away, to be traced back to me?

And didn't I want the cops to have them so they'd be able to solve the murder? Though I was afraid that Detective Rivera seemed to be pretty comfortable with me as his perp of choice.

I quickly copied the last names and addresses into my Droid and wrote down their addresses. At the last minute, my mother *noodged* me to add their email addresses.

"You never know what could be useful," she said. "Remember all those plastic bags and string I used to save? And buttons, I had a whole tin of buttons."

"The buttons maybe, but what use was all that string? And the recycled waxed paper?"

My mother could never bring herself to dispose of waxed paper. Her kitchen cupboard had been a waxed paper museum.

"Stop sassing me and finish your list," she said.

Which I did, not wanting to have stolen property in my possession any longer than necessary. I handed the files back to her and closed my eyes, not relishing the thought of witnessing her disappearing act again. I heard a grunt and felt the air rustle. I kept my eyes closed, counting my breaths. On my eighty-second inhale, I heard her panting, and she descended heavily on the sofa.

"Ma, all this activity is not good for your health. You're not a spring chicken, you know."

"I'm just not used to all these ups and downs and sideways. They should have warned me." She lay there, breathing hard for a few minutes. "I appreciate your concern, darling. But that's what I'm here for, to help you. Don't worry, I'll be okay in a little while. And you know I never had a very good sense of direction."

That I knew. Turn her around the wrong way, and she'd get lost in her own kitchen. No inner compass or something. I remembered the time she decided to take me to Brighton Beach to swim when I was about six. We got all dressed, with our bathing suits under our clothes, packed a picnic lunch and towels, and ended up in the South Bronx. She made a regular routine out of getting lost in department stores. I had to be the only kid who had to have salespeople find her mother. And unfortunately for me, I inherited her directional disorder. The last time Toniann and I went out for dinner, and I walked into the lobby to go to the ladies' room, I opened a door and ran straight into a man at a urinal.

My mother was sitting up again, with a bit of color back in her cheeks. Not that she had as much coloring as she'd had before she…died. It was kind of a paler version of it. And she had even less of it when she overly exerted herself.

"We better conserve your energies, Ma, for when we really need them," I said.

Drawing herself up, she said, "The rainy day is here. Who do we tackle first?"

"Tackle?"

"Interview, interrogate," she said. "Like what that Rivera should be doing, only he's probably not bothering because he thinks you did it."

"We're going to be police persons? How are we going to do that?" I shuddered. "Should I call Otis Pinckney? Do you think they're getting ready to arrest me?"

She brushed this aside. "What we have to do is find the real murderer ourselves. Before you are in need of that Otis's services. And just where would you be without me, sweetheart? In jail, that's where. Waiting to be tried for murder, that's where."

"Okay." I didn't need any more convincing. "But just how are we going to do that?"

My mother had a gleam in her eye. She was actually enjoying this, the callous soul. "By detecting, by figuring it out," she said. "Like Jessica Fletcher on *Murder She Wrote*." She had a far-away expression on her face, probably reliving steamy episodes involving horny septuagenarians. "And who knows who you could meet—"

"This isn't Century Village," I said. "And you shouldn't get too excited. It's not good for your…condition."

She grinned. "A little romance never hurt anyone. Anyway, we need a plan." She tapped her teeth with the marker. "Get someone on your side first. Who's the easiest?"

"Chris," I said without hesitation. At least she wasn't violent and seemed to like me.

"Okay. Call her and tell her you want to come over to talk about Dr. Ditstein, to commiserate with each other, over coffee," she said.

"Probably herb tea, since she's a healer," I said.

"Okay, over a cup of flowers, then," she said, handing me my phone.

I scrolled down to Chris's number. I got a machine. But not your ordinary machine. She—it—said, "Relax. All will be well. Though I am not physically present, I am very nearby spiritually. Let me know you are nearby, too, and we will connect very soon." After some tinkly bell sounds, I left my name and number.

"Now what?" I asked my mother.

"Now we eat," she said, lifting herself off the sofa and moving into my kitchen.

When she took the cover off the pot, I smelled lamb, a substance I'd considered to be inedible for years. Besides the fact of its innate greasiness, I'd had an unforgettable experience with a sheep at a 4-H show in upstate New York ten years ago. After that sheep had fixed me with a homicidal look from its blazing red eyes under a mountain of black wool, I was done for. I swear it had been a serial killer in a previous life.

But there was one of its relatives, stewed, on a plate, being served up to me. Maybe I could plead a touchy stomach. "What else are we having, Ma? Do you need any help?"

Lifting the cover off another pot, she brushed my offer aside. "Green beans and peas and carrots, I made a medley."

Those, I knew, were fresh from the can. When I was a child, I thought all vegetables grew in cans or, if they were really fancy, in freezer bags.

Salad consisted of iceberg lettuce—who actually eats iceberg lettuce?—a tomato still redolent of its plastic carton, and bottled French dressing. Fortunately, she'd put out seltzer water to wash it all down.

This was why I tended to avoid any restaurant that advertised itself as "Mother's" or "Home Cooking." For now, though, I was so hungry I wolfed down the salad and veggies and managed to pick at the stew when she asked me why I wasn't eating it. I figured the sheep encounter excuse wouldn't go over too well with her.

"Are you becoming a vegetarian these days?" she asked, sipping her seltzer. "I don't think it's so healthy, not to eat meat. After all, we were meant to be meat-eaters, from our earliest days." She belched delicately. "Aahh. Who needs Maalox when you've got seltzer?"

I was trying not to think about a number of things about this meal as I ate. As in, for starters, how did it happen? Did she waft into the meat counter in Fairway, picking out the best cut of lamb with invisible fingers and spiriting it away? The same with the produce?

"It all works somehow, sweetheart. Most of the time, anyway," said my mother-the-mind-reader.

Then there was the fact that she was diving into the food—well, maybe not so heartily—but eating, all the same. Not to mention guzzling the seltzer. She needed food and drink? Or was she just keeping me company?

She evidently had developed ESP along her travels, so to speak. "Yes, I'm eating, though I admit, I'm not enjoying it as much as I used to." She heaved a sigh. "But that's to be expected, I guess," she said, gnawing away at what used to be part of the leg of a live sheep." Swallowing, she said, "Thank God, I've still got most of my own teeth."

I chugged some seltzer, trying not to look at what she was devouring, when the phone rang. It was Chris. I asked her if I could come to her place, for her convenience. Putting it this way was my mother's idea, to, as she said, "grease the skids," while we snooped around. I suggested to Chris that we might lend each other support in our mutual grief, a prospect she damply embraced. I heard the sound of nose blowing. Since tomorrow was Saturday, we settled on eleven o'clock, and she promised to serve me a special new tea made from twigs and bark. Yum. I was really looking forward to that.

After dinner, I went over to Sam's with some audio books. He settled me in the overstuffed chair in the living room with a cup of Swee Touch Nee tea. I never knew what he did to the tea, but it was always absolutely delicious.

"Okay," he said, dropping onto the sofa on the other side of the coffee table. "So, tell me, how are you doing?"

I recounted the story about Dr. Ditstein's murder.

When I got to the part about Detective Rivera's suspicions, he grew indignant.

"How dare they treat you like that?" He pursed his lips. "Why aren't they out there looking for the killer, instead of questioning a nice girl like you?"

"Thanks, Sam," I said.

"Nothing to thank me for, Marabella. It's not right, that's what it is." He got up, came over, and patted me on my arm. "As if you didn't have enough heartache, with your mother gone."

I choked a little on my tea, as he sat back down.

"What's the matter, is there maybe something wrong with the tea? I'll make a new cup." He was starting to get up again.

"No, no, it's fine, Sam. Really." I waved him back onto the sofa. "Delicious as usual. I'm just…a little nervous, that's all."

He leaned back. "And no wonder, you poor girl. Why do the nicest ones have all the trouble, I'll never understand."

I felt positively bathed in fatherly concern. I really loved this man. But it was time to get back to my mother, who, by the way, I was sure would have preferred to be sitting in Sam's chair herself.

I got up and kissed Sam on the cheek. "Thanks for the tea and sympathy, Sam," I said. "It was just what I needed."

He walked me to the door. "Whenever you need a shoulder or a cup of tea, you don't have to ask. I'm always here."

Chapter 10

Lucy's cough was definitely worse, and her cheeks looked sunken. "Lucy, you've got to go over to the clinic," I said.

"It'll pass," she said, smiling at me before another coughing fit took over.

I shook my head and dropped a dollar into her cap. I added another after my mother shot me a look.

"Give her another one, don't be so stingy," my mother muttered.

"Ah," Lucy said. "You're a good girl, you are. I bet your mother would be proud of such a daughter."

My mother squeezed my arm. I beamed at her, which caused Lucy, even in her feverish state, to give me a funny look.

We would have taken the subway to the Village but I was worried about my mother's fragile state, so I got us a cab whose insides smelled like a humongous ashtray. We couldn't get the windows open so we were stuck with the smell for company. I was practically gagging by the time we got out at Chris's street.

Chris lived on a street chockfull of fancy-schmancy

brownstones. Strange, I thought, that a masseuse—all right, a body worker—could afford such a lifestyle.

"Must have been family money, or else something very illegal," said the mind-reader.

Chris's apartment was a second-floor walkup in a brownstone. I buzzed the speakerphone to tell her I was here. I walked behind my mother while she made her way up slowly, gripping the handrail.

"You all right?" I whispered.

"I just need to catch my breath." She stopped half-way up the stairs.

At the top of the stairs, a door opened and Chris poked her head out. "Marabella! I'm so glad to see you!"

"Me, too." I realized I had to make it look like I was having trouble negotiating the stairs. "Old ankle injury," I explained.

"Good thinking," my mother mumbled, clambering up the rest of the way ahead of me and going inside.

A puzzled expression appeared on Chris's face as I walked inside with her. "I felt a...presence...come in with you," she said. "Did you feel it, too?" She shivered, drawing her glittery purple shawl, which matched her glittery purple top, tighter around her shoulders.

"Probably a draft," I said. "Getting windy out. Strange weather this time of year, isn't it? Unpredictable. Could be hurricane season. Feels like anything could blow its way in."

She giggled. "Just like Oz. That's one of my all-time favorite movies."

This was an understatement. Chris's living room could have taken up residence in Emerald City. There were plaster busts of Dorothy, the Lion, the Scarecrow, and Tin Man, a mural of the tornado scene complete with a dead witch's feet sticking out from under the house, blow-ups of the Wizard and the good and bad witches, and a large plush Toto. A pair of red patent-leather pumps hung from a mirror. Glass and silver art deco objects served to gild the lily.

"There's no place like home," I murmured.

Chris nodded then said, "This isn't where I do treatments, of course. That room is very professional and rather severe."

"Tell her you'd love to see where she does her work," my mother hissed in my ear.

Chris stopped and seemed to sniff the air. "You know, I really feel…something…" She shrugged. "Well, it's probably harmless, whatever it is. I don't feel anything negative in the air. So don't worry." She smiled at me.

"Negative, huh?" my mother said in my ear.

Harmless, huh? I thought.

"Marabella, I'm so sorry, I forgot to ask you. Your mother…"

"Um, she…" It was all I could do to nod my head.

"Oh, it can be so difficult to deal with a loved one's passing," she said in a soothing voice. "I'll get us some tea. I have water brewing. Be right back."

"Now's our chance," my mother said, full of energy again. She whipped over to the delicate little white desk in the corner and began rummaging through the drawers.

"Ma," I said, shocked.

"Shhh, let me work," she said, quickly sorting through papers.

I walked over to her. "Not only is this illegal or whatever, the important stuff is probably all locked up." I pointed to the deep-set bottom drawer, which was, indeed, locked.

"Turn your back," my mother said.

I obeyed. "Hurry up, she'll be coming back in a minute."

"Aha! Oho!" came from behind me.

I turned around, and my mother swept the papers back into the desk with two seconds to spare before Chris made her way in with her tray of goodies, which she set before us as if it were a banquet. We sank into silver-trimmed armchairs in front of a huge silver-and-glass coffee table. I decided to move cautiously, since nothing on the tray remotely resembled any species of food I'd had even a nodding acquaintance with. There were giant white things that looked like man-eating plants, a fleshy reddish pulpy substance surrounded by a grayish sauce and bits of dark green that looked like seaweed—for garnish, I guessed.

"It's all natural, and this—" She pointed to the pulp."—is my own recipe. It's good for you, trust me."

I declined the food and accepted a cup of the *eau de tree*, instead, with plenty of milk and sugar. Both substances were raw, of course, and I tried not to imagine zillions of bacteria saying, "Ready, Set, Go!" as they took off for a great adventure in my insides.

"Chris," I set down my cup and got to the point. "How do you feel about what happened to Dr. Ditstein?"

Her eyes filled, and I could see her fingers trembling. "I still can't really believe it. Who'd want to harm such a beautiful person? I can't talk about it." She sniffed and reached into the pocket of her flowered purple pants for a Kleenex, dabbing her eyes.

"I'm sorry to upset you, but I think we need to talk about this. After all, somebody killed that beautiful person," I said.

She flinched. "How can you be so cruel? I thought you were a good person," she reproached.

"I didn't cause Dr. Ditstein's death," I reminded her. "But someone did. Don't you think that someone should be punished?"

Mopping her wet face, she stared at me a few minutes, then something flickered behind her eyes. "Yes," she said, her voice hard, "very definitely, absolutely, they should be punished."

"So, what we need to do is first establish our own whereabouts on that night," I said, trying to lead her in the direction I wanted her to follow.

My mother was patting my back behind my chair.

"That's my girl," my mother said.

"This way, we can use a process of elimination. Of course," I added, "we know that we didn't do it."

"Elimination?" Chris said, looking a little dazed. "You think one of *us* did it? One of the group?"

"It's possible," I said. "In fact, it's pretty likely."

"Why do you think so?"

"Look at the timing. Because who else would have such access to her apartment but one of us, one of her group?"

A few years ago, Dr. Ditstein had cut way back on her patient load because of her commitments to research on children, she'd said. So we—the members of her group therapy sessions—were it. "And because who else would have a reason?" I asked.

Of course, there was also Dr. Ditstein's boyfriend. And Dr. Shokum. But I didn't need to discuss them with Chris.

"What reason?" She had her hand against her mouth. "She was helping us with our problems. That's like, uh, killing the goose, you know…"

"That laid the golden eggs," I said, trying to be patient about her logic, though it set my teeth on edge. "Well, maybe one of us didn't think she was such a hot…goose. Anyway—" I segued into my trap, "—you didn't happen to be anywhere near her office Thursday, did you? Because you might have seen something suspicious."

Her eyes flew open. "Oh, no, Thursday isn't my appointment day. I go on Tuesday at ten a.m., before my first client. My clients never come in before noon, usually. I mean, who wants to get a massage first thing in the morning? You don't start getting stressed out till the afternoon, so that's when they start piling in. Sometimes I've got them back-to-back, so to speak, till eight at night." She giggled. "Of course, they're not really back-to-back. That was just an expression. I give a very personalized, individualized service. Very client-oriented." Narrowing her eyes, she gave me an appraising look. "You know, speaking frankly, I hope you don't mind if I speak frankly, but you really look stressed out and I mean really. I bet you could really use some good bodywork. Not that I'm trying to sell my services." She giggled again, a habit which was beginning to stress me out.

"Gee, thanks for noticing," I said, giving her a wide smile and nod of appreciation. "One of these days, when I have time. Speaking of time," I said, though we hadn't been, but I figured she wouldn't have followed the sequence of conversation too closely, "do you have clients back-to-back on Thursdays?"

Chris wrinkled her forehead in concentration. "Thursdays, well, usually I have Marcy at one, she comes while her kids are at school, you know how stressed out you get with little kids." I didn't know, but I nodded to encourage her. "But she couldn't come because her middle one, that's the nine-year-old, had an earache. That must be so painful. Have you ever had one?"

I gritted my teeth. "No, can't say I have. But who came after Marcy didn't?" I tried to smile, but it may have come out more like teeth-baring.

"Uh, my two-thirty, that's Tom, he comes before he

starts his shift at the hospital. He's an orderly, and he threw his back out trying to get a patient on a stretcher into an elevator that closed its doors on him." She shuddered. "It must have been awful. And you'd think at a hospital, they could fix him up, but nobody could take the pain away, until I started working with him," she said, beaming.

"You must be really good at your work," I said, after my mother poked me in the ribs, muttering, "Keep her talking."

She grinned, trying unsuccessfully to look modest. "After Tom, there's Mrs. Reilly, my four o'clock. She's sixty-five and such a sweetheart. She calls me her little dolly." I geared myself up for the forthcoming giggle. "She says I make her feel like fifty again."

"Amazing," I murmured.

"Ken comes at five-thirty." She made a face. "I wish he didn't, between you and me and the wall."

I never did understand this expression but nodded at her as if I did. "What's the problem?"

She sighed. "Most of my clients are, you know, just so into getting relaxed, feeling good, and really respecting my work."

"As well they should." I actually heard myself using one of my mother's expressions.

"Well, Ken doesn't...seem to respect that," Chris said, wrinkling her nose. "Or me. I mean, he's always making suggestive remarks, just a hint, nothing that I could really catch him on. But it's not very pleasant."

"That must be..." I searched for a word.

"It's very painful to me," she finished. "As a professional, I mean."

"I understand," I soothed.

She looked mollified.

"And your seven o'clock?" I asked.

"Oh, that's Harmony Light. She's another body worker, and we work on each other to give ourselves a break. Otherwise, *I'd* get stressed out, you know?" Giggle, giggle. "I go to her on Mondays. She's just down the street, so I don't have to take a lot of time out."

"Harmony is your last appointment on Thursdays?" I asked.

She nodded. "After that, I'm ready to collapse. So I just turn on some really soothing music that just blends in with my surroundings and sit on the floor in the lotus position for about twenty minutes. It really does the trick."

"I know just what you mean," I said. "For me, it's the sofa and TV."

"You'd really be better off with a little meditation or at least some quiet time," she said. "Much better for your poor jangly nerves, I'm sure."

"I'm sure, too," I said. "Oh, by the way, you wouldn't happen to have Harmony Light's phone number, would you?"

She looked shocked. "That's therapist-client confidentiality," she said. "By the way, how did you get my phone number, Marabella?" The softness seemed to melt before my eyes.

"Tell her you looked in the professional section of the phone book," sounded in my ear.

"Oh, I found it in the phone book."

She looked pleased. "Oh, didn't they do my ad up nice? You should have seen the one they did in last year's phone book. Awful. I tried to get my money back, but no go. You know how big corporations are, you can't win."

"I know," I said.

I took another sip, which was just about all my stomach could stomach, and put my cup down. "Aaah, that was good. Thank you so much for the tea and goodies." I got up from the chair. My mother followed suit.

Chris looked a little upset. "But you hardly ate a thing. Didn't you like it?"

"Loved it, but I don't want to ruin my lunch." I patted my stomach and winked. Walking toward the door, I said, "Oh, just one more thing…"

"Shades of Columbo," my mother said.

I wanted to smack her.

Chris looked startled. "What?"

"Um, how long are your sessions? Just in case—" I thought quickly. "—I can schedule one sometime."

The relief spread over her face. "Oh, about fifty minutes. You know, the fifty-minute-hour. Just like—" She sniffed into her handkerchief. "—poor Dr. Ditstein."

She closed the door as we made our way down the stairs, not quite as slowly this time, since going down was easier on my mother than going up. Less strain on her cardiovascular system, which was not exactly in great shape.

As soon as a cab, whose windows were fortunately wide open, got us home and we were safely ensconced in my apartment, I settled my mother on the sofa. Then I pounced.

"Okay." I planted myself in front of her and assumed my best questioning position: arms folded across my chest. "What was all that 'turn your back' stuff back there when you were rifling through Chris's papers? And what was the 'Aha, Oho,' business?"

Her eyes had a definite gleam. Ignoring my first question, she said, "What do you suppose I found in that secret drawer of hers?"

I sighed. "Ma, I'm no good at *Jeopardy*, either. Why don't you just tell me what you found?"

She was really enjoying this. Leaning back against the cushions, she said, "I found a birth certificate."

I was getting a tad irritated. "Okay."

She was grinning from ear to ear. "An important birth certificate."

"Everyone has a birth certificate, Ma, that they usually keep in a locked drawer," I said, enunciating clearly, "because they don't want people looking at their private papers."

She snorted. "Not this kind of birth certificate, sweetheart."

"What, already?"

She was playing my nerves like a beginning violin student.

"A birth certificate that belonged to a baby boy, sweetheart," my mother said triumphantly. "Your Christine is really a Christopher."

Chapter 11

It took me a few minutes to digest this information. But as I absorbed it, it made sense to me. There had always been something nagging at me about Chris, something not quite kosher. Then it hit me: that something was her Adam's apple. Men have them, women don't.

"Okay, so what does this mean in terms of Chris's status as a suspect?"

She picked up the marker lying on the coffee table and tapped her teeth. "Hmmm, I can see some interesting possibilities here."

"For instance?"

"Maybe Chris was being counseled by Dr. Ditstein, and she didn't like the counseling. And another thing. Just because you're a therapist, doesn't necessarily mean you know everything."

"That's not grounds for murder," I said. "It's grounds for malpractice. Get real, Ma."

She threw me a wounded look and shook her head. "Such a mouth on you." Tapping a tune on her teeth, which, by now, were probably contaminated with ink, she said, "Okay, try this for size. How about blackmail?"

I stared at her. "I always knew you were jealous of her, but how could you sink so low?"

She did not look at all abashed. "Think about it. Christopher-Christine has a sex change operation, which comes out in therapy. Now Christine has a boyfriend, who she doesn't want to know that she used to be a he. Dr. Ditstein sees a way to make a bundle. Christine gets tired of paying for silence. So, bang! Or—" She nodded. "—maybe they were both interested in the same man. So Dr. Ditstein decides to fix Christine's wagon good, and tells the boyfriend that his girlfriend was a boyfriend. And then she/he does her in."

"You've been watching too many TV movies," I said.

She gave me a reproachful look. "I haven't seen TV in—"

"A week," I finished for her, feeling like a slug for reminding her.

"I still like the blackmail idea," she said.

The idea that Dr. Ditstein would have done such a heinous deed was such a betrayal of my trust that it was totally unthinkable. I reminded myself that there were other, more likely possibilities. The other members of the group, for instance.

Then I remembered why I'd asked Chris about the timing of her sessions. Even to my math-o-phobic mind, her fifty-minute hour left forty minutes in between sessions, since her sessions were scheduled every hour and a half. I did some calculations. Forty minutes was time enough for her to get to Dr. Ditstein's apartment on the East Side, do the dirty deed, and hurry home to work on the next body, so to speak. Not only that, I recalled, she'd had a one o'clock cancellation, the woman whose kid had the ear infection. But that was way too early. With a shudder, I remembered that Dr. Ditstein's body had still felt warm when I found her.

But now there was something else. Why would I think that Chris was necessarily telling the truth about her clients as to who showed up and who didn't that day, since she'd lied—okay, omitted, the truth—about her sex change? What about Chris's colleague, Harmony Light? If she didn't show, would she lie for Chris? Was there a massage therapist code of silence? I made a note to look up her number in the yellow pages and ask the cops to check out Chris's alibi.

And wasn't it a bit odd that Christine hadn't ever talked about her previous gender state in group? After all, wasn't group the place to unburden yourself? *Whatever happened to trust?* I wondered. *Who knows what other secrets have not been bared in group? There could be all sorts of serious nuttiness bubbling underneath, never rising to the surface, just waiting to come to a furious boil. Speaking of nuttiness, what about Dr. Shokum?*

No one from the group had ever seen him, and as far as the rumor mill had it, none of his patients ever had, either. But that didn't mean that he didn't go out when he thought no one else was around. Or that he didn't have something against Dr. Ditstein. Something bad enough to kill for.

Chapter 12

The rock music was blasting away as usual when I rushed into the Healthy Woman Fitness Center after work the next night. Julie-the-svelte, as Toniann and I referred to her, was frowning prettily at me at the front desk.

"Bad girl!" she shouted over the music. "You haven't been here in a long time!"

I looked properly ashamed. "I'll make up for it tonight!" I shouted back.

Toniann and I had tried for years to get them to tone down the volume, to no avail. According to Julie, the other customers, whom she referred to as clients, loved it. Of course, most of them had barely reached drinking age.

Julie gave me her perfunctory smile. "Class is starting, better hurry up, hon!"

I ran into the locker room, fiddled with the combination lock, which always gave me trouble, and finally got it to unlock. I changed out of my work clothes, hung them up in the locker, and changed into the only sweats I owned that my mother wouldn't wear. She hated Kelly green. I thought it brought out my green eyes.

Toniann waved at me across the exercise floor, and I walked over to join her. She was dressed in spotless white, from head to toe. Even her sneakers were sparkling white.

"How do you do that?" I asked, looking down at her feet.

"Shoe polish," she said. "Once a week. Easy."

"I'm lucky I even made it to class."

Chloe, the aerobics instructor, clad in a skin-tight silver leotard, danced across the floor to the front of the room. The walls were lined with full-length mirrors, the better to motivate us, I guess. Or to scare the hell out of those of us who weren't among the svelte. I was one of those unfortunates. No matter how much I dieted and exercised, I still had what was politely called a "full figure." Translation: a bit too much figure, especially around the hips. I'd give my eyeteeth to have Toniann's long, slender body.

"It's in my genes," she told me. "The Nordic side. They're all pretty leggy. But I wish I had half your chest."

Generous bosoms and hips were my genetic portion. A slim body and long legs weren't.

Chloe barked at us over the music. "Let's go, girls! Remember, your body will thank you!"

Not my body, I thought. *My body will curse at me.* Before I grabbed the painkillers I kept in stock for after exercise.

After we warmed up with neck, shoulder, and side stretches, we went into aerobics, my ears pounding from the music. Toniann and I had tried ear plugs. That didn't work, because we couldn't hear the instructor. I couldn't believe that even the nymphets in the class actually liked it, but they were grooving on it, snapping their gum to the beat.

"Jumping jacks!" Chloe screamed, leaping into the air like a gazelle.

I huffed and puffed. "Maybe we're getting too old for this!" I yelled to Toniann.

"No way!" Toniann yelled back. "Just keep on going!"

"Heel pumps in four, rocking horse in four!" shrieked Chloe.

I pumped and rocked.

"Cross over into grapevine!"

I grapevined, wondering whatever happened to the California raisins. Probably keeled over and collapsed from all that grapevining.

Chloe put us through a bunch of squats, kicks, and knee lifts. When I was about ready to drop, she cooled us down. I checked to see if I still had a pulse and trailed Toniann into the locker room. I huddled in a corner as I stripped and quickly covered myself up with a beach towel. Not only was I a locker-room prude, but the sight of all these great bodies didn't exactly make me want to strut my stuff. Toniann always told me I had a really sexy figure, and I should stop wishing I looked like someone else. It wasn't easy when the national ideal these days was Ms. Anorexia. Jane Russell was fifty years out of date. Hell, even Marilyn Monroe would be considered fat by twenty-first-century standards.

After Toniann and I showered, we put on bathing suits and settled into the whirlpool. "Aaah," I said, as my body collapsed in gratitude.

Two women lounging across from us were communicating in a language I'd never heard before. Whatever it was, I was positive they were making fun of us in it, because they kept looking at us and giggling to each other. I glared at them, but it didn't do any good. The giggles got even louder.

"This is the life," Toniann said, closing her eyes.

"Speaking of life, I haven't heard anything from the cops."

"No news is good news," she said.

"Yeah, right. But I don't suppose they're straining themselves to make a big effort to find the real killer."

She patted my shoulder. "They'll find him or her, don't worry."

"What, me worry?" I tried to laugh.

"One day at a time." Then as if trying to change to a more promising subject, she said, "Hey, what's with the animal—" She made some lascivious growling sounds. "—doctor?"

The mention of John made me think animal thoughts, too. "We're going out Friday night. A long, lovely dinner at Le Bijoux."

She sighed. "How romantic. I wish Peter and I could do an evening like that. I'm lucky if, these days, we get to a pizza joint."

"But it'll all be worth it when he graduates from law school," I said. "You shouldn't complain. You're the one who encouraged him to go back to school in the first place, remember?"

"That's because I thought he was wasting his potential as a paralegal."

"You were right," I said. "So—one day at a time."

We laughed and clambered out of the Jacuzzi.

Chapter 13

As for the next suspect on my list, Shokum, I figured getting inside his apartment would take a minor miracle. After I discussed my theory with my mother, I had to forcibly restrain her from turning into the Cheshire cat and wafting over to his apartment that minute.

"Rest for a while, first, Ma."

By the time I finished tucking her up with the afghan and pillows on the sofa, her eyes were drooping with sleep. I went into the bedroom and did a crossword to clear my head. At the point where Indonesian metal product intersected with Australian insect, the wheels began to turn.

Besides her exhaustion, there was another reason not to rush my mother into a break-and-entry at Shokum's. It might be more productive if I first attempted to gain lawful entry and talk to him in person. This way, I could hopefully soften him up enough to get some information out of him, such as what he'd been doing just before I found Dr. Ditstein. Then I realized he probably wouldn't tell me a damn thing. As a shrink, albeit possibly only on the phone, even he had to be clued in enough to know what I was fishing for.

But there was still a good reason to try to do the in-person scene first. I'd get some sense of Shokum *in situ*, in his own claustrophobic little habitat, and maybe that could answer some questions. I could always send in the heavy artillery, i.e., my mother, later. And she really did need a rest.

Convincing Shokum to let me in behind his peephole was going to take some doing, though. Like what?

I had it. I'd tell him I needed another therapist, ASAP, to help me work out my feelings of grief and loss about Dr. Ditstein. And, though I'd heard the rumor that he only treated patients on the phone, I was interviewing replacements, and that had to be done in person. The idea that I was an eight-year-therapy veteran ought to tempt him. Think of the phone mileage he could get from another eight years. He could become a major shareholder in AT&T.

I opened the phone book and turned to the Yellow Pages marked "Psychologists." I half expected Shokum to be listed in his own little esoteric sub-category— "psychologists-phone"—but there he was, in alphabetical order, right in the mainstream. Then I punched in his number.

"Dr. Shokum, here." An incredibly sexy voice came on the line after one ring. Must have been waiting for customers, willing it to ring.

"Dr. Shokum," I breathed, using my best "flies with honey" manner, "I'm Marabella Vinegar, a patient—a former patient—of Dr. Ditstein's. I'm so glad I found you in." I figured it would be better if he thought I wasn't aware of his little peculiarities.

A silence ensued. Then a throat clearing. "Ah, yes, tragic, tragic thing," he murmured. The voice deepened, became more honeyed: "How are you?" The effect was as if he were blowing directly in my ear, taking little bites, nibbling delicately, licking around the edges with his probing tongue. *What a wonderful instrument the telephone is*, I thought, trying to press it harder against my head.

"I—" I had to remember that I was supposed to be interviewing him, not getting an ear-job. "I haven't been feeling very well," I said, trying to stick to a description of my general state of mind, not my raging hormones. This was not easy.

"Tell me how I can help," he purred. "Anything I can do. Anything at all."

Oh, the possibilities that conjured up. I tried to concentrate: *Marabella, remember your purpose. This man could have done in Dr. Ditstein. Not to mention be neurotic as hell*. Or was he? Maybe this was all just crazy gossip, started by some disgruntled patient. Or maybe it was part of an image—not leaving his apartment, doing therapy on the phone. Part of a Dracula-type fetish, perhaps? A walk on the dark side? The man could be keeping some very strange objects in that apartment. Whips and chains? A satin-lined coffin to sleep in?

"Um, I'm kind of stuck, that is…" I fumbled for the right words. "I was a longtime, a very longtime patient of Dr. Ditstein. And now…"

"I understand completely," he crooned. "You need someone to talk to."

"Yes, someone to talk to," I said, trying unsuccessfully to ignore the waves of heat racing through my body. It was—he was—too much for my right ear and the rest of my poor, sex-starved body. My body couldn't remember the last time I'd had any, and was obviously on a roll. Finally, I gave up and sank down on the bed, the phone glued to my ear as he continued to murmur deep, heartfelt nothings into the receiver. My innermost parts began to twitch and tingle, my breathing rapidly reached a crescendo. "Yes, oh, yes, yes, yes, to talk to," I gasped. Molly Bloom had nothing on me at this moment. Finally sated, I unstuck the phone. God, this was embarrassing. What would he think?

I got my answer soon enough. "I hope it—I—was good for you," he whispered.

"Uh," I said, trying to clear the mucous from my head and everything else, "I don't usually…"

"No need to explain," he intoned. "I was with you, all the way."

This was his phone therapy? Did this fall under the category of sexual harassment? Sex with a patient's ear?

"I need to see you. I mean—" I said, thinking rapidly, "—I'm starting to interview therapists, you know, to continue treatment. And also," I threw in, "to work on my feelings of loss and grief about Dr. Ditstein."

Another silence. Then, "I do not generally hold sessions in person. My patients," he oozed, "generally find that my telephone sessions provide complete satisfaction."

"Oh, I understand—completely." I matched his tone. "But I need to at least have an initial interview in-person. In order to make a more responsible choice and comparison. After all, I've been with Dr. Ditstein for eight years. And," I lied, "I already have three other therapists that friends have offered me whom I'm scheduled to interview. This week," I threw in for good measure, turning the screws. He would not want to lose such a potential reach-out-and-touchable gold mine. "And it would have to be after work. I'm at Chelsea College till around five."

Another silence. I could hear his little gray cells busily pondering the big question: To keep my door closed or to entice this potential cash cow?

A throat clearing. "Well, I suppose I could make an exception and allow you to conduct an interview. But you must appreciate that this is not normally my practice. And that I have an extremely tight schedule. So I can squeeze you in for…" A rustling of paper. "…about thirty minutes this afternoon around five-thirty. I have a cancellation."

"Fine, terrific," I said. "I appreciate you taking the time. But, you understand, I have to be able to know what—whom I'm getting."

A low, throbbing chuckle, which set my ear to vibrating again.

I bid him a hasty goodbye and hung up. Dripping wet.

Chapter 14

I never made it to Shokum's inner sanctum that day. I spent most of the afternoon and evening getting booked, photographed, and fingerprinted at the police station. And charged with second-degree murder.

Turns out that some scumbag—somebody in my group?—informed Detective Rivera that I had been heard screaming at Dr. Ditstein. That someone, it seemed, had been early for his—or her—appointment and was waiting in the foyer that led to Dr. Ditstein's room for individual sessions. He or she heard me accusing her of ruining my life. Yelling that it was all her fault. Shrieking that I hated her guts.

"Not only that," Rivera informed me. "We found the threatening letter you sent to Dr. Ditstein, in her mailbox."

"I never sent her any letter," I said. "And what makes you think it was from me?"

"Maybe because it had your address on the envelope," he said, with a smirk.

Pushing aside thoughts of getting revenge on the scurvy slime who was setting me up, I remembered what happened with the so-called argument I had with Dr. Ditstein. That was the day her old white noise machine died, and my loud and angry voice could be distinctly heard, yelling and screaming about my problems with my mother that had yet to be resolved in therapy. Dr. Ditstein had encouraged me to "let it all hang out," in terms of my rage and fantasies. She was an active supporter of role playing, which, in my case, meant that she stood in for my mother.

"Feelings are always healthy," she'd said. "Venting them in a safe place is a good way to let them dissipate without hurting you or the person you feel rage about."

Good old Dr. Ditstein. I'd felt so much better after that session, I'd even been able to talk to my mother the next day without either blowing up at her or gobbling peanut butter out of the jar with a tablespoon, my usual method of dealing with my post-anger-at-my-mother-syndrome.

Now it was coming back to haunt me, pardon the expression. And maybe hang me, thanks to some ratfink from the group. I explained to Rivera what happened. He asked if I had any proof. Of course I didn't, I said. Unless, it dawned on me, there might be something in Dr. Ditstein's files—that I must have missed when my mother kidnapped them. Rivera reminded me that those files were confidential. Of course, the fact that I was rapidly being hung out to dry by some helpful member of the group—who?—didn't matter.

He went off to consult with the prosecutor about the charge against me, while I was interviewed by somebody from the Criminal Justice Agency, to decide whether or not I should be sent to jail.

Since I had no previous criminal record—I guessed being caught smoking pot at a couple of rock concerts in the park didn't really count—and wasn't about to flee, maybe I could throw myself on the judge's mercy.

Rivera decided that I'd threatened to kill my therapist, instead of my mother, about whom I'd been having serious homicidal thoughts. To him, this, plus finding me with the corpse, qualified me as perp of the month.

Never mind that Rivera said Dr. Ditstein was killed with a .38 caliber pistol. And that the only gun I'd ever owned was a water pistol in second grade, which I employed to fight back against the boys who were always squirting water down my back. As for motive—what was mine supposed to be, anyway? An unwholesome attachment of eight years? Fear of her blabbing my deep dark secrets? I was more than ready and eager to blab them myself whenever a crisis struck. On occasion, I had actually been accused of treating my friends as a giant ear, there for the sole purpose of hearing me out.

The subject of ears evoked very warm memories of the telephone episode earlier in the day, which I quickly squelched.

Getting all hot and bothered in a police station was probably not a great idea. I switched to thoughts of Otis Pinckney, which had the immediate effect of a cold shower. I'd used my phone call to call Toniann, who said she'd call Otis, promising to drag him down here as fast as she could. That was an hour ago.

I began thinking about why somebody would've called the cops about me. Maybe he or she was trying to frame me because he or she did it?

Since my behind was getting sore from sitting in a hard-backed chair, I got up, popped a Xanax, and paced for a while. The room was small and dank, smelling of mold, with vile yellow paint peeling off the walls.

Probably it was about the size of a jail cell, I thought, except there would also be a metal cot and a toilet, with no lid. Was there a sink? Where did they keep the toilet paper? I'd lay bets it wasn't Charmin, either, but some cheap, scratchy gray stuff.

Toniann was racing down the corridor with Otis huffing and puffing in her wake, like the Queen Mary. She blew into the room, hugged me, and wailed, "This is terrible!"

"No shit," said Otis, heaving his green-plaid-suited bulk into a chair that protested by creaking and wobbling underneath him. He mopped his moon face with a large green handkerchief then took off his steamed-up tortoise-shell glasses and polished the lenses. I knew better than to rush him into anything. Otis would never be accused of rushing into anything, except maybe where a lot of money was involved. Since I would be a charity case of Toniann's, he wasn't moving any too quickly.

"Otis," I said, trying to control my impatience, "I want to thank you for helping me out here. I truly appreciate it."

"Not at all, not at all." He waved his meaty hands in a gesture worthy of a duke addressing his serfdom. "Otis Pinckney for the underdog. That's his motto."

One of Otis's less-endearing traits was his habit of referring to himself in the third person. As for his so-called social conscience, it was nonexistent, except for those who might possibly be able to do him some good if he ran for office. Maybe he was hoping to get some mileage out of defending me. Selling his story to a TV movie of the week, maybe? "Woman kills therapist after eight-year-relationship," or, "Too much therapy can kill"?

Toniann was crossing and uncrossing her rose-colored pant legs, something she did when she was either trying to show off her best feature or was agitated. I figured it was agitation in this case, since she'd hardly waste it on Otis. "Let's get her out of here, Otis. Do what you have to do. And hurry, please," she said.

Telling Otis to hurry was like telling grass to grow faster. He eased his plaid bulk off the chair, one butt-cheek at a time, and got to his feet. "Okay, we gotta talk to the detective." He ruffled through some papers, "They said unpremeditated, okay." He plodded to the doorway and down the corridor. A minute later, I heard him say, "Hey, who do we gotta see for my client here, the Murder Two."

I willed myself not to move. Otherwise, I was going to kill him, which would make me a Murder Two, Two. "He might as well be working for the DA," I said to Toniann. "He's got me tried and convicted already, after being here for five minutes."

Toniann patted my arm and clucked her tongue. "He's trying to negotiate with the cops, he's just talking their language, that's all. Don't worry, he'll take good care of you."

I had profound doubts of that, but I thanked her for her support. "If it wasn't for you, I'd be a total mess right now." I grabbed her hands. I could feel my hands trembling and the rest of my body starting to shake with huge sobs. Tears poured down my face, and I couldn't stop them. I just couldn't take one more thing, that's all. My rope had just ended.

She squeezed my shoulder and dug out a Kleenex. "Here, blow," she said. "It's good that you're crying. You needed a good cry. After all, you lost your mother, and then your therapist. And then all this happened."

"And then there's—" I stopped in mid-sentence. My mother must be worried sick about me. How was I going to let her know I was all right, well, at least, not in agony? Not only that, there was my missed appointment with Shokum. Probably my only chance. What was I going to tell him? "Oh, sorry I couldn't make it, I was busy being fingerprinted?"

"What?"

"Um, my…shrink," I said. "I miss my therapist."

"Yeah, I'm sure. I missed mine for a while, too, after he was indicted for having sex with his patients. You know," she said, looking puzzled, "I often wonder why he never approached me, you know, that way."

Sometimes I couldn't believe this was an otherwise intelligent, hip woman of the twenty-first century. "It's not quite the same," I said.

"Oh, I know." She nodded her head. "I only saw Dr. Charles for a couple of months. You saw Dr. Ditstein for a long time, and you had a really good relationship with her," Toniann said. "How many years was it? Three? Four?"

"Eight," I said, feeling my face get hot. She gaped then looked away. "Some of us have a lot to work out," I said.

Clumping sounds signaled Otis's return. "Okay, we've gotta get to the arraignment." He pointed to me. Turning to Toniann, he said, "Wait here. It shouldn't be too long. Camino likes his cocktails early."

I followed Otis and the prosecutor out of the precinct office over to the courthouse building next door. Judge Camino's courtroom, which was on the second floor, was a veritable Sleeping Beauty's castle. Camino's elegant white head was propped up in his hands, his elbows on a huge pile of papers on his desk. His eyes were half-closed. Probably bored to death. I didn't know whether that was a good or bad sign. The gray-complexioned court clerk down below was shuffling papers in slow motion.

After Otis had a brief discussion with the prosecutor, he clumped back to me. "Cripes, he's gonna to be in a helluva mood, especially if I startle him," Otis whispered, indicating the judge. He shook his head and shambled to the bench. "Good day, Your Honor," he said quietly.

"Whuzzat?" Camino jerked upright, his robe rustling, looking furious. Probably embarrassed at being caught half-asleep. Not a good omen. "You were saying?"

"Good day, Your Honor," Otis repeated.

"Not that, you fool," Camino said. "What's the case?"

"Right. My client, here, Ms. Vinegar—"

I could see Camino trying to stifle a grin. Turning to Otis, he said. "So, give me the papers for the name change. I don't blame you one bit, miss," he said, with a smile. "Though I must say, I thought it was another one of Pinckney's feeble attempts at humor."

Otis sighed. "Your Honor, Ms. Vinegar here has been charged with murder in the second degree. The charges are ridiculous—"

"I'll be the judge of that." Camino stared at me, his mustache twitching. "Geez. It's always the quiet, good-looking ones."

"I didn't—" I started to protest.

Otis pinched my arm. "Your Honor, sir, Ms. Vinegar is not guilty of anything. There isn't a shred of evidence. And she's never been in trouble with the law."

"Except for a couple of pot-smoking incidents when I was little more than a mere child," I muttered under my breath.

"Shhh." Otis glared at me. "She's regularly employed at Chelsea College, in the…" He looked at me.

"Public relations department," I said.

"Right. Where she's worked for…"

"Nineteen years."

"Right. She lives in the area, in an apartment on…"

"West Ninety-sixth Street."

"Right. Where she has lived for…"

"Nineteen years."

"Right—"

Camino interrupted, "All right, you two, cut the Alphonse and Gaston routine. Give me the paperwork."

Otis handed up the file. Camino opened it, flipped through it, gave an "Mmmmm," and an "Ummmm," and closed the file.

He motioned to the prosecutor to come to the bench. A short period of low-voice discussion among the three of them was next, followed by Otis and the prosecutor returning to their seats.

Camino harrumphed. "This case is cockamamie crap. They've got an anonymous typed letter in an envelope with a typed address. And the other thing, she's accused of what, yelling? This is evidence?"

I let out my breath. He was on my side?

"Young woman," Camino said, "go home and don't get into any more trouble, please. Like finding any more bodies. And, uh, try not to yell anymore." He actually seemed to twinkle at me.

"Right," said Otis.

Camino checked his watch and stood up, drawing his robe around him. "Scram. I'm late."

"Right."

"Shut up, Pinckney." Camino looked down at some other papers on his desk. "Michaelson, file these under Wooten versus Wooten, damn their eyes. Another damn stupid waste of my time…"

The gray-faced clerk got up from his chair with a groan and plodded to the bench.

"Thank you, Your Honor, sir," Otis said, practically genuflecting.

We made our way back to Toniann at the precinct office.

"Okay, we're done," Otis told her "Those cops were

wasting everyone's time. There's no case."

"Thank God," Toniann and I said in unison.

He turned to Toniann. "And I wasted my time."

"I really appreciate this, Otis," I said. "A lot."

"Just try to keep out of trouble," he said to me.

I got to my feet. "How soon can we leave?" Not only was I not thrilled with the ambience, but I was worried about my mother. She could be *in extremis* before I got home. My nerves couldn't handle another death scene at this point.

Otis looked annoyed. "These things can't be done in a minute. There's paperwork. Which I have to take care of."

"Sorry," I said, abashed. "Look, Otis, thanks a lot, from the bottom of my heart. Otis Pinckney is the best." I laid it on with a trowel.

He beamed, which turned his moon face into a jack-o-lantern.

I tried to make conversation. "So, how's the campaign going?"

He stuck his thumbs into the bands of his green suspenders, snapping them. "Of course, we still have money to raise." He warmed to his subject. "You can't have enough money for an election campaign these days. Goddamn outta sight expensive TV spots. Even radio." He lumbered to his feet again. "Don't go away," he said to me, chuckling as he went out into the corridor.

"This is whose hands I'm putting my life in?" I said to Toniann. "Mr. Cheap Yuks?"

"He's taking care of everything, that's the important thing."

I could feel exhaustion creeping over me like kudzu. I had trouble even keep my eyes focused and I felt dizzy.

"What's the matter?" Toniann leaned over me anxiously, trying to sit me up in my chair.

I shook my head, trying to clear it out. "Just very tired. I need to go home and crawl into bed for about two days." Of course, I wasn't going to be able to do that, since I had to deal with my mother when I got home. And then call Dr. Shokum and try to reschedule. And somehow have the energy to go to work tomorrow. That brought up pleasant, animal-like thoughts involving a certain animal doctor. I sighed. How could I think romantic thoughts at a time like this? Was I sick?

"Are you sick?" Toniann was asking.

"Yes," I said, not really listening.

"Should I call a, whatever they have here, a matron?"

I grimaced. "Not yet."

Otis finally came back. "Okay, you can go home now," he said. "But don't—"

"Leave town," I said.

He nodded solemnly. "Right."

Toniann looked at him. "You just want to make sure Marabella's okay, right? Because Otis Pinckney really cares."

Otis bobbed his head up and down, making it look like a beach ball. "Right. Otis Pinckney always cares."

"Let's get out of here," I said.

Chapter 15

Toniann and Otis dropped me off at my apartment building. Clutching my sleeve, Toniann peered into my face. "Are you sure you don't want me to come over? So you won't be alone?"

"I'll be okay, thanks anyway, for everything." I shut the cab door and waved goodbye. I'd have company enough once I got upstairs.

She was wearing out the living room rug in my cut-off gray sweats which fit her perfectly at the bottom and barely, at the top.

"Hi, Ma," I said.

She clutched her chest, saying, "I was worried sick. It would have killed you to pick up the phone?"

I went over to her. "Are you okay? Come sit down. You don't look too good."

She allowed me to lead her to the sofa. "And how am I supposed to look with my daughter God knows where?"

"I'm sorry I couldn't call you, but they only allowed one phone call from the police station."

"You were in jail?" She looked like she was about to faint.

"Let me get you a cup of tea first and I'll tell you." I took off my jacket and headed into the kitchen. "By the way," I said, "any messages on the machine?"

"Dr. Shokum. He wanted to know why you didn't keep your appointment. What a peculiar voice that man has. It almost seems to be vibrating."

I choked.

"What's the matter?"

"Nothing, Ma, just water that went down the wrong way."

"Take a teaspoon of sugar, or you'll get the hiccups," she said.

"That's an old wives' tale," I said. "It doesn't give you the—" Hic. I opened my canister of Sweet 'n' Low.

"It has to be sugar, artificial sweeteners won't work."

"Not true. Anything granular should do it—including sand, ground glass." Hic. But just in case, I opened the cabinet and poked around in the back, behind the boxes of cereal and cocoa. I might still have some of the real stuff from the last party I had. God, that had to have been years ago. It could have grown fuzzy mold by now. Or maybe the roaches ate it. No, there it was, wedged in between the English breakfast tea and the diet cocoa. I sniffed, and it seemed okay, so I swallowed a spoonful.

"Take two for good measure," she said.

"Grrr," I said, taking two and resuming my tea making without hiccups. I couldn't stand it when she was right and I was wrong about things.

"Mothers are supposed to know about such things," came the voice from the living room.

Now she was reading my mind. Well, she was always pretty good at knowing what I was thinking, which, I recalled, when I was a teenager, had been extremely hazardous to my incipient sex life. How was a boy supposed to enjoy making out with me after my mother had taken him aside and told him that I had a very contagious virus which, though it wasn't a venereal disease, could be transmitted through intimate sexual contact and would permanently affect his ability to have children? She only stopped after I found out and threatened to leave home and support myself through prostitution.

I brought in two mugs of tea, strong enough to grow hair on the chest for me, straight, and weak for my mother, with plenty of milk.

"Thank you, sweetheart." Taking a sip, she said, "And just the way I like it. You remembered." She beamed.

One thing for sure, she had definitely mellowed. I was actually beginning to enjoy her company. Sort of.

"Well?"

"Well what, Ma?" I said, slurping because I was trying not to burn my tongue.

She frowned. "A lady doesn't slurp her tea, Marabella."

"You'd rather I got second-degree burns on my tongue?" I put down my mug.

"Fresh, fresh," my mother said, waggling her finger. "Your father would never have put up with that. He had rules, you know."

I sighed. Did I just say I enjoyed her company? To get her off the subject of my father and his legion of rules and regulations, I said, "I'm sorry I couldn't call, but I could only make one phone call."

"Hmmph. So it shouldn't be to your mother?"

"It was for a lawyer, Ma." I didn't even try to explain the problem of calling my home with a cop overhearing me having a conversation with someone who wasn't supposed to exist. As far as they knew, I lived alone.

"Oh." She nodded. "That's right. You need a good lawyer. Who did you call?"

I tried another sip, blowing on the spoon, trying to ignore her disapproving look. "Good may not be the operative word here, since I had to hire Otis Pinckney."

She shook her head. "You told me yourself that you think he's an ambulance chaser, a sleazebag. Why not a real lawyer?"

"Because he took me on as a favor to Toniann, that's why. Everyone else would be out-of-sight expensive, which I can't possibly afford."

She puckered her lip. "Don't you have any savings? Didn't Daddy always tell you to put money aside for emergencies? I'm sure he would never have imagined an emergency like this. Not for his daughter."

I took a big gulp of my tea, which made tears come to my eyes, it was still so hot. "Ma," I said, when I could talk again, "I have two hundred dollars in the bank, that's all."

"Why?"

"Because," I said. "I get paid a barely livable wage, and I have to live."

"Oh," she said, in a small voice. "You never told me you were having a hard time managing. I wish I could help. But there was never much from Daddy's insurance. Only just enough for you and I to live on until…" She lifted her hands, palms out.

"I know, and that's why I never told you. Don't worry, I'll be all right," I said with a lot more confidence than I felt at the moment. "At least I'm out of the joint." I tried to joke.

She narrowed her eyes. "Never mind the jokes. We've got to get this thing solved in a hurry. We're running out of time." She lay back on the cushions.

Was she talking about herself? I could see that she seemed to have gotten a little paler. And sometimes she had to stop for breath in between sentences. With a talker like my mother, that was not an easy task. "Okay, let's get to work. What next, Ms. Marple?"

She practically preened. "Hmmm. Well, why don't you call someone else?

The boyfriend, maybe?"

"Right." But what to say to Mr. Zoltan Karyoli? "*Hi, I'd like to check you out as a murder suspect?*"

"Tell him that you're planning a memorial for Dr. Ditstein," said the-mind-reader.

"Good idea, but do you think he'll go for it?"

"Why not? Especially if you sound very sincere about the whole thing," she said.

"And I have to call Dr. Shokum back. But what am I going to tell him about why I didn't show up?"

"Tell him you came down with a twenty-four-hour bug, and you didn't want to give it to him."

I thought about what a call to Shokum would entail and decided to call Zoltan first. I'd do Shokum, figure of speech, of course, when my mother was sleeping or otherwise occupied. I looked up Zoltan's number, added it to my contact list, and made the call.

"Hah-lo," a voice answered.

"Zoltan Karyoli?"

"Who vants to know?"

I could tell this was going to be fun and games. "Hi, there," I said in my most innocent tones. "I'm Marabella Vinegar, a longtime patient of Dr. Ditstein's."

"Yaas?"

"I'm trying to organize a memorial for her. We members of her group therapy all miss her terribly."

"Yaas?"

"I wondered if I could meet you to talk to you about it," I said. "I thought that you, being a…friend of hers, might be able to give us some ideas on how it should be done."

A long silence. I thought the line had gone dead. "Hello? Are you still there, Mr. Karyoli?"

"I don't know…vhy do you…ho-kay," he finally said.

I pounced. "How about eight tomorrow night at the bar around the corner from Dr. Ditstein's? I'd be sooo grateful for your help, and I'm sure the others will, too."

Another long silence. This time, I shut up and waited.

Another sigh. "Ho-kay. I suppoze it vouldn't kill me to mitt with you."

Hopefully, it wouldn't end up killing me.

After my mother and I ate the dried-out reheated meat loaf, which, she pointed out had been delicious and moist when she first cooked it hours ago, and I apologized again for not calling her from the police station, I settled her on the sofa with a new paperback of an episode of *Murder She Wrote*, and went into the bedroom to prepare for my call to Dr. Shokum.

This time, I wouldn't let him get to my ears. I had a strategy up my sleeve. I turned on my phone, plugged in an earphone, stuck it in my poor defenseless left ear, and found some heavy metal music. I left the right ear open so I'd be able to hear what he said. Then I picked up the land-line phone and punched in his number. That was all I wanted to do, just have a conversation with the man. Not a session, you should pardon the expression.

He answered while a band did their thing to someone's mother, father, and chickens. "Hel-lo," the Voice hummed.

I jacked up the volume on the radio. "This is Marabella Vinegar."

Silence. "I can't make you out."

I bet you can't. "It's Marabella," I yelled. "Sorry I couldn't keep our appointment," I made sneezing and coughing noises, "but I've been really sick."

"I'm sure that noise can't be good for your...well-being," he breathed.

Oh, yes, it can. "Sorry about that. It's a noisy neighbor. Can we reschedule?"

"Strange, it sounds as if it's coming right into the phone," he rumbled.

"Very close quarters," I yelled. "Can we make it Wednesday, say, six o'clock?"

"I'm finding the background noise really disturbing. We'll have to talk about how you can improve your living situation," he purred.

"Fine," I yelled. "Wednesday, six o'clock?"

"All right. But if you cancel this time, we cannot reschedule."

"Don't worry, I'll be there," I said, clicking off. My left ear felt as though it had lost its hearing. Or was probably wishing that it had. Even so, it was better for my equilibrium than certain other types of pollution.

Chapter 16

On my way to the bar to meet Zoltan Karyoli, I popped a Xanax and glanced at the paper, hyperventilating while I conducted a search for my name as a murder suspect. It was there all right, but buried on a back page, and spelled so badly, my own mother wouldn't recognize it. I sent up a prayer of thanks for my bizarre name.

Zoltan didn't notice me when I walked into the bar. He was too busy admiring his reflection in the mirror across from the booth. I hated to break up such a happy couple, but we had business to discuss.

"Hi, I'm Marabella. Thanks for coming."

He glanced at my barely combed hair, my spotty sweatshirt, and jeans, valiantly trying to conceal a look of utter disgust. Even though he made me feel like an inferior being, I had to admit that he was gorgeous.

His white skin had a wonderful sheen to it, almost translucent, giving him an otherworldly, ethereal appearance. The pallor set off his deep-set eyes, which were coal-black and fringed with thick, sooty lashes. They matched his brows and hair, which was waved into a pageboy that rested on his slim shoulders. I couldn't take his eyes off his lips, which were full, red, and pouty. They kept reminding me of someone. Ah. They were clones of the lips of Rudolf Nureyev, who had been gifted with one of the more lustful set of lips in creation. A pure sexual organ. The whole effect was enough to immediately make a woman want to jump Zoltan's bones. And he knew it.

He was done up in a black suede jacket, black pants, and black silk shirt. With studied casualness, he shot the left cuff to accidentally-on-purpose reveal his gold Rolex. Or to indicate how valuable his time was. Or both. When he motioned for me to sit down, the diamond rings on his thin manicured fingers winked at me. I wished I had some place to hide my bitten fingernails and cuticles.

He set down his drink and bestowed a dazzling smile on me. Somehow, I didn't quite trust it. It seemed practiced. He asked me if I wanted anything.

"Um, white wine, please." My eyes were so glued to that mouth, I could barely open mine.

He silently acknowledged my worship. "Ho-kay. Vat you like ve should do about memorial?"

A waitperson came by, and he gave her my order. "I know how much you must miss Dr. Ditstein," I began.

"Uff cosse." He pursed those luscious lips. I fantasized that he was blowing kisses.

"All of us, from her group, feel the same way. So I thought we should have a memorial, a…you know, a sort of a remembrance of Dr. Ditstein, to show our affection for her. Maybe we could all say a little something about what she meant to us, or read a poem or sing a song."

"Vary nizze." He dipped his lashes at me.

"So I thought since you were a…friend of hers…you might like to be there, too."

He put the tips of his fingers together and flashed me

another brilliant smile. It was almost scary, that smile. "Ve vere much more than frandss. Ve vere plenning to be married."

The waitperson brought my drink. "Oh," I said. "Then you must be totally, absolutely devastated."

"Yass." He nodded. "Todally devastated." He whipped out a handkerchief and made dabbing motions at his eyes.

For some reason, I wasn't really convinced. "Please excuse me for intruding on your grief," I said. "But when were you two going to be married?"

"Thiss month," he said, adding, "vy do you esk?" His eyes bored into me.

I shivered. I let out what I hoped was a girlish giggle. "Oh, I'm an incurable romantic. I just think it's so terribly sad, thwarted love, Romeo and Juliet, you know," I babbled, hoping he'd dismiss me as an airhead. I sipped my wine.

He folded his arms across his chest and glared at me. No more Mr. Sexy Nice Guy. "Vat you vant from me?"

"Well," I thought quickly, "we'll need somewhere to hold the memorial. Could we possibly use your place?"

"Ha!" His laugh sounded like a bark. "I live in small rhooms, like for mouze." The beautiful lips twisted in a snarl. "In dis contry, impossible to get daycent plaze to liff. Excapt for millionaire."

"Oh, I know, I know." Sympathy dripped from my pores, despite my raging curiosity as to why someone with such heavy jewelry couldn't afford a daycent apartment. "Well, would you be willing to come and share some personal memories of Dr. Ditstein? I'm sure what you have to say would mean so much to all of us."

The dazzling smile was back in a flash. "Uff cosse. I vould be most heppy and delighted to obleege."

I stood up, reached for his hand, and shook it.

"Thank you so much for agreeing to see me during this terrible time for you," I said.

He put his lips to my hand with a flourish. Right out of the movies. I sighed. Even if it was all an act, it felt damned good. No wonder Dr. Ditstein fell for him. Any woman with hormones would.

"It is vary, vary hard to loose somevone zo pracious," he said, looking at me with sorrowful eyes. "You kennot i-maghine."

"I'm so sorry," I said. "I'll be in touch with you about the memorial."

I started out the door, feeling bad for him, almost believing in his grief. Until I turned around and caught him gazing into the mirror again.

Chapter 17

I stopped off at Sam's the next morning on my way out and told him about my arrest. After offering me whatever money I needed for legal expenses, which I declined, he begged me to let him help somehow.

"Please, Marabella, let an old man be useful. Whatever I can do? There must be something, anything," he said. I could see tears in his eyes.

"I'll think of something," I said, patting his shoulder. "And don't worry. I'll be all right." *Who are you kidding, Marabella?*

When I got outside, I looked around, but there was no sign of Lucy. She hadn't been at her usual corner for a couple of days. Remembering her bad cough, I was worried about her. But who was I going to ask? I only hoped that, being a tough old bird, she'd kick whatever ailed her.

When I got to my office, I found a bouquet of pussy willows sitting outside my door. The note said: "To a very special lady, for a terrific in-depth interview. Looking forward to Saturday night. Call me when you get in. John."

Hopefully, I wouldn't be back in the clutches of Rivera and company by the weekend, I thought, patting the pussy willows and bringing them inside,

I rummaged around in my file cabinet for something resembling a vase and came up with an ancient bottle of iced tea that had long outlived any possibilities. I trotted to the ladies', dumped the contents down the toilet, rinsed out the bottle, and filled it with water. The pussy willows now sat on my desk, brightening it and my spirits.

Donna had her door closed, which meant that she was either on a personal phone call—intensely discussing her current diet or hairstylist or both—or talking to somebody in administration about stuff she didn't want me to know about. But I didn't care. Unlike the number one public relations job, the number two was seen as so unimportant a function that it was ignored during the college's history of administrative changeovers. So I had a certain modicum of security. Which Toniann used to say was like a jailbird's. Of course, that was before my possible encounter with the real thing.

Besides calling John and thanking him, I needed to take care of the messages on my desk. If I didn't deal with them soon, I could end up being unemployed. And I had to write up the interview on John. And pick up the intercom from Donna, which was making annoying buzzing noises right now.

"Yes, Donna?"

The squawks from the box were loud and angry. "Get your ass in here, toot sweet," my boss said.

Her sense of refinement was equaled only by her ear for language. I hustled down the corridor to her office and opened the door cautiously. You never knew with Donna's rages.

After scoping out UFOs, I slid into the room, which was enormous, with four big windows and built-in shelves that held Donna's collection of doggy knick-knacks. The real dog, her toy poodle, Twinkie, lay in ber-ibboned state on a satin blanket next to Donna's chair, chewing on a rawhide bone. Its piggy little eyes glared at me when I sank into the chair in front of the desk. I glared back.

Donna pushed her leather swivel chair back from the desk and folded her broad arms across her chest. A bad sign. "Well, what have you got to say for yourself, miss?" Her blood-colored lipsticked lips twisted in a sneer. I glanced at her nails, which were, as usual, done to match in the same ugly color.

"Well, what?"

This was not the right approach, I soon realized. She got even madder, if possible. "About the cop that was on the phone asking about you, a..." She picked up a piece of paper. "Detective..."

"Rivera."

"Right. So, what's going on? Why are the cops after you? And why are they calling here? Calling me? If this gets out, our office will be in deep shit. *I'll* be in deep shit. Are they going to arrest you?"

I took a few deep breaths, tried to clear the mucous from my brain that Donna always inspired. "Thanks for the vote of confidence, Donna. Okay, I guess you have a right to know."

"Damn straight."

"Okay, okay." I started to tell her the story. But when I mentioned Dr. Ditstein's name, she turned ghastly pale.

"What's the matter?" I asked. She was looking weirder by the minute. "Are you getting sick?"

She fumbled in her drawer, pulled out a bottle of as-pirin, and popped a couple in her mouth. Without water. "Splitting headache," she mumbled.

I wondered what the hell was going on. But before I

could process it, she recovered enough to revert to her usual charming self. "Oh, goody, so you're not in jail—yet. Then I've got absolutely nothing to worry about, right? No scandal, no president or board of trustees breathing down my neck about my criminal staff member." Her little eyes glared exactly like Twinkie's.

Would tossing her a chewy bone improve her disposition? "Donna, I hired a lawyer, even though everything seems to be okay now."

"Who?"

This I didn't want to start with her. She was still sore about Toniann's leaving, which was six months ago. "Somebody who was recommended to me."

"Who?"

"Otis Pinckney."

Her eyes got even smaller, and her face turned an ugly shade of red. She looked apoplectic. "That—"

"Not in front of the dog," I said. "And I agree with you one-hundred percent. But he gave me a break on his fee, and I can't afford anyone better."

She ignored the pointed hint about my lack of raises for the past two years, when she kept saying that Chelsea College didn't have money to spare for staff raises, except for important ones like hers, of course. "But can he keep you out of jail? More to the point, out of the papers? That—" She threw a quick glance at Twinkie. "—is always looking for publicity."

"Don't worry, he's been told," I lied. I'd have to get Toniann on the phone right away and tell her to tell him my job was on the line if this got out. Even though he'd want to blab it all over the papers that he was doing such a good deed. Otis Pinckney really cared and all that jazz.

"I don't know why you don't just go to a twelve-step group instead of all that therapy garbage," she said, leaning down to stroke the dog, which made her washed-out blonde hair fall over her face. Twinkie closed his eyes and made snorting noises, one of his charming responses to being petted. The other was breaking wind. "It's free, someone isn't telling you what to do, and you get to vent all you want. It's such a release."

Donna was so anti-therapy, I sometimes wondered if she'd had a bad experience with a therapist. What she did believe in was ACOA, Adult Children of Alcoholics. She'd been going to meetings religiously, she said, to cope with her abusive childhood at the hands of her alcoholic parents. So far, I hadn't seen a shred of evidence that her weekly vent-fests had turned her into a less-hostile person. But just the thought of what an untrammeled Donna might be like made me bless Bill W. and his Friends on a daily basis.

"Different strokes, Donna," I said, as the dog rolled over onto its back and Donna rubbed its disgusting little belly.

"Oh, by the way, our boy Lionel is back among us, so you don't have to do the science beat anymore," she said, cooing to her little beast. "You can give him your notes on that new dog-and-pony-show guy, and he'll fix them up. Somehow," she said with a cackle.

Though her opinions about my science-writing expertise were true, I was upset, since I had a couple of reasons to write up this one myself. Follow-up questions and points from the interview would give me the excuse to Donna that I needed to see him during the day. And I wanted to impress him with my brilliant writing. Though I had the feeling he'd probably be more impressed if I could be around a horse without passing out, which was probably what would happen if I got up the courage to try. Maybe I should ask Donna about a twelve-step group for large animal phobia, I thought, as I made my way back down the corridor. Or maybe I could enlist Lionel's help, I thought, as I caught a glimpse of him, bandaged ear and all, bending to pick up a pile of papers from his office floor.

I strolled over to him, casually. "Hey, how's it going, dude?" I tried to be as hip as possible when talking to people Lionel's age, though I was afraid it never quite came off. But he tolerated it. At least I tried.

Poor Lionel looked like a bad imitation of Van Gogh. Except that his hair was sleek and black, not wild and red. Same with the dark fuzz where the beginnings of a beard kept threatening to erupt underneath his acne.

"Unnh," he groaned, standing up.

"I take it that means you're not quite up to par yet," I said, reaching up to pat his shoulder. Every time I saw him, it seemed like he grew a couple of inches. Or it could be that I was shrinking. "It looks really horrible," I said, pointing to his ear.

"Gee, thanks, Mom," he said, throwing me a dirty look. He called me Mom when he was annoyed with me. Otherwise, it was Marybelle.

"Sorry, young'un. I'm just concerned."

His face softened. "And I've got a date with Tiffany this weekend. Unnh."

"Tiffany," I said, trying to remember which one of the drop-dead-gorgeous young things Tiffany was. "She's the, um, dancer?"

"Actress," he said. "The dancer was Brittany. She's history."

The dancer, as I recalled, was three weeks ago. *Ancient* history.

"The worst thing, though, is that my mom says I've got to put Izzie down." His face scrunched up, and he looked about to cry. Izzie was his pet iguana, which had recently taken a liking to Lionel's left ear and had nearly bitten it off. It took fifteen stitches and a highly trained plastic surgeon to keep Lionel from becoming a permanent Van Gogh look-alike.

"Geez, Lionel, I'm sorry," I said, really meaning it. Though I wouldn't want to get anywhere near Izzie or any of Lionel's other reptilian pals, if he had them, I felt sorry for him. The poor kid never really had a chance to be a kid, since he was so intellectually advanced for his age. All he'd had to relate to, that was, until being discovered by girls, were his scaly friends. "Won't your mom give Izzie another chance?"

A bitter laugh. "She'd say, 'What, give that thing'—she calls Izzie a *thing*—'a chance at your other ear?'"

"Do you think it would help if I talked to her?"

Lionel's mother, whom I'd never met but had had occasional phone conversations with, thought of me as kind of Lionel's on-the-job babysitter, watching over her son during the day when she couldn't be there. Of course, if he knew that, he'd never talk to me about anything again.

"I doubt it," he said. "But go ahead. It can't hurt. And thanks, Marybelle."

I was back in his good graces again. Now was the time to press my luck. "Lionel, would you do me a favor?"

"Sure, what?" he asked over his shoulder, digging around in his file cabinet, mumbling to himself. "Where did I put that—"

"Especially since I know you've got a lot to catch up on from when you were out," I pointed out.

"You got that right," he muttered into his file cabinet.

"So, Lionel, how about if I finish up the article on Dr. Adriance? You know, the new veterinarian?"

He picked up his head. "Boy, that would be a big help, for sure." Then a worried look spread across his face as he flashed on my science-writing disability. "Uh, Marybelle, I don't mean to, uh, criticize, but—"

"Not to worry. I practically have it written already." A bald-faced lie. "And if I come to any roadblocks, I'll knock on your door, okay?" I'd be breaking it down, for sure.

He looked vastly relieved. "Thanks," he mumbled, before sticking his head back into the file cabinet.

What makes you think you can write a good science piece, Marabella? Thinking had nothing to do with it. Unless I'd suddenly started thinking with my hormones. I walked back to my office and closed the door behind me. The pussy willows sure brightened up my gunmetal gray desk.

I sat down and gently stroked one of the pussy willows, thinking about John Adriance, which led to a few sweaty moments. I had to call him to thank him. I reached the college's main operator, who seemed to be barely functioning, as usual, and asked her to connect me with Dr. Adriance's office. She informed me that Dr. Asian did not have a permanent office or phone number assigned to him yet, and I could leave a message for Dr. Ayju in the biology department and that Dr. Haitian would be sure to get it. She transferred me to bio, where I left detailed messages for Drs. Adriance, Asian, Ayju, and Haitian. Hopefully, one of them would get back to me.

I got Otis's voice mail and left explicit instructions to call my direct line and not to reveal his identity to anyone else, especially the operator. She might be barely able to do her work, but her gossip ability was off the charts. They didn't call her Flashmouth for nothing. It was bad enough that Donna knew about my little problem with the NYPD. I could live without the rest of the college, including John Adriance and Lionel, knowing, too. As soon as I clicked off, Professor Myra Newsome, whom I privately referred to as Nasty Nuisance, walked in.

"I left a message. Which you have neglected to return. Causing me to have to get up and come over to your office." Glare, glare. Dressed in an outfit years too young for her—short plaid skirt, thigh-high white boots, fluffy sweater—she was in high dudgeon.

The trip from her office to mine was a whole couple of yards down the hall. "Sorry, Professor Newsome." I tried looking abject. "I just...I had an emergency at home."

"Not my problem."

I sighed. "What can I do for you, Professor?"

Among her other lovely qualities, she wouldn't deign to answer unless you addressed her by her title. The good professor was also a card-carrying bigot: race, creed, color, sexual orientation—it was all the same to her. Something to sneer at.

"What you can do is at least, at least, spell my student's name correctly. Don't they teach spelling in whatever school you went to? Or do you just rely on Spell Check?" Spittle appeared at the corner of her mouth.

Deep breaths, Marabella. "Professor Newsome, I'm afraid the student you're referring to had such bad handwriting that I must have mixed it up. I'm—"

She was on fire. "If that were the case, Ms., Ms..."

"Vinegar," I said helpfully.

"Then the proper thing to do would have been to check with me. Is that too much to ask, Ms..."

I figured she might take even more offense if I said "Vinegar" again. "No, Professor, you're perfectly correct." Grovel, grovel. I even flashed a smile. "Please accept my apologies. It won't happen again."

"Damn straight, it won't," she snarled, and stormed out of my office.

I put my head down on my desk and stayed there for a few minutes. When I picked my head up, I fished in my pocketbook for my pill box and popped a Xanax. Then I remembered my promise to Lionel to call his mother. Poor kid, he really related to that iguana. I scrolled down for Mei Lee Yung's number.

She answered and was glad to hear from me, she said. I expressed sympathy for her recent trauma with her son's ear in the ER. Then I pled Lionel's case for keeping Izzie happily thrashing about in her terrarium, or whatever it was you kept amphibians in these days. She agreed with me that it was a shame to put the iguana down, especially when it had been her son's best friend for so long. Geez.

But she really couldn't take a chance, at least not right away, with her son again. Izzie, it seemed, had really done quite a job chomping away at Lionel's earlobe.

There was a solution, Mei Lee said, if I'd agree to it.

I didn't like the sound of it already. But what could I do? "What?" I asked, not wanting to ask.

"You could bring Izzie to your house," Mei Lee said. She added, before the shock could set in, "Just for a little while. Just till she gets over her new taste for Lionel's flesh and goes back to her usual diet of chopped leafy greens. And don't worry, she's never tried to bite me. It was probably her way of expressing affection to Lionel."

I didn't answer, hoping she'd think I'd died.

"Pleeeze," she said. "Lionel could come over and visit Izzie and help you with her." Then she brought out the ace in the hole: "You wouldn't want that poor kid to be miserable, would you? I know how much you like him. And since you'll be keeping her in her tank, and she can't get out, there's nothing to worry about. She hurt Lionel's ear when he took her out to pet her."

This was not fair. I didn't even like green food, let

alone green pets. And the whole idea of petting a reptile made me want to heave.

But then again, Izzie might be a good conversation piece for my date with John. As in, "I think my iguana is looking a bit off-color." How could you tell, anyway? Did it turn blue or purple, like those stress cards that turned various colors, depending on how warm or cold you were? But weren't iguanas cold-blooded animals anyway, so maybe they were always cold. Or warm. I couldn't remember which.

Mei Lee was still begging and moaning on the phone, waiting for me to respond. Finally, she pulled out all the stops. "Marabella, I'll send over a five-pound box of my fudge brownies with Izzie."

This was clearly taking advantage of my good nature and total lack of willpower where brownies were concerned.

"Okay," I said to her, looking down at my hips, which waggled back at me. "I'll do it. But could you make them low-fat brownies?"

A snicker on the phone. "Sure," she cracked, "And I'll make them no-calorie, too. But thanks so much. Lionel will be so grateful. And I'll sleep better, without worrying about what part of Lionel Izzie will acquire a taste for next."

She told me she'd have Lionel bring Izzie and her equipment over tonight. I clicked off and decided to not even think about my mother's reaction to Izzie. Hell, it was my apartment, wasn't it, and if I wanted to share it with a flesh-eating reptile, it was my business, right?

Thinking of slimy creatures, what about the ratfink who'd ratted me out to the cops. Who could it be? I ran through the list in my head. But there was something else, too: Donna's reaction to my mentioning Dr. Ditstein, never mind telling her about the murder. I needed to have that checked out. A task for super-ghost-mother, for sure.

The phone rang. Tommy Woods, the director of our community substance abuse program was eagerly awaiting my presence that afternoon at the one-month sobriety party for recovering students, BS. (Bring soda.) I'd have to pick up the soda on my lunch hour, since I'd forgotten all about it because of my little weekend distractions.

I collected my pocketbook, told Donna I was going for lunch, and went out to pick up soda for the party.

Chapter 18

The banner taped on the wall said, "Congratulations on One Month Sobriety!" in gold letters. A CD player was playing oldies. Nice and mellow. The table was nicely decorated with a paper tablecloth, paper napkins, paper plates and cups and plastic silverware—cheap, because the college bought paper goods in bulk. The coffee machine was brewing up a storm. And there was a wonderful sweet smell from a pile of doughnuts, which I was trying very hard to ignore. Without much success. As I finally succumbed to a chocolate-covered one, Tommy Woods loped over to me.

He did not look happy. Neither did the partygoers. "Marabella, I appreciate you bringing the soft drinks. But…" He shook his balding head.

"What's the matter, Tommy?" I liked him and admired the work he'd been doing here for years, helping people in the community get their life back together.

"You got the wrong kind of soda. And the wrong flavors for my guys here."

I looked around and didn't see anybody drinking it down. They were eating their doughnuts dry. I was worried somebody could choke on doughnut crumbs. God, I sounded like my mother. Scary.

"Tommy, I'm so sorry. But I had to get what was on sale since the college doesn't believe in name-brand buying. And those were the only flavors the generic came in."

Then I started coughing. Whether it was from doughnut crumbs or the smoke-filled room—the only one allowed on campus—I didn't know. I went over to the table and poured myself a cup of generic. After a couple of swigs, I realized why the people were boycotting it. Good for them.

I told Tommy the smoke was too much for me and left. Well, it was their party, so if they wanted to celebrate by promoting the growth of carcinogens in their lungs, so be it. The big question for me was how to get the smoke out of my hair. It smelled like an ashtray. All I needed was for my mother to think I'd started smoking again. I'd never hear the end of it.

I called Toniann. "What's a quick, easy way to get smoke out of your hair?"

"Whadja do, set it on fire?"

"Ha, ha. It was the chain-smokers at the sobriety party. I can't go home like this."

"Why not? Afraid you'll run into the hunk?"

"Um."

"A-ha. You really like him."

"Well, yeah. But c'mon, what about my hair?"

"Bathroom spray."

"What?"

"Takes it out right away. Just overpowers it. Of course—" She gave a raucous laugh. "—you might smell a little like Lysol for a while. But that's got to be better than smoke."

"Thanks. And I called Otis and left a message this morning, but I haven't heard a thing."

"You know Otis. You can't rush him."

I gritted my teeth. "I know that. But I need to make sure he keeps my recent troubles out of the papers. Otherwise, I'll be in deep doo-doo with Donna. My life is complicated enough these days. So, could you please make sure he got the message?"

"Okey-doke. Not to worry. But I'll have to be delicate about it. We wouldn't want him to think he's a publicity hound, would we?" she chortled.

"Who, him?" I said. "Anyway, thanks. For being there." Wonderful. A lawyer who was not only a gross sleaze but who had to be handled with kid gloves. And Toniann used to complain about the people at Chelsea College. "How can you stand him?" I asked.

"Easy," she shot back. "He's not Sawicki. Talk to you later, he's buzzing."

CC's former PR director, Joe Sawicki, used to regularly chase Toniann around his desk and down the corridor. Once he even tried to follow her into the ladies' room. She managed to slam the door on his fingers. One thing you could say about Otis, he wasn't a sexual harasser or a chauvinist pig. He was just a pig.

We said goodbye, and I went to the ladies' room and pried open the cabinet under the sink, a place I would not ordinarily risk putting my ungloved hands into. I pushed back the cleansers, which were still unopened and covered with roach crap. Shuddering, I reached behind them and unearthed a can of Lysol spray. I cleaned it off with a wet paper towel and sprayed my hair. Now it smelled like disinfectant and smoke. I gave the Lysol back to the roaches, went to my office to gather up my briefcase, and left, shouting goodbye to Lionel. No need to say goodbye to Donna, she had already taken off like a bat out of hell.

Monday was her after-work tennis date, meaning a shorter-than-usual workday.

Speaking of Donna, why would she practically faint when I told her about Dr. Ditstein? This would not have been due to her being a person of tender sensitivities, feeling horrified that someone had been murdered. Not our Donna, whose favorite reading matter was the *National Globe*.

Then I thought about my mother and the imminent arrival of Izzie, my latest roommate. The question was, should I tell my mother now? Or did I just let it slide until Izzie got there? Which, of course, would save me explanations, of sorts.

I opted to call my mother before I left the office. I didn't think her heart could handle the shock. Luckily, I'd kept one land-line phone, with an answering machine. We'd worked out a signal: She'd pick up and not speak, unless she heard my voice. Hopefully, she was sticking to it.

Even though I was expecting Izzie and her accoutrements to be delivered tonight, I wasn't sure I could count on the Yungs to wait till then to deposit Lionel's boon companion. By now, who knows what part of Lionel's tender flesh Izzie could be fancying?

Well, my mother always said that if you had to have a pet, if it couldn't be stuffed, at least let it be something that didn't shed or need to be housebroken. She never said anything about scales and claws.

Her reaction was more or less what I'd expected. "They're bringing a what?"

"It's only temporary, Ma. I feel sorry for that poor kid, losing his only friend."

"Tch, tch," she clucked. "What's the matter with him that he can't make real friends? Is there something wrong with him?"

"Ma, he's a very bright young man, too bright for his age, so he has trouble fitting in with his peers. Except, somehow, for females."

"Ah," she said, "a genius. Oh, well, that I can understand. You remember Cousin Albert, the one who was too smart for his own good? Aunt Evelyn's first husband's nephew?"

I dimly recalled a pale, pudgy boy who was always sneaking around corners, spying on everyone's conversations so he could torment them about what they said later. I occasionally wondered what had happened to him.

"He died," she said. "He was investigating a story for a tabloid and decided to listen in to one conversation too many of the wrong kind. So they bumped him off."

Not only did this give me the shivers, but—I couldn't believe it—she was practically drooling with excitement. But I didn't have time for this. I had to find out what made Donna the unflappable freak out when she heard about Dr. Ditstein.

"Ma, I need you to swipe the files again," I whispered. Even though I was positive Donna was gone for the day, I couldn't risk her coming back and overhearing what it was I needed to know.

"I'd be happy to, sweetheart, but what do you want it for? Didn't you get what you needed already?"

"I can't tell you now," I said. "But it's important."

"Will do."

"Thanks, Ma. Will you be okay? About the iguana, I mean?"

She groaned. "Don't worry, I can handle it."

"But what about—"

"And don't worry about me giving myself away, either," she said. "I'll be quiet as a mouse. They won't even know there's anyone here. I can be discreet," she said.

As far as I was concerned, discretion and my mother had never occupied the same universe.

Chapter 19

The huge glass tank was parked outside my front door on a red wagon next to the brownies and a large box, with a note attached. The note read:

Please take good care of Izzie. She has been a loving and faithful companion. She needs plenty of veggies and/or fruit, preferably chopped up leafy greens. Here's a supply to get you started. The plants in the cage need to be misted every day, so she can drink the water. And sift the gravel in the bottom of the tank every few days. She doesn't like a mess. She also needs lots of light and to be kept warm. Everything she needs is in the box. Thanks, I owe you, Lionel.

Izzie was very big, very green, very ugly, and very scaly. She gave me a beady-eyed once over and turned her back on me. We were off to a jolly start. Not trusting her one inch, I grabbed the handle of the wagon, keeping an eye on her to make sure none of my body parts were within reach of her vicious-looking jaws.

I stuck my key in the door and pushed it open with the wagon.

My mother jumped up from the sofa. She was wearing my red sweater and matching tights, that I must say, looked a lot better on her than on me.

"Hi, Ma," I said. "We have company." I grinned in Izzie's direction, and she flicked her tongue at me. Thinking this was her way of testing the waters before snacking on my tender flesh, I pushed the wagon to the farthest corner of the room in a hurry.

My mother just stared.

"Don't worry, she's locked up," I said. "And so far, she only seems to like to nibble on her owner, so I think we're relatively safe."

Izzie began moving up and down the tank, acting as if she were in a prison yard. Maybe I was identifying, but I actually started to feel sorry for her.

My mother was still staring. Neither of us had ever seen a reptile that size before, except for the ones at the Museum of Natural History, which were very dead.

Then my mother closed her eyes.

"Are you okay?" I asked, peering at her.

Her eyes snapped open. "Of course, what do you think, I'm some kind of weak sister? Have you ever known me to shrink from something just because it's distasteful?" She threw a meaningful look in Izzie's direction. "Or difficult?"

"It's not easy being green," I murmured, hoping to get on Izzie's good side. I stole a glance. She hadn't stopped pacing.

Then I got a glass of water for my mother, some extra for Izzie's water dish, and a Xanax for me. At least it got her to calm down. My mother, I mean. Not Izzie.

My mother took a few sips, and her color came back a little.

"Are you all right?" I asked.

"I'll live."

I wasn't even going to try to process that one.

"Here's the files," she said, pointing to the coffee table.

"Thanks."

I sank down in the rocker opposite the sofa and almost tipped over backward. I'd forgotten that the rocker had developed an annoying squeak, a sound that, unfortunately, it seemed Izzie was sensitive to. She leaped into the air, banging her head on the roof of her tank. Just what I needed, a reptile with a sensitive soul.

My mother was cowering on the sofa, peeping over at the cage.

"Don't worry, she can't get out," I said, not really believing it.

I had visions of Izzie roaming our apartment in search of tasty body parts while we slept. I didn't want to wake up missing any of my digits. Or my mother's. Maybe I'd be better off trying to find another foster home for her. But who?

I flashed on Maxine. She'd once told the group how reptiles had been her favorite pets when she was a kid. She'd gone into positive raptures about a boa named Jezzie, short for Jezebel. Beth, with her usual sarcasm, had retorted that the only boa she'd ever related to was the skin of a dead animal, a forties-retro-fashion thing.

I looked at Izzie. She bared her teeth and swiped a claw in my direction. Shuddering, I picked up my phone, scrolled through my original list of contacts, and pressed Maxine's. This could kill two birds at once, or, at least, keep one of them from inflicting bodily harm.

She answered on the first ring.

"Maxine, it's Marabella, from the group."

"Oh, hi." Her voice was warm and friendly. Didn't sound as if she'd killed someone, but what was that supposed to sound like?

"I'm calling you with kind of a strange request."

She laughed, a creaky sound coming from the depths of her throat. I realized I'd never heard Maxine laugh before. "What's up, doc?"

"It's about something you once said in group."

I could hear the shift in her breathing. "What? What did I say?" Her voice was shrill.

"That you used to like reptiles when you were a kid."

She let out her breath. "Oh, yes, and especially—"

"Jezzie."

"You remembered that?" Her voice was incredulous. "I guess you really listen, don't you? Not like *some* of those people in the group."

"Um, right. Anyway, Maxine, I wonder if you'd like to play foster mother to a lovely—" I squinted at Izzie, who, I could have sworn, stuck out her forked tongue out at me. "—good-sized—" That was putting it mildly. "—iguana for a little while. Very well-behaved." I crossed my fingers and eyes. "Very low-maintenance."

She didn't hesitate. "I'd just love to. I've always wanted to get to know an iguana. They're such unique animals."

I let out my breath. *Thank you, gods*. "Thanks so much. I'll bring her over tomorrow morning, if that's okay with you."

It was more than okay with her, and she gave me her address, thanking me profusely for thinking of her.

My mother looked definitely relieved.

Anyway, tomorrow I'd get to poke around Maxine's place while she was making nice with Izzie, who was now no doubt plotting an attack. I felt a moment's twinge for the unsuspecting Maxine but brushed it aside with the thought that Maxine could be guilty of far worse things. Besides that, Maxine liked reptiles, so presumably, she knew something I didn't about how to calm them down.

Too bad I didn't know whether or not Xanax worked

on reptiles. I could have mashed a couple into her veggies, and maybe it would have helped. Right now, I could only hope and pray the locks and the bars were strong enough to hold out till I could get Izzie to her new foster mama. Maybe a little extra food to hold her over would stave off her lust for human flesh for a while.

I thought of the one thing a city dweller never ran out of. I hightailed it into the kitchen, squashed a bunch of roaches that were marching into my cabinet, and handed them to Izzie with a flourish. She pushed them out of her tank with a grunt. Okay, wrong choice. I opened the box Lionel had left. Ah, there it was: lots of leafy greens and fruits and a mister for the plants in the cage. I didn't see why she couldn't just nibble on the plants, but what did I know? I shoved the greens at Izzie. She tore into them.

"Marabella," my mother whispered, "what is that reptile doing?"

"Having a snack," I said. "Speaking of which, I'm starving." I picked up the files and the brownies, which I offered to my mother, and she declined. Then I headed for the kitchen.

"There's cold chicken and a salad in the fridge," she said. "Help yourself. Take some dressing from the bottle of French's"

Ugh. "Thanks, Ma." I realized I'd been eating, if not better, at least more regularly, since my mother moved in.

While gnawing on a drumstick, I went through the files, till I got to the "T's." Ah. There it was. Donna Tomiello. With a notation: "Terminated." Who terminated who, I wondered? Was it remotely possible that Donna was such a difficult patient that even Dr. Ditstein, who never lost her cool, couldn't deal with her? Or was therapy so scary to Donna-the-Hostile that she couldn't take it? Or did something else happen, something more…sinister?

What did I really know about Donna, anyway? Besides being the world's bitchiest boss, I mean. And that she'd had a miserable childhood and had a hate-on for her alcoholic parents and the world in general.

I opened the box of brownies and thought about what I knew so far about everyone else. Not much, actually.

Chris was transgendered, which didn't make her a murderer, only someone with something to hide. Dr. Shokum was a killer phone porn artist, but again, that didn't make him a killer killer.

Henry was a nutcase, who'd freaked out on one or more occasion in group, and seemed to be violent. Violent enough to kill? Ron was a pig, and Maxine had a lot of anger, some of it transferred to Dr. Ditstein because of Maxine's feelings about her sister. Zoltan's relationship with Dr. Ditstein didn't ring true. As for Beth, being a narcissist didn't make you a killer, as far as I knew.

The brownies were pure heaven. Lionel's mother had outdone herself this time, unfortunately for my hips. I bit into my third, but who was counting?

What did all this add up to? Not enough to get Rivera off my case and onto somebody else, that was for sure. Maybe when I delivered Izzie to her new home, I'd find something really incriminating.

I could hope, couldn't I?

<h1 style="text-align:center">Chapter 20</h1>

Next morning, I called Maxine and told her that her new reptilian friend and I were on our way. She responded with squeals of delight, at least, that was what they sounded like. Then I left a message for Donna that I'd be delayed with a medical emergency. This was true, in a way, since if I didn't get Izzie to her new babysitter, one of us was going to need serious medical help.

Not only had Izzie terrorized my mother all night, with her thrashing about, when I tried to tempt the beast with some nice, fresh watermelon this morning, the ungrateful thing spit the seeds at me.

Needless to say, my mother, who had circles under her eyes and was huddled in a ball in my robe on the end of the sofa farthest from the tank, breathed a sigh of relief that Izzie was leaving.

"Sweetheart, I really didn't mean what I said about you not having a pussycat. Even a dog would maybe be nice."

"It's okay. That was when I was ten," I said, grabbing the handle of the red wagon under the tank while

Izzie did another of her swats. "Stop!" I snarled. Izzie snarled back. "Besides, I'm afraid of dogs. And they don't allow dogs in the building."

"They allow those?" She pointed at the tank.

"Not exactly," I said, dragging the wagon and myself out the door.

My poor neighbor, Sam, dropped his trash and almost dropped his teeth.

"Don't worry," I said, hoping he wouldn't have a coronary. "She's safe enough in there."

Unfortunately, Izzie chose that moment to begin thrashing in earnest.

Sam stared. "I can understand you wanting something to keep you company, my dear, but—"

"No, no, she's not mine. I've been watching her for a friend." Izzie was banging her head against the tank. I could only pray it was stronger than she was. "I'm taking her to someone else's house."

Sam looked very relieved. I pushed the button for the elevator, hoping it would be empty. It wasn't, but after my neighbors got a look at what I was dragging behind me, it emptied out fast.

Though I worried about her absence from her favorite corner, I was glad Lucy wasn't around this particular morning. One look at Izzie would have sent Lucy into the DTs, for sure.

I finally got a cab by offering to pay double the fare, a deal, I was sure the poor cabbie wished he'd never made for any price. Evidently, rock music wasn't Izzie's thing and whipped her into a frenzy. She tried to make a break for it, banging the tank non-stop, saliva dripping from her horrible tongue, while the cabbie mumbled something that sounded like prayers, dodging in and out of traffic.

By some miracle, the cabdriver, Izzie, and I arrived

at Maxine's in one piece, no thanks to his maniacal driving. I gave him the double fare and pulled the cage into Maxine's building, a splashy new condo. The monthly rent for an apartment here could probably feed a poor family and all its relatives for their entire lifespan. The doorman widened his eyes at my traveling companion, but was probably too snottily well-bred to make a comment. Peasants, after all, had strange habits. I tossed him what I hoped was an engaging grin, buzzed up Maxine, and proceeded inside to the elevator bank as if I were schlepping nothing more unusual than a few tasty treats from Balducci's. Again, we had the elevator to ourselves, while the crowd chose to wait for a reptile-free one.

Maxine was lying in wait when we tumbled out. The sight of Izzie sent her into raptures.

"Oh, she's just such a sweet baby, she is," Maxine cooed to Izzie as we traveled down the corridor. Sweet and baby were two words I would not have used to describe Izzie.

For her part, Izzie was emitting what must have been the reptile version of a love song, in return—a series of god-awful guttural sounds, in combination with oh-so-sexy tongue thrusts. I controlled my gag reflex by reminding myself that everyone had his or her own predilections, bizarre as they may be. And far be it from me to criticize Maxine's passion, since it was responsible for ridding me of another roommate I needed like a city garbage strike in July.

I followed the lovebirds into the apartment. It was stupendous, magnificent, gorgeous. Everything that money and excellent taste could buy. I hoped Izzie would agree.

The huge living room was graced with a baby grand at one end and a deep velvety conversation pit at the other, facing the incredible view from the thirty-fifth floor.

A few African sculptures were grouped on a table, just enough to be interesting, not overwhelming. The lighting was low and inviting, the sound of the jazz on the stereo superb. I could live here happily for the rest of my natural life, given a salary at least triple what I made now. Although, I recalled, at the last group sessions, Maxine had been making noises about getting a smaller apartment, taking less expensive vacations, getting into the "simple" life, yadda, yadda.

Even on a comptroller's salary, it was hard to imagine how Maxine, or anyone engaged in a legal occupation, could afford this place. Which led to my next thought: maybe she had another source of income. What?

"What a gorgeous place. Could I have a tour?" I asked, interrupting the billing and cooing.

"Huh? Oh, sure, just take a look around while I get her settled," Maxine said, making revolting kissing noises in Izzie's general direction. "Don't go away, sugar. I'll be right back with some yum-yums for the tum-tum."

I quickly went through the other rooms, trying to scope out as many details as I could. At this point, I was heartily wishing I weren't the type who walked into walls because I never noticed things that were staring me in the face. It was a case of my having an auditory style of learning, rather than a visual or kinesthetic. Toniann would have had everything down pat in two seconds: position of furniture in bedroom, types of materials used for windows and bed linens, what items were on the bureau, etc.

I did my best, given my limited noticing ability and time frame. The kitchen was galley-style, the only small room in the apartment. The bedroom was almost as big as the living room, with a king-sized bed, a large French style armoire, and enormous closets. The other wall had a huge, floor-to-ceiling antique-style mirror. Hmmm. I had a suspicion that it was covering up…something. I managed to peek behind it, not without banging my head against the wall. But it was worth it. The something turned out to be a wall safe. Why would she need a safe? What was she hiding in that safe?

I headed back into the living room, where Maxine was hand-feeding Izzie dainty little morsels of what, I shuddered to think.

"Got to get to work," I said to Maxine, who barely broke stride to wave goodbye in my direction. Izzie gave me her best snarl. "Thanks so much. I'll let Lionel know she's in good hands," I said and went out the door.

Chapter 21

When I arrived at work, Lionel practically attacked me. "Is Izzie okay? Is she eating? How are her spirits?"

"Yes to one and two, and she certainly seemed very…um…spirited at my apartment," I said.

"That's great." He grinned. "Oh," he added, "did she give you any trouble?"

"Nothing that I couldn't take care of," I said, bringing him up to snuff on Izzie's new foster mother.

He looked pained, as if I'd personally rejected him instead of his unholy reptile.

"Believe me, Lionel, Izzie's much better off. Maxine has a thing for lizards." I gave him Maxine's phone number and address so he could pursue his parental visiting rights.

He brightened and swung off to his office. I tried tiptoeing to mine, hoping to avoid an encounter with Donna, who, I was sure, would ream me out for being over an hour late.

"Marabella." Donna's dulcet tones said. This was not my lucky day. Well, any day that began with transporting a vicious reptile in a New York City cab promised to be less than ideal. I braced myself and trudged into her quarters.

Her eyebrows shot up when she saw me. "You look like hell," she said, tapping her pen on her daybook. "Don't tell me you're really sick. You're not, are you?"

Like, how dare I? For all the concern in her voice, she might have been discussing the weather. I wondered what I could find out about her relationship with Dr. Ditstein. I couldn't come right out and ask her about her therapy sessions, could I? Maybe I could. I plopped down in the chair, facing her. "For one thing, you know I've been very upset about—" I took a deep breath, to emphasize my next words. "—Dr. Ditstein."

She dropped her pen.

I pretended not to notice. "After all, I had a long-term relationship with her. We really got quite *close*." I hoped that would get her rattled.

It did. She seemed to choke. "Dry throat," she muttered. Then she fumbled around on the floor for the pen, actually missing it when it was right in front of her hand. Wow.

When she finally retrieved it and got back into her chair, her face was bright red. Whatever it was with her and Dr. Ditstein, it must have been really something. And maybe that something was so bad that she totally lost it and offed Dr. Ditstein. As far as I could tell, Donna had never had any problem letting her inner angry child out to terrorize those around her.

"Well…uh…you…what happened this morning?" She was practically stuttering.

I wondered how much of this morning's escapade to tell her. None, I decided. The only believable thing would be a lie. "I had to have a…test," I said. I cast my eyes down, partly to keep a straight face, partly to evoke a few morsels of what passed for sympathy with Donna.

"Whatever." She shrugged. "Time's a'wasting, kiddo. I've had to answer your calls, take your messages. I'm not your secretary, y' know."

"Couldn't be helped, Donna," I said, picking up the pink message slips she handed me.

I walked to my office, shut the door, and stuck my tongue out in Donna's direction. I looked at the messages. Bob from the art department, Harold, the European Studies chairman, John Adriance.

Work before pleasure. I phoned Bob and the European Studies chairman, a royal pain-and-a-half who looked down his nose at us lesser beings who did not possess advanced academic degrees.

My duty done, I called John. Dancing before my eyes were visions of dark curly hair in places on his body that I was looking forward to exploring.

"Dr. Adriance, here," the voice answered.

It was the first time I'd heard his voice on the phone. It was low, musical, and enormously sexy. Not like Dr. Shokum's, which was phony baloney sexy, commercially sexy, sexploitative. John's was genuinely male-animal-high-testosterone-level sexy.

"Hi, it's Marabella."

"Ah, Marabella. I've been missing you."

"I miss you, too," I said, feeling tingly all over.

"About dinner tonight, I'll pick you up at your place, seven-thirty. Tell me how to get there."

Shit. Why does my life have such lousy timing? Here I was, just itching to seduce him on the couch that happened to be currently occupied by my mother. "Um, I'll meet you at Le Bijoux," I said. Then, realizing I must sound pretty peculiar, paranoid or something, I said, "I'll be in the neighborhood, anyway."

Chapter 22

I zipped home to check on my mother and change into something a lot less comfortable and a lot more sexy. My mother's coloring and spirits, you should pardon the expression, were a whole lot better since the exodus of Izzie. I gave her the scoop about Maxine's apartment. Namely the safe.

Then I went into my bedroom to rummage in my closet.

"What would a young woman living alone need a safe for?" my mother mused.

"Her deep dark secrets?"

"Speak up if you want me to hear you. My hearing isn't what it used to be," she yelled.

"If I wanted you to hear me, I would have," I muttered.

My clothing selection was pitiful. I hadn't been out on a real date in so long, my wardrobe was basically limited to work clothes and sloppy hanging-out stuff. Pawing my way through sweaters and blazers, I finally found a soft-looking, rust-colored silk blouse that brought out the chestnut highlights in my hair. A delightful little shiver ran through me at the memory of John playing with my hair at our first meeting in the cafeteria. Our only meeting. Till now.

I searched the closet some more and unearthed a black velvet skirt that I hadn't worn since…the last winter formal occasion at Chelsea College, probably the last president's holiday party, two administrations ago. Fortunately, it still fit—barely. For shoes, an old pair of black pumps would have to do. By turning the bottle of Chanel No. 5 upside down, I eked out the last few drops. I was ready for action. I presented myself to my mother for her inspection. And got the usual warning.

"Don't get too close on the first date, and don't let him—"

I cut her off in mid-warning. "Mother, I'm an adult. In fact, I'm almost—" I couldn't bring myself to say the word "forty."

She smiled. "You're not too old to be careful, sweetheart."

My mother, the mind-reader. Tucking her up on the sofa, I set off for Le Bijoux, trying to exorcise the lascivious thoughts racing through my brain so I wouldn't arrive at the restaurant dripping wet.

After fifteen minutes of being practically knocked over attempting to get a cab, I succeeded by diving for the door handle before the driver screeched to a halt. Having my body plastered to the door didn't exactly help the state of my hair, let alone my clothes. But at least I was in, I thought, giving the finger to the disgruntled cab-seekers still on the curb.

Breezing into the restaurant, I tried and failed to appear nonchalant while craning my neck to catch a glimpse of John before he got a load of me. I had to deal with the wreckage of my hair.

I scooted into the ladies' room and fixed my mop the

best I could. When I came out, my nether regions did a dance as I spied him at a table in the corner. I took a couple of deep-nostril breaths and floated over to John's table.

His eyes lit up, and so did my privates.

"Ah," he murmured, pulling out my chair and giving the back of my neck a quick nuzzle.

"John, no—" I tried to sound stern as my hormones laughed at me. "—not here." I picked up my glass of water.

He grabbed my hand. "I've been thinking about you a lot. In fact, while I was spaying Serena today—"

I choked on the water. "Spaying a…"

"Beautiful Irish setter mix," he said.

"Made you think of me?"

"With a mane almost exactly like…" He reached over and touched my hair.

I sighed. At least John's other love interest didn't appear to be dating material. Hopefully.

The waiter appeared, reeled off the specials and his name in an equally haughty manner befitting Le Bijoux's ambience. John ordered beer for himself and seltzer for me, the steak for him, and chicken Marsala for me.

"If I drink, I'm warning you, I become a different person," I explained.

He looked hopeful. "Less inhibited?"

I shook my head. "I fall asleep or throw up until I pass out."

"That sounds just like Harry," he mused.

"Is Harry, by any chance, a horse?"

"A Clydesdale, no less. Every time his owner tried a new feed on him, Harry would—"

"Throw up until he passed out?"

Turned out that John finally diagnosed poor Harry-the-horse's problem as an allergy to a certain type of oats.

"That has to be very hard to do, diagnosing animal problems," I said. "You must be really good."

He tried to look modest. "You have to have a real feeling for the animals. Once you get inside their skin, you can figure it out."

"How did you get into animal doctoring? Did you have a favorite pet when you were a kid?"

I really wanted to know. This trait of mine, asking questions, had its up and down sides. Some people accused me of interrogating them for information. And, would you believe that some people thought I was just downright nosy? Of course, I interviewed people all the time at my job. But I was actually one of those people who really wanted to know all about you, if I was thrust in a common space with you for a period of time. Even if you're not someone I'd end up being close to. And in John's case—

He settled back with his glass of beer. "I grew up in the country, on a farm in Nebraska. Good-sized place, a couple hundred acres."

"So, what about the animals?"

"The usual. Cows, sheep, chickens, pigs, dogs, cats."

"But…"

The waiter ambled over with our salads as if we were hardly worthy of his attention.

"Didn't growing up with cows make you upset about eating beef? Not that I'm casting aspersions. Cluck, cluck."

"The cows weren't pets, any more than the chickens or pigs," he said. "They were the family business. I never got to know any of them personally. Not like…." He turned his face away.

I reached for his hand. "It was a horse, wasn't it?"

He nodded. I could see tears in his eyes. "A Shetland pony. He was my eighth birthday present. Merlin."

I smiled. "You were reading…"

"*The Knights of the Round Table*."

"I bet he was beautiful."

"The most beautiful pony in the world, to me. I'd race home from school and go out to the barn. I'd feed and water him and brush his coat till it shone. Then we'd ride through the fields."

"It sounds like every little boy's dream."

"It was. Until the day that he ate something, somehow, somewhere…" His lips twisted.

"And he died," I said.

"The stupid vet couldn't figure it out. He could have saved him." He took a swig of the beer. "That's when I decided to learn everything I possibly could to be able to help the animals I'm entrusted with."

I squeezed his hand. "I'm sure the animals and their owners really appreciate you." I almost added, "And so do I," but gave him a dazzling smile, instead. "So, other than being the good animal doctor, what do you like to do?" As soon as the sentence left my lips, I knew it shouldn't have.

He gave me the most loving leer I'd ever received.

"Ah," I said.

My hormones were practically shouting. Our waiter appeared with our dinner, which he presented with a flourish and a belittling look.

"Seriously," John said, cutting into his steak. "Not that I wasn't serious…" A mini-leer. "I'm an outdoor type, fishing, hiking, skiing. No hunting, though. I couldn't bring myself to hurt an animal. What about you?"

The only outdoor activity I'd ever enjoyed involved stripping off my clothes and doing it in the woods or even on the beach, for that matter. Somehow, I didn't think that qualified as an outdoor sport. "Um," I said, in between forkfuls of chicken, which was quite good. "I'm really a sit-by-the-fire-and-get-cozy type of woman," I said. "Preferably with a good book or a new puzzle."

His eyes lit up. "Crossword?"

I couldn't believe it. Another buff. Turned out we also shared a love of old movies. And classical music, which he listened to with the Marx Brothers, his three large, hairy dogs. Groucho, Harpo, and Chico. At least he had good taste in names. I speculated on how I was going to broach the subject of my large-animal phobia.

"You've got to meet the boys," he was saying. "You'll love them. You just can't help it." He fished in his wallet and pulled out a picture and handed it to me, beaming like a proud father. I stared at the huge beasts, looking like carbon copies of the same dog. With identical big, sharp teeth. The better to bite me with.

"They're very…cute," I said. "How do you tell them apart?"

"Oh, don't you worry. Even though they're littermates, they each have very distinct personalities. You'll see, once you get to know them."

I was hoping this wouldn't be any time soon, so I'd have time to find a hypnotist who specialized in phobias. Or at least a book on self-hypnosis. But on the other hand, if we were going to get to know each other, it would have to be at his place. Unless I wanted my mother to watch.

Of course, there were always motels. Or even a big, shady tree. Fond memories of my last outdoor exercise bubbled up, and I grinned.

"See? I knew you were a dog person, the minute I met you." The enthusiasm in his voice nearly killed me with guilt about my deception.

I just smiled.

"But what about you?" he asked. "Tell me your story."

Which part? I thought wildly. My dysfunctional childhood? My eight-year-dependency on Dr. Ditstein? My unsuccessful love relationships? My status as a murder suspect? My mother, the ghost? This was going to require my best efforts as an editor.

I carefully picked and chose incidents that sounded vaguely normal and not overly wimpy. For instance, I left out my two disastrous weeks at Girl Scout overnight camp, which I spent nursing a wounded knee—slipped on pine needles. Then there were the bee stings on my arms—stuck my hand where I shouldn't. A near-drowning and an ear infection when the swimming counselor tried to teach me to swim. And a sprained wrist from arts and crafts—don't even ask.

I glossed over my years in therapy and sort of lied about how long it was. Okay, downright lied and said it was a couple of years. But, hey, everyone's definition of a couple could be different. I also neglected to mention my mother's present incarnation. I didn't think he could handle it. At least, not until we knew each other a little better. I also decided not to mention my intimate relationship with the NYPD. I figured that would come out in time, if it was meant to. Or not, if I somehow managed to get myself cleared.

I told him about my father's death when I was twelve and he took my hand. "That must have been so hard on you," he said.

His parents, it turned out, were still alive and in amazingly good health, thanks to the family's great genes. His grandparents on both sides lasted until their upper nineties, dying from things like being thrown off a horse or run over by a tractor. In other words, natural causes of death on a farm. The family still had the farm, which John's older brother, Jim, ran.

"What about your mother?" he asked.

At that, I excused myself to go to the ladies' room. After I removed several choice bits of salad greenery from between my front teeth, I took a couple of deep-nostril breaths and practiced various responses: "She's not well." "She's really ill." "She's dead." None of which exactly described the situation.

When I came back to the table, there was the distraction of dessert, which I declined even though it looked sinfully delicious. I was afraid of bursting the zipper on my skirt. I didn't want to lose the skirt until we were alone.

Unfortunately, he remembered the thread of our conversation. "Is your mother…"

Right. I cleared my throat and looked down at my cup. He looked so concerned, I felt guilty. But not quite guilty enough to give him the unexpurgated version of the truth. "She…died…" At least that much was true. "…of congestive heart failure a couple of weeks ago."

"That's terrible. Why, you're still in mourning. Maybe we shouldn't be—"

Not a chance. I smiled bravely. "She was sick for a long, long time. It was…" I didn't dare finish the thought, "a relief," since I never knew how far her powers could reach. Plus, somehow, I thought it could sound funny. Heartless, even. Though, God knew, I didn't mean it that way. She had suffered for a long time and had been in considerable agony. A horrible thought occurred to me: Did she still—in her present condition—have pain? I shuddered. I fervently hoped not.

"Are you cold?" John asked.

"I'd feel a lot warmer sitting by your fire, if you have one." I gave him a suggestive smile.

"You're on."

He paid the bill, helped me on with my coat, and whisked us outside to the parking garage where he'd left his car. We drove in comfortable silence to his place in Larchmont.

In the full moonlight, the white house seemed peaceful and serene. Until the barking and howling started, that was. It was coming from inside the front door. Through the glass, I could see giant paws scrabbling at the door.

Oh, God. I took a few surreptitious alternate nostril breaths, fished in my pocketbook for a Xanax, and popped it. *Help me get through this, Dr. Ditstein, wherever you are*, I prayed. *Please don't let them eat me.*

"They're so excited," John was saying. "Wait till they meet you."

Oh, God.

He turned the key, and the three beasts leaped on him. "Guys, guys, I missed you, too," he said, an ecstatic look on his face.

I tried to pretend I was invisible, wishing my mother had taught me her trick. I was sure I was giving off fear hormones, or pheromones, or whatever it was that animals could smell on someone who was deathly afraid of them.

They charged. I fainted. Something wet sloshing on my face revived me. I figured it was John with a cold washcloth. "Thanks," I murmured.

It was one of the triplets, slobbering all over my face with his big pink tongue. Being up close and personal with those huge white teeth was threatening to make me pass out again.

"Um," I said, trying to sit up and finding it impossible with the dog's feet planted firmly on either side of my body. "Excuse me, please." I tried a gentle shove, but he was glued. He'd taken possession, as if I were a choice hunk of meat. In fact, when one of the other dogs approached, he kicked him away with his hind foot while continuing his relentless dribbling on my face.

John was beaming. "He really took to you. I knew it, I knew it in my bones, from the minute I saw you. I knew you were a dog person."

I suppose you could call it a romantic evening, that was if you liked the idea of being romanced by a dog. Harpo, my new significant other, stuck by my side all night, not even letting John near me. Growling, in fact, whenever John tried to make a move on me.

John thought it was hilarious. I thought it stunk. But who was I to try and change the minds of either of them? I pretended to act like a good sport and go along with my doggy date, while plotting my next encounter with John in an animal-free zone.

Thank the gods, he was thinking along the same lines. He proposed a night beginning with dinner and dancing at the Millefleurs Inn, a quaint little hideaway with a firm no-pets-allowed policy, about twenty minutes from his house. Harpo, I swear, understood every word and pricked up his large, pointed ears. I wondered how I was even going to make it out of Harpo's clutches to get back home tonight.

I needn't have worried. John had it all planned. He went to the garage, opened a humongous refrigerator, and retrieved what looked like an entire cow, which he casually tossed on the kitchen floor. He and I escaped to the car as Harpo and his brothers tore into the carcass. At least we could cuddle dog-free on the way home.

I turned down his request to come up to my apartment for a nightcap, pleading exhaustion. "All that dog-wrestling really tired me out," I said, with what I hoped was a convincing smile.

"You'll get used to it," he said, giving me a long, slow kiss that went down to my toes.

Somehow, I managed to stumble out of the car without falling into the street. As soon as I let myself into the apartment, I heard my mother snoring away on the sofa. At least she didn't think she had to stay up for me these days after a date. While I undressed, I recalled some of my not-very-fond memories of her doing this in my youth, which was a bit less than exciting, thanks to my mother's constant interference. I remembered her parking herself on the sofa in between me and Jerry, my heartthrob at the age of fifteen. Come to think of it, it was sort of like what Harpo did.

That made me smile. But was I smiling because of thinking about John? Or because I didn't consider man's best friend Public Enemy Number One anymore? Maybe dog-wrestling had not only worn me out but addled my brain. Turning out the lights, I scrunched under the covers. I fell asleep as soon as my head hit the pillow, dreaming wild and woolly dreams of a creature that had John's gorgeous face—and Harpo's less-than-gorgeous body.

Chapter 23

My mother-the-ghost detective was to meet me at Shokum's after her nap. Munching on one of Mei Lee Yung's brownies for fortification and trying not to look across the hall at Dr. Ditstein's office, I rang Shokum's bell. We went eyeball-to-eyeball at the peephole for a few seconds. Figuring maybe he didn't recognize me, I yelled, trying not to choke on brownie crumbs, "It's Marabella Vinegar, Dr. Shokum!"

The door creaked open, and he stood there, a hand clapped to his ear. "No need to shout, young woman," he said in a stern tone that, unfortunately for my juices, didn't disguise The Voice.

"Sorry," I mumbled, hoping that The Voice wouldn't get to me. We inspected each other. He peered at me.

I was underwhelmed. He was a nebbishy little guy who had maybe a couple of inches on me—which wasn't saying much since I'm only just over five feet—with those yucky strands of hair plastered over his balding head. Eyes hidden behind dark-tinted glasses. Shlumpy posture. And a graying goatee.

What a prize. No wonder he preferred being king of

the phones, with his one asset. At least, his only visible one. I wondered idly if he confined his dates to the instrument, too. The thought of Shokum whispering unspeakable things into some woman's unsuspecting ear began affecting my nether regions. *Stop it!* I told myself. *You're here on business.*

I followed him inside, down a dim hall into a poorly lit living room with heavy, drawn drapes. The man couldn't afford more than forty-watt bulbs? Probably no one ever entered this sanctum, so he didn't have to bother. But what about him? How could he see? Ah, that might explain things.

"To answer the question you haven't yet asked," he said, with a smirk, "I have a degenerative eye condition in which light bothers my eyes. Any light."

The man was a goddamn mind reader, like my mother. *Let's hope that the powers of good outweigh evil in this case.* "I'm sorry," I said, hoping I sounded like I meant it.

He shrugged. "But tell me, Ms. Vinegar…may I call you Marabella?" he said.

I nodded, figuring that even though it was unequal, it would make him more comfortable.

"What can I do for you, my dear?" he crooned.

The Voice was in full throttle, and I had to keep my wits, not my hormones, going. A real challenge which I hoped I was up to. Keeping in mind that he might be a murderer should help.

"Um, I want, I need, to think about a relationship with a new therapist," I said in a tentative voice, hoping I sounded sincerely in need of his services. The psychotherapeutic ones, that is.

"What do you have in mind?" he purred.

God, please help me. I shook my head, trying to clear it of salacious thoughts. *C'mon, Marabella, think of Dr.*

Ditstein, cold and dead, lying on the floor in her own blood.

I did a quick scan of the walls, as much as I could in the near-dark. Not a diploma in sight. "Um, where are your credentials? Not that I'm questioning them, of course."

He frowned at my impertinence. How dare I doubt him? "They're in my desk." The Voice had developed a distinct chill. "Since I conduct my...sessions..." He flicked his tongue at me. "...on the phone, there's no need for them to be in evidence. And with the lights being so dim..." He lifted his hands. "What would you like from our sessions? If we decided to go ahead, that is."

I heard a faint rustle behind me and my mother said, "Get him out of the room."

Shokum peered around the gloom. "Must be a draft," he said.

"I think I'd be able to concentrate a lot better with a cup of tea," I said, smiling at him. "It helps me focus."

With an exasperated look, he shuffled off into the darkness. "Let's go!" my mother muttered.

"I can't see a damn thing in this dark," I mumbled, groping along what appeared to be built-in bookcases.

"I can." She was flitting in and out of nooks and crannies, opening and shutting drawers.

I realized that seeing in the dark was another of her new powers. I heard a kettle whistling and the clink of silverware on china.

Crash! She tipped over a drawer onto the floor. I heard him making his way down the hall. "He's coming!" I hissed.

"Not to worry, sweetheart." She dumped everything back in the drawer.

"What was that?" Shokum appeared in the shadows, bearing a tray.

"I banged my knee into the lamp, trying to get up," I said, rubbing my knee for emphasis. "I was going to help you."

He sniffed. "That didn't sound like a lamp to me. Sounded more like a table or a desk." He walked over to the desk and peered at it, then glanced back at me. "You wouldn't be trying to snoop around, would you, my dear?" The Voice had turned sinister.

I drew myself up in righteous indignation. "What a thing to say to a future patient! Maybe we're not right for each other, after all."

I could see the dollar signs clicking in his brain. "Now, don't get exercised, my dear," he said. "Relax. Drink your tea. Have a cookie." He set down the tray with a teapot and a plate of stale-looking cookies.

My mother landed next to me. "One bite, it won't kill you. Then let's get out of here."

He looked around and shivered. "Funny, there's that draft again. Guess I'll have to call maintenance."

Washing down the cookie with my tea, I said, trying not to gag, "I think you seem to have the…um…" I searched for the right word."…empathy I need from a therapist."

He preened. "My patients all seem to be well-served. When do you want to begin our phone sessions?"

I wanted to rattle his cage again. "There's just one little thing I need to know," I said, putting down my cup.

"Yes, Ms. Columbo?" my mother said.

He frowned. "What?"

"What do you charge?"

He looked relieved. "The usual, same as what Dr. Ditstein was charging. Reimbursable by your insurance company, of course."

"Of course," I murmured, wondering what the insurance code was for phone ear sex therapy.

He opened the front door with a flourish. Probably taking up his place at the peephole as soon as we got out the door. What a creep.

"That's not even the half of it," my mother muttered in the elevator.

I still wasn't used to her reading my mind. This could turn out to be pretty damn embarrassing, depending on how far it—she—went. About which I had absolutely no idea.

"It all depends. Sometimes it's a yes, sometimes, a no," she whispered.

I waited until we were back at my apartment and she was settled on the sofa. "Okay, what about him?"

She grinned. She was getting downright sassy these days. "You really want to know?"

"Ma-a-a-a."

"Okay, I was just trying to make a joke. I don't really get to have too much fun these days." She sniffed.

God. "What did you find out?"

"Okay, all right, already. Your Dr. Shokum—isn't one."

I was getting testy. "Isn't one what?"

"Isn't a doctor," she said triumphantly.

Maybe her brain wasn't working too well anymore. "Of course, he isn't," I said with a bit of impatience. "He's a shrink, a psychologist. Not a medical doctor."

"He's not a psychologist either." She lay back against the pillows.

"What?"

"You remember all those credentials that he said were in his desk?"

I nodded.

"*Nada*. No PhD, no diplomas, no license, no nothing."

I pondered this information for a moment. "But that doesn't necessarily mean he's not—"

"What he claims to be?" She sat upright. "Then why, my darling, would he first say they're out of sight and then lie about them? Unless he has something to hide."

Chapter 24

As soon as we finished her overcooked pot roast the next night, my mother picked up her pad and marker.

"Okay, let's go. What about that Henry person?"

I groaned. Confronting Henry the nut case was not something I was eager to do.

"Go on, get it over with."

She was right. I had no choice but to hold my nose and jump in, something Toniann said when she had to deal with someone particularly onerous.

I picked up my phone and scrolled down to Henry's number.

He answered on the first ring. "Nusbitt, here."

This didn't sound like Henry. Or maybe he'd developed a second personality. I wouldn't have put it past him. "Henry, it's Marabella. From Dr. Ditstein's group."

The voice instantly changed to the Henry I'd known and feared. "Oh, the group. Oh, Dr. Ditstein. Terrible, terrible. Death. Evil."

I heard snuffling sounds. I couldn't tell if he was laughing or crying. This was going to be fun. Too bad I couldn't deal with his more rational alternate personality. I wondered if there was any way of conjuring it up. Like, "Would the rational self of Henry Nusbitt please come out now?"

The irrational side was making more gross noises.

Since I couldn't summon up his rational side, I tried to summon up whatever patience I could, though the disgusting sounds were getting to me. "Henry, I need your help," I said. "We're planning a memorial for Dr. Ditstein, to honor her memory."

Louder snuffles. "Dr. Ditstein," he said. "Terrible, awful—"

I cut him off in mid-babble. "Henry, can I come to your place and talk to you about the memorial?"

Blessed silence, for a moment. Then the noises were back, full force. "No—my place—no good!" His voice was agitated.

Who knows, maybe he didn't want me to see his collection of shrunken heads in the apartment. Or body parts in the refrigerator, like that serial killer. Or maybe he was just paranoid about visitors, like Shokum. Whatever the reason, I'd better calm him down in a hurry, or I'd lose my chance to talk to him.

"All right, Henry," I soothed. "We don't have to meet at your place. We can meet in the little park across from Dr. Ditstein's old office. Is that okay?"

"Okay." He sounded a little less crazed.

"How about tomorrow night, around eight?"

"Okay." Snuffle.

We hung up.

What have I gone and done? I thought. *What if something I say gets him violent*? Even in a public place, like the park—

"Don't worry, sweetheart," my mother said. "I'll be right there with you."

I glanced over at her. She was lying on the sofa, looking thoroughly exhausted, stretched out like a…corpse. I shivered. What could a seventy-year-old ghost with congestive heart failure do if Henry went bonkers and started attacking me?

"Plenty, just you wait and see. Believe me, I can take care of everything," she said, reading my mind again.

"But how—"

"It's the surprise element, sweetheart. Works every time." She winked at me.

Okay, I told myself. She had her mysterious ways. What did I know, anyway, about what she could or couldn't do, these days? And I'd never been able to psych her out before.

She grinned from ear to ear. "Trust in Mother, sweetheart."

Chapter 25

On our way out of the apartment, we ran into Sam, heading to the trash room.

"Marabella, how is everything? I worry about you." He patted me on the shoulder.

"He's looking good. Really good. And nice sweater. Good color for him. Matches his eyes," my mother said with, I swear, a note of lust.

Since I couldn't tell her to behave, I poked her with my elbow. When I saw Sam staring at me, I realized I'd better do something about my arm, so I moved it up and down. "Too much aerobics," I said, with a laugh. "Anyway, everything's on hold right now, Sam. About the case, that is."

"Have they tried to find the real—" He lowered his voice. "—killer? Have they made any progress?"

I shook my head. "I don't know."

He looked so dejected, I thought I'd better say something positive. Even if it was probably a lie.

"But who knows? They could be pursuing all kinds of leads," I said. "They're not going to discuss strategy with me, right?"

Unfortunately, Sam was too perceptive to buy it. He folded his arms across his chest and looked me straight in the eye. "Marabella, don't say things to try and get me not to worry. Or because you're afraid I'll have a coronary. I can take it, whatever it is."

"I always liked a strong man," she said.

I longed to tell her to shut up, but I realized what I'd sound like. Talking to myself. Embarrassed at my pathetic attempt at dissembling, I said, "I'm sorry, Sam. I shouldn't have tried to fool you. Or maybe," I said, with a sigh, "I was trying to fool myself."

He gave me a hug. "What you need is a decent lawyer, kiddo."

"I can't afford one. I've got Otis instead," I tried to joke.

"We'll just see about that," he said, opening the door to his apartment.

"Sam, don't do anything, please," I said, as he shut the door behind him.

I banged on the door, but he wouldn't answer. Stubborn old man! The last thing in the world I wanted was for Sam to get involved in my legal problems.

"Such a sweet man. If only…" My mother sighed heavily.

I couldn't deal with any of this now, especially the thought that Sam might think it was me who was lusting after him. And I was going to be late for my date with Henry. "Let's go, Ma," I said.

Luckily, we got a cab right away, didn't hit traffic, and made it to the park just a few minutes after eight. Henry was pacing back and forth under a tree.

"What's wrong with him?" my mother said.

"Who knows?" I steeled myself and walked toward him.

Henry stopped in mid-pace and stared at me blankly,

his mouth open. He looked worse than ever. His hair looked like it hadn't been combed for days. His shirt was torn, his pants were filthy, and on his left cheek there was a large scratch.

I took a deep breath, exhaled, and did it again. I marched up to him and stuck out my hand. "Henry, it's Marabella. You remember me, don't you? From the group?"

He stared at my hand as if it were a foreign object. I made myself grab his and shook it. It felt lifeless, like a dead thing. I had to force myself not to shudder.

"Poor man," my mother said, clicking her tongue. "He doesn't have all his marbles."

No kidding. But I didn't share her sympathy for his mental misfortunes, having been on the receiving end of his episodes in the group a couple of times. "Let's sit down on a bench, Henry, where we can talk." I led him over to a bench that was fortunately empty, except for a couple of squabbling squirrels and pigeons, glad that there were few other people around us at this point.

We sat down next to each other. I tried to ignore his staring at me. He switched his stare to the squirrels, who were now fighting on the ground in front of us. He moaned and his eyeballs looked like they were rolling back in his head. I was afraid he'd pass out—or worse. What was worse? He could begin foaming at the mouth. I shuddered. Then a young couple walked by us, and he switched his staring to them. The woman looked terrified and the man started to hurry her away. Henry stood up and glared at them. I shook my head, hoping they'd get the message: *Don't upset the lunatic.*

I asked Henry if he'd like a soda from a nearby wagon. He rolled his eyes, and I took that for a yes, and got one for him and a Diet Coke for me.

He seemed to concentrate on slurping the soda. Then

he started staring at the squirrels again. *Squirrels for the squirrelly*, I thought. That was better, because it was just gross, not scary.

I did my breathing exercises again. Then I plunged in. "Henry, I know how upset you must feel about poor Dr. Ditstein."

He stopped slurping. A shudder ran through his body. "Terrible, terrible, terrible."

"This is not a normal person," my mother hissed. "Just like my second cousin Gerald, may he rest in peace. Even though nobody got any peace before they locked him up."

I gave him what I hoped passed for a sympathetic look. "Yes, someone committed a terrible crime and killed a wonderful human being. Someone—" I took another deep breath. "—who must have been very angry at Dr. Ditstein." I gave him a penetrating look.

Something flickered behind those unseeing eyes. "Somebody did something bad," he mumbled. "Evil, evil."

This was going to take every ounce of courage I had and then some. "Henry, I know Dr. Ditstein upset you at the last group session. Were you very angry at her? You can tell me, it's all right," I said, in a soothing voice.

It wasn't all right at all. He jumped up, knocking over his Coke. I could feel the cold sticky liquid pouring into my lap. "Oh, no you don't! You're trying to trick me, aren't you?" he yelled.

"Please, Henry, calm down," I said, tugging at his sleeve.

Henry shoved my arm away. My mother flew up and smacked his hand hard.

"Ow!" he yelled. He stared down then up at me then back at his hand, sheer panic in his eyes. "Don't you touch me!" he yelled, and ran away.

Unfortunately, the little park was now pretty full of people, strolling and relaxing on the benches. Everyone was staring at us. I was afraid somebody would call the police, and I didn't want to be around when they showed up.

"Thanks, Ma. Let's get out of here," I whispered. I got up, my soaked jeans sticking to my legs. I forced myself to walk instead of making a mad dash, which would have looked pretty suspicious. Especially if the cops were on their way.

Chapter 26

Toniann and I were getting ourselves some well-deserved R and R in the whirlpool the next night after aerobics. In fact, Toniann was already half-asleep.

The giggling women had brought a friend with them. While the three of them giggled and pointed and chattered away in their own language, I told Toniann about interviewing the suspects.

"By yourself?" She jumped, causing a minor tidal wave. "Geez Louise, Marabella! Are you trying to get yourself killed?"

The three women glared at her, and I gave them the finger. They hissed at me.

"I hope not," I said.

"Murder—"

"Shhh!" I said, even though it was obvious the only English our companions understood was sign language.

Toniann lowered her voice. "Murder is the cops' job. You don't know anything about solving crimes. You're a writer, for godsakes."

"It may be the cops' job, all right, but do you see

them coming up with any suspects? Other than yours tru-ly?"

She slumped down, making figure eights in the water with her toes. "You're right, but—"

"Has Otis found out anything that can help me?"

She shook her head.

"So what else can I do?"

"There must be something," she said with a sigh.

The three women roused themselves as one and trooped out of the pool, wrapping themselves in large, flowered towels. Then they took turns rubbing a heavily scented lotion on each other. I tried to inhale as little as possible, but even so, it was more than my poor, sensitive mucous membranes could tolerate.

Toniann was still ruminating. I tapped her on the shoulder and stood up. "Hey, I've got to get out of here. Can't stand the strong smell of whatever they're using."

"Promise me something," she said, getting up.

I climbed out of the whirlpool. "What?"

She followed me out. "That if you're in any trou-ble—"

"Ha!" I snorted. "What more trouble could I possibly be in than I am now?"

"Real trouble. Like your life being in danger. If that happens, please tell me, okay?" She looked really upset.

"Don't worry," I said, with a smile.

"I'm worried," she said, not smiling. "I'm really worried."

Chapter 27

When I got home, my mother was lying in wait on the sofa with her notepad and marker. "What about the crummy character with the stupid jokes?"

"Ron." I picked up my phone and scrolled to his number I'd copied from Dr. Ditstein's files.

"Yo," he answered.

"Ron?"

"Yo-oo." He seemed to be salivating at the sound of a female voice.

"It's Marabella, from the group."

"Mara…oh, yeah, so, whaddya want?" His enthusiasm had taken a noticeable dive.

"Sorry to disturb you, Ron, but I wanted to talk to you about Dr. Ditstein."

"Whaddabout?" Belligerence was rearing its ugly head. "Why'd ya wanna talk to me, anyway? You think I know something? I don't know nothing."

"I know that, of course," I said. "But you were very fond of Dr. Ditstein, right?"

The voice was still wary. "Yeah, so I liked her. So? Whaddaya wanna make of that, anyway?"

"Absolutely nothing, believe me," I said. "But I'm planning a memorial with the members of the group." I had an instant stroke of genius. "And since you're a professional performer, I was hoping you could spare the time to—"

He practically purred. "Yeah, I might be able to spare a little time."

"After all, we all miss Dr. Ditstein."

"Right, right."

"So can I come to your place to talk about it? At your convenience, of course, since you'd be doing us such a big favor."

The suspicion was back. He snorted. "No way, Jose, are you gonna snoop around my place."

"I wasn't trying to—"

"Yeah, sure." He snorted again. "If you wanna talk, you can come over tonight and catch my act. It could give you—" He cackled."—a preview of coming—" He cackled again. "—attractions. It's at The Comedy Pit, East Third Street and Second Avenue, eleven o'clock."

I agreed, and we hung up. Oh, God. This was going to be painful. *Miss Marple never had to suffer anything like this, I'm sure.* Worse than that, my mother decided she was going to go, notwithstanding the late hour.

"You don't want to go there," I warned. "You'll hate it. It's got a terrible reputation. There's a reason why it's called the Pit. I hear it's the pits."

"So, I'll close my ears during the nasty," she said. "I'm not such a delicate flower. Your father once made me sit through a Jackie Mason show in Atlantic City."

"This place will make Atlantic City look like Disneyland. Believe me, you don't want to go to this skuzzy Comedy Pit with me."

"You could need some help. Who knows what could happen in such a place?" she said.

I sighed. There was no reasoning with her, as usual. Since we had a little time before we had to leave, I filled her in on the details of my close encounter with Zoltan the gorgeous.

"Those Hungarians," she said. "They're so romantic. I remember the one who—"

I couldn't believe it. She actually blushed.

"Sounds like an interesting story," I said, hoping to get her to spill the beans. No long-ago past romantic relationships were ever discussed when I was growing up. It was as if my parents had emerged from their respective wombs as full-blown adults, married for life.

She didn't bite.

"Anyway, how do you know he's Hungarian?"

She waved her hand in dismissal. "Hungarian, Romanian, what's the difference? They have an accent, and they know how to treat a woman, yes, sir." Her eyes were half-closed, and she had a dreamy half-smile. "I especially remember that really yummy one, a violinist, I think he was. Oh, boy, could he—"

"Oh yeah? Do tell," I said, still hoping for dirt.

Her eyes snapped open. She cleared her throat. "About your Zoltan, it sounds like—"

The phone rang. "I'll get it," I said, unnecessarily. By now, my mother knew the drill: don't answer the phone or the door. I worried that it was Ron, telling me not to bother. He'd sounded pretty suspicious.

"Hello?"

"You think you're so clever, don't you?" a scary voice whispered.

I couldn't tell if it was male or female. I sucked in my breath, my hand poised to hang up. But I stopped myself. I had to keep him—or her—talking, if I was going to find out who this creep was. "What do you mean?" I said, with what I hoped sounded like I had no idea what he or she was talking about.

"You know what I mean, you little bitch." The voice was a hiss.

"Now, there's no need to get nasty, is there?" I said.

An ugly laugh. "If you don't mind your own business, you'll find out what nasty really is."

"You don't scare me," I said, terrified. I heard a click.

My mother was at my side in a flash. "What's going on?"

I clicked off and stared at the phone. I realized I was trembling. "Somebody doesn't like my asking questions about the murder. Somebody is threatening me."

She pressed me to her ample bosom, nearly suffocating me. "Nobody hurts my daughter, over my dead body."

I couldn't help it. I burst out laughing and felt instant guilt at the look on her face. I gently extricated myself from her bosom. "Damn straight," I said. The fear was rapidly being replaced by righteous anger.

"Call the police." She grabbed my phone and shoved it at me.

I put it on the table and shook my head. "They'd never believe me."

"Well, anyway, that's the end of it," she said, looking grim.

"The end of what?"

"Your questions, your investigation. Let the police handle it. They've got guns," she said.

"You're forgetting something, Ma. They've also got me as their chief suspect. Until I—we—figure out who the real killer is."

She bit her lip. "Marabella, you know I don't usually tell you what to do…"

Was she becoming delusional? I decided to let that one pass.

"But this is dangerous, foolhardy. Who knows what kind of person you're dealing with here?"

"A worried person," I said. "A person who thinks I may be on to something. A person who is afraid of me." I realized I was right. That gave me a bit of satisfaction.

"But—" my mother started to say.

I interrupted. "Don't worry. I'm not going to do anything foolish. And if things get scary," I said, with a grin, "I've got you, right? What's a mother for, anyway?"

She tried to smile, but I could see she wasn't convinced.

"Showtime," I said, looking at my watch. "We've got to get going."

Chapter 28

Worrying I was going to miss my chance to talk to Ron and feel out his reactions to Dr. Ditstein's murder, we got to the club early, around ten-thirty, which turned out to be a big mistake. One shouldn't be required to spend an extra minute in a place like that, least of all to listen to the so-called comedians.

To get to this fine establishment, you had to walk past garbage dumpsters and go down a flight of stairs that stank of piss. Human, cat, or otherwise. My mother and I held our noses while I guided us.

"What kind of people would set foot in a place like this?" she practically spat in my ear.

Inside, it was so dark, you couldn't really tell what shade the walls were painted or anything else, for that matter. The spotlights overhead looked as though they were made out of tomato juice cans painted black. Which was what they turned out to be. The electrical cords running along the cement floor couldn't have passed any code, not even a Cub Scout handbook. To add a bit of class, the restroom was situated behind the performers on the stage. You had to literally go on the stage to pee.

"Lovely establishment," my mother muttered. "Even so, the rent is probably a fortune."

"Probably."

There were about a half dozen of those little tables that were just big enough to hold drinks. Only two were occupied, by guys who looked as if they came in to get out of the cold. The tables wobbled, and spilled drinks seemed to be the order of the day. A sour-looking waitperson with black fishnet stockings was moving around behind the bar. It was obvious that cleanliness wasn't high on the list of priorities here. The floor was so gunky with God knows what, the soles of my shoes stuck to it when I walked.

My mother shuddered. "They can't get someone in to do the floors cheap?"

The stage had barely room for even one performer, with a mic stand and a beat-up piano in the back.

Some pimply guy was pleading with the manager to let him perform that night. "Please lemme go on, I'll just do three minutes."

Of what?

"My act isn't very long."

"One minute, not a minute more."

The manager was very short, fat, and bald. He wore a red tee shirt that read: *Bald men have more testosterone.* And was obviously out to prove it.

"Excuse me," I said. "Can I get something to eat?"

He chortled. "You gotta be kiddin'."

"Not even if you were starving, sweetheart. Even then," my mother hissed.

"Shh," I said. Of course, the manager thought I was speaking to him and stared at me. "Oh, sorry, I didn't mean—"

"Okay, what can I get for such a lovely young woman? Just let me know, and I'm at your service." He looked me up and down.

I fled to the restroom. Big mistake. I was afraid to sit down.

"Don't sit down." My mother was spreading toilet paper on the seat.

"I can do that myself, goddammit," I said. "In fact, I'd prefer a little privacy, if you don't mind."

She gave me a hurt look but stood her ground. "I'm not leaving you alone for a minute in this place with these disgusting people."

The restroom had the old-fashioned kind of toilet where you pull the chain—very noisy. I was afraid to flush, although it wouldn't have harmed the act that was on at that time. Would probably have improved it, as a matter of fact.

The so-called act was a woman who looked like an assistant librarian who was reading her jokes off index cards. The next act, I think, was supposed to be a parody of S and M.

This woman was wearing black leather, black lipstick, and white pancake makeup, with long straight black hair that must have been a wig. She was carrying a cat-o-nine tails that she lovingly stroked across her shoulders and sported a huge, hopefully fake, bruise on her thigh. Yuck.

Finally, the moment I had been waiting for, in breathless anticipation. Ron came out on the stage, wearing skin-tight pants, a muscle tee shirt, and a grin. Wasting no time, he started right in on us. Badda-bing, badda-bang.

"Got a question for you: Why is divorce so expensive?" He stared out at us. "C'mon, folks." Then he sighed. "Because it's worth it. Ha, ha. Get it?"

No one laughed. The waitperson yawned.

"Here's a dinner joke. Very ap-pro-paw, right? Did you hear about the restaurant on the moon? Great food, but no atmosphere. Not like this classy establishment, right? Especially the cli-en-tele."

One of the winos at the table started hacking away and finally coughed up a lunger. Ron shot him a dirty look. "My wife is such a bad cook, the dog begs for Alka-Seltzer."

"That one's so old, I heard it on Milton Berle. And he stole from everyone, George Burns, Jack Benny, everyone," my mother muttered.

"How do crazy people get through the woods? Wait for it. They take the psycho path, ha, ha. Hey, sorry to disturb your sleep, asshole," he said, nodding at the other wino who had slumped down in his seat.

"'S'awright," the wino said, starting to snore.

"A patient at the mental hospital said to another patient: 'I'm not myself today.' The other patient replied: 'That makes four of us.'"

My mother snorted. "Dumb."

"I called my acupuncturist last night and told him I was in pain. He told me to take two safety pins and call him in the morning. Hey, what's with you people, anyway, are you dead or something?"

"How can people sit here and listen to this *dreck*?" she muttered.

"My shrink told me I'm crazy. I wanted a second opinion. He said, 'Okay, you're ugly, too.' Get it? Get it?" He glared, as nobody even cracked a smile.

My mother groaned. "They *hire* people to do this? In *public*?"

None of the people in the room had moved a muscle or batted an eye during his so-called performance. I was stunned into oblivion. I had no idea that human beings would actually choose to do this. Neither had my mother.

"I used up my sick days, so I'm calling in dead. Like you people. That's all, folks." He glared at us. "It's been—real—swell." He strode off the stage.

My mother shook her head. "Much worse than Berle or Henny Youngman, even. And not even funny. Henny Youngman, at least, was once in a while funny."

Ron sauntered over to my table. "How'd I do?" He slid into the rickety seat opposite me. Sweat streaked his face.

"Terrible," my mother hissed in my ear.

"It was very…a real experience," I said, forcing myself to smile brightly.

"Yeah." He leaned back in the chair, grabbing his crotch and scratching his balls. "I try to give 'em what they want."

I nodded, and my mother made a face.

He signaled the waitperson. "A glass of beer. And make it cold, will ya?"

She gave him a dirty look and walked to the bar.

My mother glared at him. "Can't even be nice to the help."

"I know you're probably tired, but can we talk about Dr. Ditstein?" I asked.

The waitperson walked back to our table with the beer, foam sloshing over the glass.

"Shit, they can't do anything right here," he said, taking a sip. "This is warm, dammit!" he yelled over to the bar. "Throw some ice in it, for godsakes."

The waitperson stalked back to the table with a couple of ice cubes in her hands, which looked none too clean. She threw them into his glass, which made the beer slosh over again.

"Shit, get me a fuckin' rag to wipe this mess up!"

"Such foul language, and to a woman yet." My mother covered her ears.

The waitperson brought over a towel and made a couple of half-assed passes at the puddle on the table.

He glowered at her. "Gimme that, I'll do it. Shit!"

He finally settled into his beer, legs spraddled, crotch up. I figured he was comfortable enough to talk.

"I'm sure you miss Dr. Ditstein, like we all do," I said.

"Yeah, yeah." He slurped his beer.

"Such a terrible tragedy to happen to such a wonderful person," I said. "I guess it's like, you know, when bad things happen to good people."

"Yeah, a terrible thing," he said.

"It must be especially hard for you," I said.

His eyes narrowed. "Why is that?"

My mother poked me with her elbow. "Make nice."

Grrr. I knew that. "Well…" I had to word this carefully. Ron might be pond scum, but he wasn't stupid. "She seemed especially fond of you."

He smirked. "Yeah, women always seem to feel that way about me. Sometimes, I swear, I practically have to peel them off me. No shit." He hiked his crotch and gave his balls another scratch.

"I can see why," I said, batting my eyes and trying not to gag.

He stared at me with new interest. "Yeah, yeah, it happens. Say, if you're not doing anything tonight…" He leered in my general direction.

"Over my dead body." A hiss in my ear.

I gave what I hoped was a girlish giggle. "Oh, I'd just love to, but I've got to get home soon because I have to be up early tomorrow. But maybe another time." I batted my eyes again.

"Okay, whatever." He shrugged, losing interest already.

"Smart thinking," she whispered.

"About Dr. Ditstein," I said, "who do you think would want to hurt somebody like her?"

"Beats the shit outta me," he said. His eyes narrowed again. "Why're you asking me, anyways?"

"You seem to be pretty perceptive." I laid it on with a trowel.

He ate it right up. "Pa-ceptive, right, I guess I am. People say I have a certain jay-nay-say-quay, you know what I mean?"

I nodded. "Sure." Flattery seemed to be getting me pretty far here. "I started to think that maybe, it could be one of the members of the group who did it. What do you think? Present company excepted, of course." I batted my eyes again.

He slugged his beer. "Yeah, yeah, I see what you're thinkin'. Sure, it could be. Maybe that fat bitch Maxine. Or Beth. She thinks her shit don't stink."

I nodded encouragement. "I hate people who think they're better than everybody."

"Yeah!"

"What about Christine?"

He let out a loud belch, without excusing himself. "Christine, yeah, I could see that. There's something a little funny about her, ya know? And I never did trust them quiet ones. They're usually up to something sneaky."

"Right. And Henry?"

He gave a snort. "Now there's a bona-fidey nut case, if I ever saw one. Yup, he prob'ly should be locked up, and they should throw away the key. He coulda done it, fa sure."

Not getting much information out of him and not wanting to stay there another minute, I stood up. "It was really good to talk to you, and catch your act."

He looked up at me. "Hey, what about the performance, for the memorial thing?"

"Oh, of course. I'll be in touch as soon as we have a time and place." We made our way out the door, stumbling into the dark. I was grateful to be able to draw in fresh, clean air again.

Chapter 29

My second date with John went off like gang-busters. We began our deliciously dog-free evening at Millefleurs, an excellent Continental-style restaurant. John got us an intimate little table in a dark corner. So dark, in fact, that we could barely see the menu and each other by the light of the rose-scented candle. A prime opportunity to engage in a little groping under the table. Knees, thighs, that sort of thing. Especially after we'd downed a couple of glasses of wine with our chicken cacciatore.

"I think they expect that sort of thing," John said. "That's why it's so dark. Not that I mind." He squeezed my knee, which sent tingles down through my black satin slip all the way to my black lace panties.

"I didn't know you were that kind of guy," I said, with a giggle, realizing I must be a little drunk.

"That's my girl," he said, starting to refill my glass.

"Whoa! If you keep that up, I'll either throw up or fall asleep on you."

He shook his head. "I forgot. Let's get out of here, okay?" He set the bottle down, signaled for the waitperson, and paid the bill. Helping me on with my jacket, he shepherded me outside and hailed a cab. I sank into the back seat, settling myself against his shoulder.

"Don't worry, I'm not sleeping," I said, instantly nodding off. Next thing I knew, John was gently shaking me awake. "Huh?" I said. Then I felt my face get hot. "I wasn't really asleep, you know. Just resting my eyes a minute."

He laughed. "Not only were you fast asleep, but snoring like an elephant."

"I never snore!"

"I love women who snore. Because they can't complain when I do it." He led me out of the cab and into Lincoln Center's Avery Fisher Hall.

"Humph," I said, feeling grumpy. Falling asleep in places other than a bed always did that to me. Well, at least I didn't throw up.

"Anyway," he said, with a grin, leading me to a box seat, "the music should wake you up in a hurry."

It did. The Philharmonic was playing Mendelssohn's Hebrides Overture, Beethoven's Eroica and Dvorak's New World Symphony—three of my favorites. So far, it had been a perfect evening. John kissed the top of my hair, and I nestled in his arms. Hopefully, the best was yet to come.

After the concert, another cab delivered us to the de Courcey Hotel, a study in Victorian grace. "How did you know?" I murmured.

John just smiled and checked us in. We took the elevator to the fourteenth floor and found our room, which I barely had time to look at. We ripped off our clothes, barely making it as far as the king-sized canopy bed. Then we tore into each other like beasts.

"Delicious," he murmured afterward. He began licking my body from my toes up.

I thought I had died and gone to heaven. Though the thought did cross my mind that maybe he'd been spending a bit too much time with his dogs.

"You bring out the animal in me," he said.

"Thank the gods." I looked at his dark curly chest hair, which matched the hair on his head and the hair between his legs. "You're the same all over," I said with a giggle.

He nuzzled at my breast. "I'm getting hungry again."

"Me, too. But I shouldn't eat again."

"Why not?"

I gestured at my hips.

He stroked them fondly. "Don't lose a pound. You're just right, perfect, in fact."

Unbelievable. A man who appreciated my long-scorned hips. And fortunately, my screw-up mechanism with men seemed to be in remission. Or maybe all those years with Dr. Ditstein had finally done the trick.

Thinking about Dr. Ditstein sure changed my mood. I sighed and started chewing on a raw cuticle.

"What's wrong? Did I do something to make you upset?" He looked so worried I could have eaten him up.

"No, of course not. It was heavenly. It's just a little problem of my being under suspicion of murdering my shrink." I tried to sound nonchalant.

"*What*?" He jumped up. "Tell!"

"Sit and I will," I said. He sat. I patted his head. "Good boy."

He held my hand, listening quietly to the first part of the story, about my finding the body. When I reached the part about being arrested, he was furious. And when I got to the last part, about my questioning suspects, he went ballistic. "One of these people is probably a murderer," he said. "And once somebody kills once, what's to stop them from killing again?"

"You mean like, 'Stop me before I kill again'?"

He scowled. "It's not funny, Marabella."

Good thing I'd had the presence of mind to leave out the threatening phone call I'd received, or he'd really freak.

"You're not taking this seriously."

"Oh, yes, I am. Very seriously. But it's either try to find the real killer myself or end up doing time."

He rose and began pacing up and down. "Not necessarily. You don't know what your lawyer is going to do or—"

"Ha!" I said. "Otis is barely competent. And even if he were, I don't know how much any lawyer could do, with the mindset that Rivera has about me."

"Then we'll just get you a better lawyer, that's all."

"John, that's very sweet of you, but—"

"No buts." His voice was determined. "I'm going to get you out of this."

"John—"

"On one condition," he said.

"But I don't want—what's the condition?"

"That you promise me you'll give up this crazy investigation that could get you killed."

"John, I—"

"Promise?"

"I'll think about it," I said.

He put his arms around me. "I'm beginning to really care about you, you know." He buried his face in my hair. "God, that smells good."

"Apricot shampoo," I murmured.

He ordered crackers and cheese and fruit and a pot of tea from room service. We climbed back under the covers to eat.

Munching on biscuits and Brie, I thought that, maybe at some point in the future, when I trusted myself more about our relationship, I'd tell him about my mother. But not yet.

Chapter 30

What about that actress one, what's her name, Beth?" my mother asked during what passed for dinner on Sunday. After she'd unsuccessfully tried interrogating me about my overnight disappearance.

"Yeah," I said. I finished as much of my mother's tuna casserole as I could stand, fetched my phone, and scrolled down to Beth's number. I got lucky.

She answered in breathy tones. "Hellloooo, this is Beth."

Unfortunately, I just had my regular old voice at my disposal to answer back. "Beth, it's Marabella."

Silence.

"Marabella, from Dr. Ditstein's group."

"Yes?"

This was not going to be easy. "I'd like to talk to you about the whole thing about Dr. Ditstein."

Silence again.

"I thought we could maybe help each other deal with our feelings of loss."

"How did you get my number? It's unpublished. And there's a reason for that. So that I don't get calls from every Tom, Dick, and Harry who wants to talk to me."

This called for some fancy footwork. "I'm not every Tom, Dick, and Harry, Beth," I said, in a soft voice. "We were part of the same group, we shared our innermost feelings, we bonded. And—" I threw in a sweetener. "—I always felt close to you, especially when some of the others weren't being very nice to you—"

"Nice to me?" she squealed. "You mean that warthog, Maxine? God, what a despicable, disgusting pig-like creature she is. I swear if I looked half that bad, I'd kill myself."

"You could never let yourself go like that," I soothed. Thankfully it got her off the phone number kick. That was the thing about the queen of narcissism, that mind of hers was easily diverted. Probably because there wasn't much in there to take up the slack. "Never in a million years," she breathed.

"She's just jealous," I said. "But you can't really blame her, with her looks."

A snort. "You know how they always say that a fat girl would be pretty if she lost weight? Well, even if that pig dropped fifty pounds, she'd still be a horror."

"Some of us are just born that way," I said. "And a few of us are lucky enough to be gorgeous. Like you." This was making me physically ill, but it had to be done.

"Little-old me?" she trilled. "Why thank you, sweetie."

Strike now. "So, do you think we could get together for a little while, just to talk, you know?"

"Sure thing, baby. How about tomorrow night? Monday nights are always dead time for me, anyway. I usually use them to catch up on things like tweezing the old eyebrows, hot waxing the legs and the bikini line, stuff like that. So if you don't mind watching," she said, with a girlish twitter.

She was letting me know she was doing me a huge favor. "Of course not," I said, figuring, *"I'd love to watch you get the hair off your various body parts"* might be misconstrued.

She gave me her address and directions on how to get there, and we agreed to meet at six-thirty tomorrow. "For a real girlie night at home," she promised.

Making nice to Ms. Narcissism and trying to snoop around while she defuzzed herself promised to be a real treat.

Chapter 31

Thanks to good subway connections, I got to Beth Hronska's apartment in a tad over half an hour. It was one of the converted warehouse buildings in Chelsea that had become trendy lately. Personally, it would give me the creeps, living in what looked like a deserted factory area, with nothing visible but shops all around. But I heard that if you were looking for a place that was bigger than a closet, this was the place to be.

Beth's apartment was a third-floor walkup above a second-hand comics store whose windows were decorated with posters of various caped crusaders. I peered in the window, which was still lighted. The stuff looked like fun and brought back a wave of nostalgia, not all of it good.

My taste had run more toward Little Lulu than the men in capes. In fact, I was such a diehard Lulu fan that I'd twisted the front of my long hair into two fat Lulu curls in the fourth grade, until Barry Spiegel yanked on them so hard, I saw stars. It was back to barrettes after that.

Dragging myself away from the store window, I went upstairs and walked down the corridor to Apartment

3M, marked "B. Hronska." I pushed the buzzer. No answer. I checked my watch. Six-thirty, right on time. Maybe Ms. Narcissist and her soon-to-be- hairless body parts were in the shower. I pushed the buzzer again, leaning on the door. And discovered that the door was unlocked, unheard of in a city apartment.

With a horrible sense of *deja vu*, I pushed open the door. "Beth?" I called. "It's Marabella."

No answer. My breath caught as I slowly walked inside.

I followed the sounds of a radio in the bathroom. Just as I'd thought, Beth had the shower on. But she wasn't in it. She was splayed on the bathroom floor, lying in a pool of blood, her brains decorating the lilac tile wall.

I started to gag and hopped over her feet past the body and blood. I just made it to the toilet. Flushing, I grabbed a couple of dainty guest paper towels from the sink and wiped my mouth and the toilet handle. Then I made the mistake of looking at the body again, ran to the toilet, and did the same thing all over again.

Trying to avert my eyes from the bloody mess on the floor, I decided that as long as I was here, I'd take a lesson from my-mother-the-snoop and poke around a bit. Though this was a sad end for Beth, for me it was nothing less than serendipity. I didn't think another chance like this one would come my way again. As my mother would say, "When opportunity knocks, don't let your doorbell be disconnected." Or something like that.

But first I needed to make sure whoever did Beth in was long gone. Grabbing another bunch of guest paper towels to avoid leaving fingerprints on anything, I inched my way out of the bathroom and into what looked like a bedroom down the hall. I gave it a quick once-over, including the closet and under the bed. Then I did the same with the living room and kitchen.

Figuring the bedroom was a good place to start looking for…what? I opened Beth's bureau drawers. Other than lacy, very-see-through undies and thongs, strapless bras and sheer pantyhose, I drew a blank. Same with the night table, although Beth's reading matter was not what I would have expected: several pop psychology books on self-esteem. Could all that narcissism have just been a big front? An old poet boyfriend of mine, Marty, used to say that inside every flower of narcissus beat the heart of a shy violet.

Anyway, poor Beth wouldn't be reading or understanding anything anymore. I replaced the books in the nightstand, carefully wiping my fingerprints off, and moved on to the closet. I pushed back the mirrored sliding door with a paper towel wad and gasped. You could, pardon the expression, bury someone in there, it was so vast. Enough designer clothes to start a Soho boutique. And shoes. And scarves, capes, shawls and every other accessory under the sun. And makeup. And jewelry.

With reverence, I reached out to touch one of the Armani dresses and froze. The material would probably retain fingerprints. What a waste, I sighed. The clothes would most likely end up in the Salvation Army. Unless Beth had a size-four relative somewhere.

Above the clothes pole were hatboxes piled to the ceiling. I dragged over a chair and climbed up. I opened the boxes and found some very ordinary-looking hats, a strange selection for someone as trendy as Beth.

Not so strange after all. Each box, it turned out, had a bunch of DVDs under the hats. I collected as many as I could carry, climbed down and searched for a DVD player. Conveniently, there was one in the bedroom. I stuck a DVD in the slot and pushed play.

There was Beth, blonde, smiling and unclothed, doing it with a well-muscled man and an equally well-muscled woman. I shut it off and stuck in another one. This one had Beth in a black wig, doing it to herself with some sort of body lotion. I shoved in the next one and started to gag again. Her privates were being licked by a German shepherd. I shuddered to think what John Adriance would have made of that one. Even I, who was definitely not an animal-lover, was ready to call the SPCA. I shut off the DVD player.

This was Beth's big acting career? What she put on such airs about? Then I realized that all of this must have taken place quite a while ago. She'd looked quite a bit younger then.

I took another look at the DVD collection. They weren't labeled, but they were numbered, though who knew what the numbers meant? I had numbers four, six, seven, nine, two, and three. I climbed back up to the hatboxes, replacing the ones I'd grabbed and gathering up the rest. Figuring I didn't need to see more of the same art form, I checked out the numbers: One, eight, and ten, which also had a note reading, "Last in series."

What was number five? And where was number five?

Maybe the killer had it. But why? Some sort of evidence? No, the top of the closet didn't look like it had been disturbed for a while. And why would Beth keep such crap, anyway? Sentiment? Didn't seem likely. Clips for future roles? Gifts for friends? A turn-on for her boyfriends—girlfriends? Pets?

After wiping off the DVDs, the player, and the hat boxes, it was time to pack it in and get out of there before somebody else showed up. I let myself out quietly, wiped off the doorknob, shoved the paper towel wad into my pocket, and slipped down the stairs, hoping no one saw me. Surely someone—not me—would call the police.

On the way to the subway, I fished out the guest paper towels and tossed them into a trashcan on the curb. Then I thought about the fact that my life, which used to make some kind of sense, no matter how bizarre, lately seemed to have gone off the deep end with a vengeance.

The question was, should I call Otis and tell him about Beth? Or wait till Rivera appeared on my doorstep again? Boy, did I wish I could talk to Dr. Ditstein. I really missed her special way of listening and her warm responses. Whoever did this horrible thing to my therapist, one of the world's nicest human beings, deserved to be punished for a long, long time.

And even though Beth wasn't in the same league as Dr. Ditstein, she didn't deserve to die, either. Even though, somebody, the killer—or killers—thought so. Maybe there were two of them, and the murders weren't related. Could Beth's murder be related to her porn career? Could somebody get bumped off for being a narcissist?

Was Beth heading for her appointment with Dr. Ditstein and saw the killer leave the apartment and the killer saw her? But then, why would the killer wait this long? Maybe Beth initiated contact, to blackmail him or her? But would she have been so carelessly dumb?

Well, call me crazy, but anyone who was willing to serve as a dog's dessert wasn't exactly discriminating.

On the way back to my apartment, I realized I'd forgotten to wipe my fingerprints off the door of Beth's apartment building. Well, I wasn't going back there. I'd just have to hope for the best.

Then I realized something even more important. If someone had now killed twice, would he or she blink about killing again? Especially if I figured out whom he or she was. And once he or she knew that I knew. I flashed on the threatening phone call I'd received. Maybe next time he—or she—would deliver the threat in person.

Chapter 32

As soon as I got home, I told my mother about Beth.

She closed her eyes. "I knew something bad happened. We've got to find that missing DVD. That's a key."

What did she say? A key? A key?

I dug my denim jacket out of the closet. I hadn't worn it since finding Dr. Ditstein, I remembered with a shudder. I stuck my hand in the pocket and fished out a tiny key.

"Ma."

"What, sweetheart?"

"I have a key, a very small key. I took it out of Dr. Ditstein's hand when I found her." I swallowed hard. "A safe deposit box in a bank. It's got to be that."

"But which bank?"

"Hmmm." I thought for a minute. "I bet it's one of the ones right near her apartment."

"Which only narrows it down to about six on just the few blocks nearby. So, it'll take a little time. But don't worry, sweetheart. Your mother is on the case. Of course,

I'll go right now, since the banks are closed. I wouldn't want to spook them." She giggled.

"Thanks, Ma."

She took off with a groan. I popped a Xanax, made myself a cup of tea and a plate of cheese and crackers, and settled in with a new crossword book. I was down to the last two words in the first puzzle, South American bird and medieval king of France, when I heard labored breathing. I immediately felt guilty about making her exert herself.

"No need to feel guilty," she said, sinking onto the sofa. "What kind of a mother would I be if I didn't help my daughter?"

"Catch your breath, Ma," I said. "I'll make you a cup of tea."

"Thanks, sweetheart, I appreciate it. But could you bring the water to a boil first? I didn't want to say anything, but I really don't like it lukewarm."

"Why didn't you say something?"

"I don't like to complain."

Grrrr. I went into the kitchen and waited for the water to boil madly before I put it into her cup. When I brought the steaming cup out to her, she sat up and beamed.

"You're really not going to like this at all, Marabella," she said, blowing on the tea. She was wearing a strangely self-satisfied expression, reminiscent of the time she'd finally figured out one of Agatha Christie's whodunits.

I sat down in the chair across from her. "Now what?"

"Remember way back right after Dr. Ditstein was killed?

"And?"

"Remember what I said, which you didn't want to listen to, of course.

"Ma!"

"What else is new? When did you ever—Oh, all right." She pursed her lips. "Anyway, I said I thought there was blackmail involved, somehow. And you, of course, wouldn't buy it."

"What kind of blackmail? Was somebody from the group blackmailing the others, and poor Dr. Ditstein, too?"

"Not exactly. But you're getting warm."

I sighed. "Okay, Ma. Let's have it."

"You're not going to like this," she said again, taking a cautious sip of her tea.

"Ma, cut it out!"

She gave me a hurt look. "You don't have to get fresh."

"For godsakes, tell me already!"

She took a deep breath. "The blackmailer—" She paused dramatically. "—is—was—your Dr. Ditstein!"

Chapter 33

I couldn't stand it. Not only had I been totally conned by my shrink, but my mother had been right all along. In a daze, I listened while she enumerated what she'd found in Dr. Ditstein's safe deposit box.

"Number one: a savings book with a total of two-hundred-fifty thousand dollars in regular deposits and a ledger with names, payments, and dates, showing amounts owed by each person. Then there was a DVD, marked 'number five.'"

That had to be Beth's missing porno DVD.

"And could you believe, a copy of Christopher's birth certificate before she was Christine? Not to mention photocopies of old newspaper stories about that sleazy so-called comedian Ron's arrest for statutory rape of his younger sister. Then we have a signed paper from that lizard-loving Maxine, admitting embezzling from her firm. And," my mother added, "you're not going to believe this—"

"What?" I asked wearily.

"There was a note about Donna, your boss, in her

ledger. Donna had a prescription drug problem. Big-time."

"Donna? Drugs?" I would have thought alcohol, if anything, because of her drunken parents. Addictive personality, I guess.

"But," she said, "there is also a notation that Donna refused to make payments and threatened to go to the police."

I was beginning to have a new respect for Donna, Her Royal Bitchiness.

"As for the boyfriend, Zoltan—"

"Yes?"

"He was in serious trouble with the immigration authorities." She smiled. "Of course, marrying an American citizen would have fixed that right up."

"Did you find out anything about him and Dr. Ditstein?"

"You bet." Her eyes gleamed. "According to his bank statements, it looks like Dr. Ditstein stopped giving him money about two weeks before she was murdered. And there's a copy of a letter she sent to him, breaking off their engagement."

Now that was interesting. What would make her do that, I wondered?

"And," my mother said triumphantly, "last but not least, medical records of Dr. Shokum's hospitalization."

"Hospitalization?"

"The funny farm. Your Dr. Shokum is a former mental patient with trumped-up so-called medical credentials," she said. "Remember that time in his office when I noticed that his credentials weren't where he said they were?"

I nodded.

"And that if he kept them out of sight, he probably had something to hide? Well, did he ever."

"What about Henry? And me?"

"For some strange reason, Henry wasn't on the list. Maybe because Dr. Ditstein already knew about his mental condition," she said. "And just what would you be doing on a blackmail list?"

"Not with my boring life," I said, with a sigh. "And it's nice to know Henry and I have something in common."

"Now that we've got the evidence on all these people," she was saying, "we can bring it to that policeman and get you out of trouble. I'll gather up the key and the box and plant it on his desk."

"Detective," I said absently, thinking about my fingerprints on the key.

"No problem," said the mind-reader. "I'll wipe off the key first."

"But all we've got is that Dr. Ditstein was a blackmailer," I said, feeling bile rise up in my throat. "We still don't have a clue as to which one of the blackmailees did her in. Or, for that matter, even Zoltan could have done it. Or Henry."

"So now what?" my mother asked.

I didn't have a clue.

Chapter 34

I figured it out after dinner the next night while pondering native Australian plant and volatile chemical compound in my crossword. I'd pretend to blackmail them with Dr. Ditstein's information and smoke out the killer. The fact that I would be using myself as bait hadn't sunk in yet.

When I knocked on Sam's door that night to drop off some audio books, I debated with myself as to how much to tell him. The less, the better, I decided. That was, unless he wormed it out of me. Unfortunately, he was very good at doing that.

Needless to say, he was terribly upset. So upset, in fact, that his hand shook when he poured my tea. I got an immediate case of the guilts.

"I wasn't going to tell you. I knew it would upset you," I said, feeling perfectly awful about causing a lovely old man to be upset.

"Upset! My favorite neighbor is running around chasing a murderer who's killed not once, but twice, and also threatened your life, and you wonder that I'm upset!" He sat down heavily on his sofa and closed his eyes.

"Now I'm worried about you, Sam," I said.

His eyes flew open, and he looked positively indignant. "About me? You think I'm going to drop dead? And I don't have a killer after me!"

"Don't worry, Sam, I'm taking care of it. It'll be okay." I sipped my tea, trying to act nonchalant.

"Oh, sure. Blackmail, murder, more murder, more blackmail, threats on your life—it all sounds just dandy to me." That was the first time I'd ever heard Sam be sarcastic.

I stood up to leave. "Sam—"

"Promise me you won't put yourself in any more danger. Please, Marabella." He gave me a hug. Playing his trump card with a grin, he added, "You wouldn't want to give an old man a heart attack, would you?"

If I didn't know better, I'd swear my mother had been coaching him.

Chapter 35

Lucy still wasn't back on her corner when I left for work the next morning. I was really worried about her. I made up my mind to ask some of the other street people about her when I got home that night.

I munched on one of Mei Lee's brownies and thought about Dr. Ditstein, the dirty blackmailer. I realized how furious I was about being conned. Thinking about needing her all those years made me even more furious. I gritted my teeth. There was nothing like being betrayed to get your juices going. And I was going to need those juices to keep me out of jail.

I had just about reached the campus when it happened. There I was, striding along purposefully, looking straight ahead, no eye-contact, a true street-wise New Yorker, when somebody shoved me sideways from behind. My body did a flying leap into the air and landed face down, with a crash, right off the curb. I guess I passed out. Somebody must have called an ambulance, and I woke up in the hospital.

And wished I hadn't. Every part of my body hurt, especially my chest, which was swathed in bandages. I tried to hoist myself up on the pillows and nearly passed out again from the pain. I must have made some pretty scary noises because three nurses came running into my room.

"Oh, you're awake!" a pudgy blonde said cheerily. "Everyone's been waiting for you to wake up."

"If this is what it feels like to be conscious, I'd rather be in a coma." I groaned.

A short dark one laughed. "Oh, she's got a sense of humor. Good for you!"

"What happened?"

The blonde looked at me with concern. "You don't remember anything about the accident?" she asked.

"Accident?"

Shorty came over to the bed and patted my shoulder, making it feel as if a ton of bricks landed on it. "You were in an accident and somehow landed off the curb into the street and got clipped by a cab. Those guys like they speak English." She chortled, giving her cohorts a huge laugh at my expense. "Good thing somebody had the wits to call an ambulance, because you could have bled to death. And three of your ribs were cracked." She shook her head.

"Which hospital?" I croaked.

"Memorial." The third one, rail-thin with graying hair, looked at me suspiciously. "Weren't you looking where you were going?"

Of all the gall. I tried to look indignant but gave up because even a small facial gesture hurt like hell. That being the case, I didn't dare imagine what shape my face was in.

My pain-fogged brain tried to remember what did happen. Then the truth slammed into me like a Mack truck. "I was pushed! Somebody tried to kill me!"

They looked at each other. I could see them trying to

restrain themselves from rolling their eyes. Yeah, right, she thinks somebody's after her.

Gray and skinny said, "Are you on any medication, dear? All you have to do is let us know, and we'll make sure you have your meds."

Great. Now they think I'm loony tunes. And if I get mad, they'll be sure of it. So talk nice, as my mother would say. "Actually, I'm not on any medication." I certainly wasn't going to tell them about the Xanax, which would only validate their suspicions about my obliviousness. "Except for the pill, of course," I said. "Better safe than—"

Blondie shrugged. "Okay, it's up to you. We can't force you to take anything you don't want to. But we find that we do a whole lot better when we continue our regular medication."

I just loved that "we." Since I couldn't do my alternate nostril breathing in front of them, or they'd rush me off to Bellevue for sure, I tried to at least slow down my breath before I answered them. "Okay," I said, with a smile. "We'll try and remember that." That seemed to satisfy them, at least for the moment, and they turned to go. "By the way," I said, "could we please have something for the pain?"

"Of course," gray and skinny said.

"Oh, God. I have to call my—" I stopped myself. They looked at me strangely. "Um, do you know where my phone is?"

Blondie went to the closet, fumbled around, and finally fished it out. She handed it to me. "Do you need help?"

I declined her offer, and they left. I hitched myself up on the pillows, a new agony in every hitch, and reached for the Droid. Luckily, it still worked. After scrolling down to my land-line number, I said in a muffled voice, "Ma, it's me. I'm in Memorial Hospital. I'll explain when you get here."

I also called my boss. Luckily, I got her voice mail, so I didn't have to listen to a harangue. Not that I expected sympathy from such a limited human being. Oh, well, at least here I'd get a little rest, which I could definitely use. If only I didn't hurt so much. I wiggled around, trying to feel comfortable. Tolerable would even be a good thing.

Trying to take my mind off my poor body, I scoped out the room. Ugh. Puke green walls hung with ersatz art—you know, the kind that was supposed to be cheery. Smiling little kid faces, puppies, kittens. Hoisting myself up to look out the window would require too much effort, and the view was probably of the parking lot anyway.

A few minutes later, an aide brought me a couple of horse pills and a cup of water, which I downed as fast as I could. The horse pills stirred up a few deliriously sensuous thoughts of my favorite veterinarian, before I drifted off to a nice, drugged, pain-free sleep.

I was rudely awakened by a hiss in my ear. "You look terrible! What happened? You weren't maybe looking both ways before you crossed the street? I thought I taught you that when you went off to kindergarten." She was sitting on the bed, dressed in one of my tee shirts and sweats, clucking like a hen about to lay an egg.

"You're not going to believe this, Ma," I whispered, in case any of the nurses were around. I struggled to sit up and gave that up in a hurry because it damn near killed me.

"Don't move, sweetheart. Just tell me what happened."

I eyed my mother. Even in my drugged, pain-wracked state, I could see that she was getting pretty frail.

"Ma, you haven't been eating. You've got to eat," I

said, "Or you'll…" The rest of the sentence was better left unsaid.

"I eat, I eat. Don't worry about me. Tell me what kind of truck hit you."

"It wasn't a truck. But it doesn't matter," I said.

"It doesn't matter? Is my daughter losing her mind as well as almost killing herself, too?" she wailed, rocking back and forth.

"You'll mess up the bed, and the nurses will get mad at me," I said sternly. "The reason it doesn't matter is that it wasn't a truck."

"What was it, then? A motorcycle?"

"Ma, it was a person. A person shoved me into the street in front of a cab. Luckily, the cab wasn't going too fast. I guess the driver didn't have a good sense of direction."

She gasped and shut her eyes.

I hoped she wouldn't faint. Then the nurses would have to take care of both of us. Both of us? Maybe I really was losing it.

She opened her eyes. "Don't worry about me. I'm worried about you." Then her face became contorted with fury. "What kind of person…"

"Would do such a thing? Think about it, Ma."

She fixed me with a look. "Don't be snotty. Somebody—"

"Is trying to kill me," I said.

"That's exactly what I was afraid of," she said. "Okay, that settles it." She folded her arms across her chest.

The gods only knew what was going on in that convoluted mind of hers. "Settles what?"

"We're stopping this investigation right now. No more sleuthing, snooping, or whatever you call it. Done. Over. *Fini*. The end."

"But why, for godsakes?" I asked.

"Because I'm the mother and I said so," my mother said.

I narrowed my eyes and even that hurt. But I could play this game, too. Only not half as well as she could.

"Because I only have one daughter and you're it, that's why. I'm not going to lose you to some cockamamie crazy killer, that's why. Let somebody else play detective." She almost looked as if she were going to cry. My mother, the stoic, who never cried. Was she actually softening in her…whatever…state?

"Ma, we can't do that." I took a deep breath and immediately regretted it. After all, almost getting killed wasn't much fun for me, either.

"Be so kind as to tell me why not."

"Two reasons. First, I told you, it won't do any good to stop now because the killer already knows who I am, remember?"

She nodded slowly.

"Second, if we don't catch the killer, I'll end up in jail." I tried to joke. "It'll be a disgrace. We've never had a jailbird in our family. Except Cousin Saul. He went away for insurance fraud, right?"

"Don't be smart. And that was your father's side of the family."

"Sorry. I was just trying to cheer us up." I tried looking pitiful. Since I felt so horrible, it wasn't hard.

She patted the only part of my arm that wasn't bruised and pursed her lips. I could see the anger bubbling up again. "Humph. Never mind the humor. Back to the subject at hand."

"Somebody's trying to kill me," I whispered. Funny. Every time I said it, it got more scary.

"Uh-uh." She shook her head. "Not if we catch him first."

Chapter 36

After my mother left, I lay there, trying to make sense of the events that landed me in a hospital bed with my body transformed into a quivering mass of pain.

At least I didn't have a roommate. Not yet, anyway. So I could try and collect my thoughts in peace without relatives from hell going on about Aunt Sally's gallbladder or turning on the overhead TV to reruns of *American Idol*.

I tried to remember what I'd been doing before my assailant had made such a valiant effort to finish me off. As far as I knew, I hadn't been doing anything abnormal, just walking to work, like always.

Walking to work. Okay, that meant that whoever it was, knew what I did every day and where I did it. Or the person had been following me. That meant following me from my apartment. That was enough to give me the creeps, the thought of a murderer knowing where I lived. Where I worked. I shuddered.

So, who? I figured the best bet was one of my potential blackmailees.

I closed my eyes. *The better to see you*, I decided. My mind's eye conjured up the members of Dr. Ditstein's group. Everyone except Beth was fair game.

Chris. I remembered the fact that, though I had once liked her, I'd always thought there was something just a little off about her. Now, thanks to my mother's great detective work—all right, snooping—I knew it was more than just a little. Hiding your gender had to be pretty high on the stress list. Though it could be a necessary thing in everyday life.

For instance, you probably wouldn't tell your massage clients, "I understand that you may feel uncomfortable about certain private parts of your body. Believe me, I can relate to any and all of it. Been there, done that."

But hiding what had to be the major experience of your life—a sex-change operation—from your therapy group? It made absolutely no sense. Unless there was a lack of trust. Would Chris think one of us would betray her secret? Somehow hurt her, damage her life?

As a group, we didn't exactly exude the milk of human kindness. But it was hard to think that even a sleazy pig like Ron or a nasty bitch like Maxine would give Chris up. I prided myself on thinking that at least we had a sense of the sacred responsibility that being part of a therapy group engendered. Dr. Ditstein had instilled that in each of us.

Right, Dr. Ditstein and her sacred responsibility. Of blackmail. Just the thought of what she really was made me want to kill her, if she weren't already dead. Or throw up. In my opinion, she'd dirtied the profession of therapist. From now on, I refused to think of her as "Dr." She didn't deserve my respect.

I shook my head, trying to clear it. Bad mistake. Moving brought a knife-like pain to my ribs. Sinking back into the pillows, I tried not to scream. I didn't have the strength to deal with that trio of helpful harpies again so soon. Fortunately, the worst of the pain subsided in a few minutes.

Back to the detective work. Chris seemed to be so tender-hearted, I had a hard time imagining her ever wanting to hurt anyone.

Unlike Maxine. Now there was a candidate for homicide, if I ever met one. I wondered how she and the Green Menace were getting along. Probably making out like crazy.

Okay, what did I know about Maxine? Besides being a reptile lover, an angry bitch, full of jealous hatred of any halfway decent-looking woman, what else?

She was rolling in dough. Embezzled dough from her firm. That was how she financed that huge apartment she lived in. Plus, she'd been taking lavish vacations every year. Until last year, now that I recalled. At the last minute, she'd canceled a trip to the Azores. Though she'd mumbled something about living a more simple life, she'd seemed even more furious after that—obviously because of Ditstein's blackmail. And given her rage-a-holic behavior toward Beth and Ditstein, especially because seeing Ditstein made Maxine remember how much she hated her slim, shrink sister.

Then there was Ron. But being a molester of your teenaged sister didn't necessarily mean being a killer, did it? Though he gave new meaning to the words "chauvinist pig," and he had tried to hit on Ditstein, though she was able to fend him off. Just the thought of that made me want to puke. And he seemed to recover, at least enough to stick with the group and continue making the rest of us squirm at his gross sexist attitude. Especially Maxine. She hated his guts so much I wouldn't have been surprised if she'd killed *him*. But as far as I knew, he was alive and well. Which made him a suspect. Not to mention the fact that he was another one of Ditstein's black-mailees.

Last, but not least, we had Henry the crazy. Now there was somebody clearly capable of murder, given the homicidal rages he'd treated us to in group. Funny, he'd never directed any of that wrath onto Ditstein. Except at the last session, of course. How could I forget about that? He'd shouted at her and slammed out of her apartment in a fury.

Henry, my boy, you're way up there on my list. Even though there was nothing in Ditstein's secret files about you. Maybe because she already knew all there was to know about your deep, dark, insane past.

But I was forgetting dear, phony Dr. Shokum. After my visit to his chamber of gloom, I thought he was as weird as Henry. Weirder, even. Now that I knew about his escape from the loony bin and his persona as a phony shrink, his weirdness made a strange kind of sense. And once Ditstein discovered the true facts about him, he must have been apoplectic. Apoplectic enough to kill?

There was definitely something scary about the man and his apartment. I shuddered. Unfortunately, I'd made a date to meet him there to collect my "payment."

Then there was Zoltan, the charmer. Whether or not he hailed from Transylvania, he was a real piece of work. Utterly self-absorbed, supercilious, and, I was sure, totally insincere about his grief over Ditstein. I didn't think he gave a rat's ass about her. So why was he pretending he did? And why was he pretending that they were about to be joined in marital bliss when she'd just dumped him? Maybe so he wouldn't look like a murder suspect?

And what about my boss? She, who practically went into cardiac arrest at the mention of Ditstein. She, who acted as if psychotherapy was something she wouldn't touch with a ten-foot-pole, had been one of Ditstein's patients. Then I remembered that she'd refused to be blackmailed. That was probably the reason why she had "terminated," as noted in Ditstein's files. I could probably scratch her off the list. After all, if she wouldn't subject herself to Ditstein's strong-arming and basically told her to bug off, why would she have to kill her?

Okay, that was the list. But how was I going to find out what they were doing at the time of my near-death experience? How could I check up on where they'd been at the time? Should I lay a trap for them? Have my mother call them about my whereabouts and the fact that the murder didn't succeed?

In other words, use myself as bait? Again?

Hold on. How the hell could my mother become my PR agent? They all thought she was dead and buried, remember? Okay, she'd just have to pretend to be somebody else. She'd probably actually enjoy it. She always did have a flair for the dramatic. She'd had the female lead in my junior high school's PTA comedy, *Twiddler on the Roof.* Yenta-in-chief. Did I say typecasting?

Okay, Ma, time for a command performance. You can do it. But wait a goddamn minute. Who was she going to pretend to be? *Think, think.* I shifted a little in the bed. It made me even less comfortable, if possible. I shifted back.

An aunt. She could be an aunt, come to visit me in the hospital. Okay, fine. But why in hell would she be calling the members of my group? *Um. Let's see…she…looked up people's names and phone numbers in my address book and called everyone. Because she thought they were all my "dear friends."*

This was not going to work.

Or, plan B. I could call them up myself from the hospital. And tell them I wasn't dead yet. *In other words, if, at first, you don't succeed….*

Then I began thinking about the fact that I didn't want to die. That I was really scared. But I also didn't want to go to jail. And I wanted to catch the killer. And, come to think of it, I was really pissed. How dare somebody do this to me?

But I wasn't going to take it anymore. And I wasn't going to stay mad. I—and my mother—were going to get even. *Don't mess with the Vinegar women. They'll toss you into a vat of brine and pickle you, soon as look at you.*

For a fleeting moment, I debated calling Detective Rivera and reporting the attempt on my life. I had a right to police protection, right? But what made me think that they'd protect me? Or even believe me? Knowing Rivera, he'd say I made it up to try and look innocent.

Right. Throwing myself in front of a cab to beat a murder rap was a tried-and-true strategy to fool the cops.

But if I didn't report it, they'd never even know about it. Or never try and think about the fact that maybe—just maybe—there could be something to what I've been telling them. Namely, that there was a real murderer running around. Who now was after me, for Number Three.

Chapter 37

I was sprung a few days later. I was so glad to get out of that hospital, even going back to work seemed good. When I left my apartment building, a cold rain was starting. I would have taken the subway, but I'd had more than enough of being confined, thank you.

So I made up my mind to slog through the streets, rain and all. Well, I wasn't the Wicked Witch of the West, so I wouldn't melt, right?

The Oz reference made me think of Chris Ragamoni's Wizard of Oz apartment. And Harmony Light, Chris's partner in mutual massage, Thursdays at seven p.m. Harmony would have to be in the phone book. Otherwise, how would she get her customers, or clients, as body workers referred to the people whose bodies they worked on? I had to check her out as soon as I had a minute.

There weren't too many people on the streets, which puzzled me, until I realized that most sensible New Yorkers took to public transportation in the rain, especially a cold rain. Or cabs, if any were to be found on a rainy day.

Well, fewer people hopefully meant less mud ending

up on my shoes. A good thing. When I got to an intersection, I heard footsteps close behind me. Too close. *Oh, my God. Not again!* I slowly turned my head, just a little, enough so I could peek at whoever was there but not let them know I knew.

I almost stopped breathing. A man wearing a long coat with a high collar and a scarf covering the bottom half of his face was right behind me. Was it Ron? Zoltan? Shokum? No, not Shokum. He never went out, right?

I started to run, dash, across the street. Against the light. Horns blared. Drivers cursed. And the guy behind me yelled and tried to—

Pull me out of the way of oncoming traffic. Not *into* it.

Out of breath, shaking, and scared out of my wits, I leaned against a shop window.

The man looked down at me. "Are you all right, miss?"

"Yes. Thank you." I tried to smile up at him.

"No problem." He smiled back and went on his way.

Deep breaths, Marabella. Deep breaths. And a Xanax. Two.

Chapter 38

Donna buzzed me before I could get my coat off. "In my office, toot sweet, Marabella."

I knew better than to expect any sympathy about the injuries that landed me in the hospital. I was not disappointed. After her initial sarcasm about my being accident-prone, she punctuated it with such lovely remarks as: "Normal people don't land in front of a moving cab when they try to cross the street, even in heavy traffic, Marabella."

I sincerely hoped that my dripping coat and shoes were making wet stains on her nice floor.

But despite herself, Donna actually sounded glad to see me. Of course, that was probably because there were several imminent disasters to head off that involved creating fictions for the press. This meant writing complete sentences, something she was totally incapable of doing.

Checking my messages, triaging them in order of importance, I decided the three from John deserved top priority.

"Where have you been?" He sounded anxious. "You know, I realized you never gave me your home phone number, and it seems to be unlisted. So I've been calling you at work—"

I filled him in about the "accident" and my enforced vacation at the hospital. He was horrified, worried, and angry at me for exposing myself to a ruthless killer and not getting in touch with him. He tried to bribe me with a romantic dinner. Much as I wanted to, I figured the multiple work crises would keep me chained to my computer late into the night, so I put him off till tomorrow. And though I couldn't wait for him to put his muscular arms around me, it would be a lot less painful if my ribs had another day to heal. Then I could relax and thoroughly enjoy his company. Hopefully, without Harpo and company.

Meanwhile, I remembered that I had to set up dates with my potential blackmailees. Something warned me not to fill John in on that little venture.

I was working my way through the pile of messages on my desk when Toniann called me. I noticed she'd left me three messages, too.

"Why the hell didn't you call me back right away?" she screeched in my ear.

"Maybe because I was in the hospital because somebody tried to kill me?" I said.

She interrupted my recitation of the gory details halfway through. "Never mind all that," she said.

"Never mind the fact that somebody wants me dead?" I tried not to scream, since the walls of my office were paper-thin. "With friends like you, who needs enemies?"

"Shut up for a minute and listen to me, will you? Something's going on. I think they might be getting ready to charge you with another murder!"

Chapter 39

The cops arrived at my apartment while I was dressing for my date with John. We were going to dinner and a concert. I was looking forward to heavenly baroque music topped off by an even-more heavenly time in John's bed. John had hired a dog walker to take the Marx Brothers for a long romp in the park before we came back to his house, so hopefully, they'd be too tired out to bother us. Though I'd bet a bushel of Purina that if Harpo had known I was going to be at John's house, he would have staged a sit-on. Probably on the dog walker.

When the doorbell rang, I yelled to my mother, who was in the kitchen preparing her dinner for one, "I'll get it." Throwing my old bathrobe over my good bra and panty set, I ran to the door.

"Who's there?" Knowing who it was but hoping it wasn't.

"Police. Open up, Ms. Vinegar," said one of them.

My mother dropped a dish with a crash. I opened the door, clutching my robe, which kept opening because I'd lost the sash years ago. I hadn't bothered replacing it, not expecting to wear it entertaining visiting policemen. Detective Rivera and two blue coats barreled their way in.

"Maybe you should get yourself dressed," Rivera said, eying the front of my robe.

"I was planning to do just that—" I said haughtily, shoving the robe back over my left bra cup, "—when I was so rudely interrupted."

"You are under arrest for the murder of Beth Hronska," he intoned. "Before we ask you any questions, you must understand…" He went into the Miranda routine, which I was unfortunately all too familiar with. "You have the right to remain silent. Do you understand?" he droned.

Out of the corner of my eye, I saw my mother slide to the floor in a faint. Good thing she was relatively quiet about it, but I was worried about her. I'd have to find an excuse to go back into the kitchen and check out her condition.

"I have to get a glass of water," I said.

"Fine," Rivera said, with a yawn. He shook his head. "Boy, you didn't even blink an eye. Were you expecting us?"

"What's the use?" I shrugged, walking into the kitchen. "Whatever you're going to accuse me of, you will." I managed to rummage for a glass while giving my mother a quick once-over. With the full glass, I dropped down, ostensibly to pick up the broken plate, and spilled water on her face. "You okay, Ma?" I whispered.

One eye fluttered open, and she nodded.

"What's taking so long?" Rivera called. "We don't have all night."

I drained my glass, wishing I could help her up, but that seemed impossible. "I need to make one, no make that two, phone calls."

"You only get one," he said wearily.

"You're going to make me choose between calling

my lawyer and canceling my date?" I asked.

"Tell your date to call your lawyer," he said. "Or the other way around."

Oh, great. Instead of murmuring sweet nothings to me at La Venezia, John Adriance got to chat up Otis Pinckney. This did not augur well for our future. I'd have to lower myself and beg. "Please, Detective," I said, honey dripping from my tongue, "I'll be brief, I promise. It'll just take a minute." I batted my eyes at Rivera and let a bit of black-lace boob slip out.

It must have had its desired effect, because he grumbled, "Oh, go ahead. But make it quick." His eyes were glued to the top of my robe.

The better to see me with, I was sure. I thanked him profusely, trying to keep from gagging, and quickly dialed La Venezia. I told the maitre d' to tell Dr. Adriance that I'd been suddenly taken ill and wouldn't be able to join him for dinner. Then I called Otis at home. After complaining about my interrupting his Beef Wellington, he agreed to meet me at the station downtown. "But," he warned, "Don't count on me to get you out on bail for this."

Right. Otis Pinckney really cares. I went into the bedroom and changed my clothes, including the underwear. Why waste black lace on jail? I packed a few things and came out into the living room. They were standing close together, like a football huddle, laughing hugely. I caught a few off-color words. Must be dirty jokes.

"So glad you're having such a wonderful time at my expense," I said, in my best snotty voice.

"Okay, let's go," Rivera said, ushering me out the door.

I thought fast. "Wait!"

"What now?" he said.

"I forgot to turn off the water in the kitchen," I said.

"You wouldn't want my apartment to have a flood."

"All right, already, go ahead. But hurry up," he said.

I got back to the kitchen. My mother was sitting up on the floor. "Are you okay?" I whispered.

A weak whisper. "Roger."

"The list of phone numbers for the suspects, it's in my desk."

"Roger."

"Hide it when you're done with it."

"Ten-four."

My mother seemed to have metamorphosed into a trucker. What the hell, when I got out, I'd buy her a CB. *If* I got out, that was.

Rivera was standing in the kitchen doorway, staring at me. "Who are you talking to? Yourself? Or the wall?"

I gave my mother a last look.

Rivera rolled his eyes and muttered, "A damn lot of good all those years of psychotherapy did, if she talks to herself."

We traveled downstairs in a clump, Rivera, me and the boys in blue. We piled into a waiting black-and-white. The blues in the front, Rivera and me in the rear. I leaned back in the seat and closed my eyes, conjuring up an image of John Adriance and me, riding home from the concert as a prelude to glorious things to come. I opened them to Rivera sitting next to me, wearing his usual sour expression.

At the station, it was *deja vu*. Booking, paperwork, yadda, yadda, yadda. At least I didn't have to deal with that horrible inky mess on my fingers again. As a known criminal, my prints were already on file.

Otis, clad in a vile lime-green suit that did not enhance his appearance, was waiting for us in the interrogation room, frowning at me, clearly disgusted. "Can't keep yourself out of trouble for a minute, can you?" he muttered. "Geez, next time Toniann asks me for a 'little favor'—"

Rivera pulled up a couple of battered chairs to the table, and I dropped into one. "Okay, let's hear the whole thing, from the top." He flipped on a tape recorder.

Otis roused himself. "Detective, my client did not kill Beth Hronska. Or Dr. Ditstein. She may be a royal pain who gets herself in bad situations." He glared at me. "But she's not a killer. She wouldn't even know what to do with a gun."

Rivera raised his eyebrows. "It just so happens, counselor, that Ms. Hronska wasn't killed with a gun. She was killed with a large, blunt object. But before the killer did her dirty deed, she decided to do a little window-shopping. The shopkeeper was away for a couple of weeks. But when he came back, he was kind enough to identify her for us. Plus her fingerprints were on the door of the apartment building."

I groaned.

Otis clutched his head with both hands. "Geez," he said. "Window-shopping! For Chrissakes, how could even you do anything so dumb?"

"You are not helping me here, Otis. I didn't do anything, damn it!" I pounded my fist on the table. "You're not going to believe this," I began.

"Try us," Rivera said, leaning back in his chair.

"I was going to Beth Hronska's house to talk to her while she shaved her legs," I said.

"Cut it out," Otis said, jabbing my arm.

I gave him a dirty look. "It's the truth. I can't help it if it sounds funny."

He sighed again.

"I decided to talk to her to see if I could find out anything about Dr. Ditstein's murder," I said.

"Like a clue, perhaps?" Rivera asked, with a smirk.

Ignoring the sarcasm, I said, "I got there around six-thirty, like we agreed, and I knocked on the door. Nobody answered. So I knocked harder, and the door pushed open."

"Just like that?" Rivera said, opening his eyes wide.

"Just like that," I said coldly.

"All by itself!" he said, with feigned amazement.

"Right," I snarled.

"Try and behave, will ya?" Otis poked my arm again. "You're not making this any easier."

I sighed. "So I went in. I called her name, and nobody answered. I walked through the rooms till I got to the bathroom. And there she was, on the floor. Dead." I shuddered at the memory.

Rivera yawned. "You already knew that because you were the one who killed her."

"Why would I do that? I didn't even really know her, let alone—" I stopped. Saying I didn't even like her wouldn't be a helpful thing to say right now.

"Let alone what? Let alone that you already killed Dr. Ditstein? And Ms. Hronska saw you and maybe you had to get rid of her, too." Rivera's eyes were steely.

I was so frustrated, I actually grabbed Otis's arm. "Help me out here, will you?" I hissed.

"Counselor, the complaint's been filed, and I met with the prosecutor. Your client will have another little talk with the CJA rep. Then you can escort her to the judge's chambers," Rivera said.

"Right," muttered Otis. "I hope to God it's not—"

"Judge Camino," Rivera said, with another smirk. "He's working night court, which makes him ve—ry unhappy."

I groaned again.

So did Otis, when he heaved his bulk out of the chair. "C'mon, let's get this charade over with," he said.

I jumped up, saying, "Have you forgotten which side you're on? You're supposed to be defending me!"

Rivera motioned me into an interview room for my chat with the CJA rep, who was definitely not as pleasant as the last one. The rep, a scrawny woman with a bristly short haircut, basically blew me off and hustled me back out to Rivera after a few questions.

Otis grabbed the paperwork from Rivera. "Go ahead," he said to me, "make my day." He motioned me to follow as he plodded down the connecting corridor to the judge's chambers, conferring with the prosecutor along the way.

At least the last time, Camino was only half awake. Now he was breathing fire, eyes smoldering, lips curled in a sneer. Probably ready to pounce and bite the heads off any unlucky petitioners to the court. He reminded me of Izzie. When he caught sight of Otis and me, he bared his teeth. "You two!"

"Right," said Otis.

Camino bellowed, "Pinckney, I don't want to hear the word 'right' again from you ever, do you understand?"

"Ri—yes, Your Honor, sir."

Camino calmed down and began stroking his chin, which made him look even more diabolical. "Just why are you two littering my courtroom today?"

Otis sighed. "Well, you see, Your Honor, sir, it's like this—"

"Get-to-the-point, Counselor," Camino hissed.

"Ri—yes. Your Honor, my client, Marabella Vinegar—"

Camino glared.

"She's been accused of another murder that she is innocent of," Otis said.

"This little lady? A double murderer?" He shook his head sadly. "Tsk, tsk."

I couldn't take it anymore. "I'm innocent, dammit!"

Red-faced, Otis twisted my arm.

"Owww," I moaned.

"Your Honor, sir, I'm sorry, my client lost her…uh, head," he said. "She didn't mean it."

"Did too," I muttered.

"Shut up! Not you, Your Honor! As I was saying, please excuse my client. She doesn't know what she's doing, she's in a state of shock. We're asking the court for leniency, since she has never committed any violation of the law—"

"Except another murder," Camino said dryly, stroking his chin again.

"Which she is completely innocent of, too, Your Honor," Otis said.

"I recall I let her off on the last one," Camino said.

Otis nodded. "And we'd be very grateful if you could—"

"Are you nuts, Pinckney? Two strikes and you're out, young lady," Camino said, rapping his gavel. "Bailiff," he called to the sad-looking man standing in the corner, "lock her up."

Chapter 40

Cuffed and chained to a bunch of other women, I was delivered in a blue-and-white Corrections Department van to the Women's Detention Center. It was a dirty, gray-colored barracks-like building with barbed wire on the roof. Several nasty-looking feral cats prowled the parking lot. A sign said: *No weapons beyond this point.* A comforting thought, until I learned this referred to the guards. I wondered exactly how the guards were supposed to protect us from each other without weapons. By using psychology? Hydrotherapy?

The van pulled in, and we were discharged, still tethered together. We did a group shuffle onto the welcome mat. I wondered fleetingly if this was how Siamese twins did their walking. As the guard opened the faded beige door, an overpowering smell of Lysol assaulted my nostrils, which was actually a relief after the too-close encounters with my van mates.

We were dumped into a small entry room and our handcuffs and chains were removed. I rubbed my sore wrists as an officer called out my name and asked my address, birthday, and mother's maiden name. After his fit of laughing—I guess the combination of Vinegar and Warmflash was too much for his self-control—he told me to step through the metal detectors and open my jacket. I left my belongings—my pocketbook, a few bucks, a comb, and lipstick—at the processing desk and was escorted into a holding pen, a large cell in the middle of the room. About a dozen women were sitting or lying on the floor, probably in substance-induced stupors. I decided to stand and stare into space, hoping my fellow inmates would think I was nuts or drugged out and leave me alone.

About an hour later, they took us out of the pen to take our picture and transferred us to holding pen number two. Shortly after that, we were taken to the shower area by a stocky, muscular-looking female guard.

"Strip!" she barked at us. "Put your clothes on the bench and bend over."

We stripped and bent. I felt hot waves of humiliation rise from the soles of my bare feet as she peered into my undefended orifices. This was infinitely worse than the cuffs and chains.

While we showered, the guard searched our clothes and gave us sickly green jumpsuits before making us strip once again for the medical exam. After putting in time in yet another holding pen, we were pulled out again, issued two sheets, a blanket, towel, toothbrush, cup, toothpaste, and comb by a guard with enormous feet. Bigfoot took a bunch of us single file through endless corridors, with gates unlocking before and after us every few hundred feet. We passed a gym on the left and on the right, some classrooms, a library and, believe it or not, a hair salon. What a relief. At least my incarceration might produce one or two good hair days.

More gates clanged opened and shut before we finally reached our cells. A central monitoring station sat at the head of the cell block that held about 100 women. My new residence, cell twenty-two, contained a metal cot, whose frame was bolted to the floor. Would someone steal it? Nah, probably it could be used for a weapon. I shuddered, thinking of how strong someone would have to be for that. There was a toilet with no lid—another weapon?—a sink, and a streaked metal mirror. A small metal locker and stool completed my new furnishings.

Welcome home, Marabella.

As Bigfoot shut the door behind me, I burst into tears.

Chapter 41

I passed up the opportunity to get my hour of "recreational exercise," traipsing back and forth in the common area in the middle of the cell block. I'd already had a taste of my fellow inmates during an earlier "rec time."

"Fuckin' bitch," the skinny streaked blonde directly across the corridor had called me, spittle hanging from her mouth. Probably just her cute way of welcoming me as the new kid on the block.

The squat woman with the butch hair next to her had a different approach, just as unsubtle. She grabbed her ample boobs, pretending to offer them to me. "Come to mama, baby," she crooned. "Come to mama."

Giving up on the local entertainment, I sat down on my cot, careful to avoid the large bump in its middle, and stared at the tiny barred window, way up on the wall. The loud voices of my sister inmates were having a bad effect on my nerves. From farther down the corridor, I could hear somebody start to sing at the top of her voice, very off-key, what sounded to be something in Spanish. Or maybe Chinese? Soon everyone was doing her own thing, whatever it was, in a veritable Tower of Babel.

I got up and decided to make my bed, figuring that it might make sitting on it slightly less uncomfortable, though there was no help for the lumpy mattress. The blue-and-white striped pillow was flattened out, and the sheets were spotted with grease or sweat stains. Or other substances I preferred not to think about.

The scratchy olive-green blanket went on top of the mess. I remembered my mother's mantra that an unmade bed was not a good start of the day. Or something.

My mother. She must be so worried. And how on earth was she going to manage without me? Silly me. I reminded myself that she'd been managing quite nicely for many years before I was even born.

What if she went into heart failure again? I shuddered at the memory.

"Ma," I said to myself. "Don't give up."

"I wouldn't think of it, sweetheart," said a voice in my ear.

I jumped up and practically fell over her. I must have been thinking so hard, I hadn't heard her land. Unless she was getting better at it with practice.

"Practice does make perfect, darling." She plopped down on the cot, landing hard on the bump. "This they call a mattress? And expect you to sleep on it?"

I shrugged. "You should see the toilet."

She eyed the lidless receptacle in the corner and grimaced. "Don't sit down," she warned. "I'll bring some paper towels. Or maybe plastic wrap." She wrinkled her forehead. "That might be better, it clings. What do you think? And don't use that toilet paper. You don't know where it came from."

"K-Mart, probably, I think it's their Martha Stewart pattern. Catching a disease from the toilet is the least of my problems," I said glumly. The noise was steadily increasing to excruciating levels. Where were the noise police?

"What's going on?" my mother asked. "You can't hear yourself think in here. It'll give you such a headache."

I shrugged again. "Fun for the inmates, I guess."

"Next time I'll bring earplugs." She sighed then brightened. "The reason I came, sweetheart. Not that I didn't want to see you, I miss you, of course—" She paused for dramatic effect.

"What? What?"

"I've got news and bad news," she said triumphantly.

I figured I'd better be sitting for this and sank down next to her. "Okay," I said wearily. "Let's have it."

"The news first or the bad?"

"Both. Whatever. I don't care."

"Well…" She took a deep breath. "You're not going to like this."

I snorted. "Doesn't look like I'm having much fun now, does it?"

She looked around and shook her head. "And it's so dingy in here. Can't they get someone in to brighten the walls?"

"Ma."

"Okay, all right. As I was saying, not good. Your picture is splashed all over the newspapers." She gave me a sorrowful look. "I think it's the one they took when they hired you at the college. Not very flattering, but I've seen worse."

I groaned. I should have expected it. What in God's name would Donna do when she saw my picture in the newspapers? Shit, she was probably the one who gave it to them.

"And your friend Henry, the nut case…" my mother was saying.

"What about Henry?"

"He's one of the splashers," my mother said.

"What do you mean?"

"Henry," my mother announced, "is not crazy. And he's not your murderer. Henry is an undercover reporter for that tabloid…what's its name?…that digs up dirt and has disgusting stories about perverts and murder and mayhem."

"*The National Globe*," I said slowly, trying to take it in.

Chapter 42

Boy, was Henry Nusbitt in the wrong profession. What an actor. All that time, he was snooping and spying on the group, pretending to be crazy as a bedbug. I was really pissed.

"What nerve, feigning craziness. Sneaking and sliming his way into our most private conversations, our deepest thoughts. Pretending to share and care. What a creep. He even had Ditstein fooled." Or did he? I wondered. Was it possible that she was in on his dirty little secret? Considering her brilliant career in blackmail, anything was possible.

"Henry's been snooping around lately, too," my mother said. "I caught him outside Dr. Ditstein's and outside our apartment."

This was puzzling. Why would he start playing detective? Unless it was more grist for his mill, for a sequel to his first article on his phony group therapy experiences.

"Guess it comes with the territory. I followed him into his apartment—" She had the decency to look abashed.

"Ma!" I shrieked. I was worried about her. What if

Henry was bonkers as well as a reporter? The two weren't necessarily mutually exclusive.

This touched off a chorus of "Mamas" outside my cell door. Great.

"You miss your mama, baby?" I figured that was my boob-jiggling pal. "Come to mama, baby."

"Tch," my mother clucked. "These are not nice people."

"You don't meet nice people in prison," I muttered.

"By the way, about that Zoltan?"

Ditstein's boyfriend.

"Not a nice man, that Zoltan character," she said, shaking her head.

"What?" I asked.

She made a face. "He lives off women."

"Aha!" I knew something about him wasn't kosher.

"He doesn't pay for his own clothes, his food, or even his rent in his hole-in-the-wall in Alphabet City. He always has an older woman to support him. They even buy his *underwear. Black silk.*" This last was said in a hushed voice.

"Nice deal, if you can get it," I said.

"Marabella!"

"Sorry."

"Not only that, he keeps a sexy young girlfriend on the side. If his patronesses only knew."

Maybe they did. Maybe that's why Ditstein dropped him.

"Maybe she found out about the young girlfriend," my mother said helpfully.

I'd never get used to her mind-reading. But something was scratching at the back of my head, waiting to be let in.

"I can't stay too long, though I hate to leave you here in this terrible place." She looked around and shuddered.

"But if I don't get back, I can't help you get out of here."

"Right, right," I said distractedly. What was it? Something…I'd have to try and remember it later. God knows, I had nothing better to do right now. It wasn't as if I was late for work or something.

Work. Oh, Geez. Well, I'd worry about finding another job when I got out. But what about John? God, what would he think? Well, at least I'd still have Harpo's affection. Dogs didn't discriminate against jailbirds.

My mother and I hugged goodbye. I could feel her ribs.

"Ma," I whispered in her ear, "Don't forget to eat, okay?"

She nodded. "Roger. Got to keep up my strength to help my Marabella."

Then, with a few groans and a couple of clink-clanks, she was gone.

<h1 style="text-align:center">Chapter 43</h1>

I couldn't remember sleeping at all. But I must have dozed off sometime toward morning, because I woke up in a sweat from a horrible dream about my group.

Beth was nude, grinning lasciviously from ear to ear, blood smeared all over her face. Maxine and Izzie were making out. Ron was pinching a pre-pubescent Alice-in-Wonderland-girl with long blonde curls and a picture hat. Chris was wearing a dress, heels, and a beard. And Henry was snooping around with a magnifying glass and a Sherlock Holmes cap. Dollar bills were floating down from the ceiling, landing on everyone's head.

But where was Ditstein? There must be some significance to all this. Dreams were supposed to tell you things. So, talk already.

I brushed the cobwebs out of my brain and tried to think. A thin strand of daylight was hovering above my cell, filtering through the tiny window. I couldn't figure out what my dream was trying to tell me about the group, if anything. I'd deal with it later. Right now, I was so hungry, I could have even eaten my mother's cooking with pleasure. I realized I hadn't had anything to eat last night, since the cops had effectively squelched my dinner date.

I closed my eyes and let warm thoughts of John flood my brain. A few minutes later, I felt myself getting a bit too warm. Not a good idea in this place, I thought, remembering my "Come to Mama" invitation last night with a shudder.

Hopefully, breakfast would be soon. And hopefully, it wouldn't be too revolting. Then I heard heavy footsteps tromping down the corridor.

"Wake up, girls, time for breakfast!" the guard boomed.

This one was skinny and ugly but looked strong enough to take care of herself and, I hoped, anyone else.

Frightful as she was, with that orange hair that must have been a wig perched on top of her head and blood-shot eyes, my stomach was overjoyed to see her. I jumped off the cot too fast and almost passed out from my weakened state. Whatever it was, I was ready to eat it.

I shouldn't have spoken so quickly.

The mess hall reminded me of my junior high cafeteria. The walls were sickly yellow, the food smells were revolting, and the seatings were large metal tables and benches bolted to the floor. The women were slouching in line with their trays, desultorily picking up plastic—of course—silverware and cups.

I ate it because I'd die of starvation otherwise. Oatmeal with skim milk—were they looking out for our health or just got it cheap?—two slices of white bread spread with greasy margarine, and a cup of coffee, definitely not Starbucks. I loathed oatmeal. Actually, any hot cereal made me gag. It reminded me of warmed-up library paste. And I complained about my mother's burned French toast? Before I could stop myself, I said, "I hate this glop."

My table companions, who had been entertaining themselves by making rude noises at me, suddenly got quiet. Then one of them, a chubby brunette, slowly drew out the syllables, "Girrlls, did you hear that? Ms. La-de-da here hates her glop."

With that, she and her pals broke into rip-roaring laughter, heaving, and snorting. Then the one to my left, a leather-faced, middle-aged woman with dirty blonde hair, poked me in the shoulder, hard. I could feel a bruise blossoming. The one on my right, who was young and sported piercings all over her arms, banged me on my other shoulder. They took turns battering me back and forth, while everyone craned their necks, this way and that way, as if they were being entertained at a tennis match.

After a few minutes of this, I jumped up from my seat, which had the delicious effect of banging their heads together. Now everyone was laughing at the two of them. Good. Maybe I could slink away without anyone's noticing—

"Where the hell do ya think you're goin'? Thinkin' a takin' a little stroll, huh?"

The plug-ugly guard was facing me, hands on the skinny hips, sneer on the lips.

"Um," I said. "No. I mean, I didn't know that I couldn't—"

"Back ya go." She marched me back to my table. "It's line-up time awready, anyways. So get yaz ass in line. Now."

"Yessir."

Snorts from my tablemates, glares from guard.

"I mean, yes, ma'am." I tried smiling at her, which had no effect.

"Watch that smart-ass mouth of yaz, too!" Her red-rimmed eyes blazed at me. "Okay, all ayaz, line up for ya fresh air—" She smirked. "—and exercise in the yard!"

I tried positioning myself between a couple of women who hopefully were too old to be vicious. I was wrong. They managed to push and poke me in my back and my ribs, all during our outdoor recreation hour. *The matron and her cohorts must be blind, deaf, and dumb*, I thought. Naah, I realized. They were smart like foxes. They knew better than to get mixed up with those murderous babes. So where exactly did that leave me?

Battered, bruised, and alone. A sob rose in my throat. I wanted my mother.

Chapter 44

Though it wasn't my mother, the next person who showed up to visit me turned out to be much more comforting.

The guard marched me out to the visitor's room. There was John sitting at one of the rickety little tables, gazing at me sadly. Even so, he was a beautiful sight.

"Marabella," he whispered, "I read about it after I saw your picture in the paper."

"It didn't show my best side, did it?" I figured a little humor would help his mood. It didn't.

"Marabella, be serious! I've got to get you out of here. Tell me what I can do."

I tried to smile at him. "Just believe in me, John. That's all."

"Of course I do." His dark eyes flashed. "But how could they do this to you? What's the matter with your lawyer? Why haven't the police looked for the real killer?"

"It's a long story." I sighed. "But I'm working on it, don't worry."

"Don't worry? You're in this place, and I shouldn't

worry about you?" He almost screamed. "I'll get you another lawyer, that's what I'll do!"

"No, no, don't do that," I said. "Actually, Otis is probably doing as much as anybody could, given the situation." I didn't really know if I actually believed that, but I certainly didn't want John to cough up money for a high-priced lawyer who probably couldn't get me out of here, either.

We spent the rest of my allotted visitor's time whispering sweet nothings across the table. Enormously sexy and enormously frustrating.

"Timezup," the guard grunted.

John and I kissed each other's fingertips. "I'll be back as soon as I can," he said.

As he walked slowly out of the room, the guard said, "Whatta hunk. I wouldn't kick that one outta bed."

I sighed. I wondered if, and when, John and I were ever going to end up in bed again. Or on the sofa. Or anyplace at all.

Thank the gods he believed in me. Maybe I was actually getting smarter about men, after all these years of Mr. Wrongs.

Chapter 45

Toniann sat across from me in the visitor's room, wearing an ecru pants suit and a worried expression. She'd brought me a couple of literary magazines. "That guard finally said it was okay to give these to you. She probably never even saw one of these in her life. You'd think it was a terrorist manual or something," she sniffed.

I actually giggled, thinking of *New York Magazine* and *Harper's* being used for secret codes. Then I thought of something much more important. Namely, how Toniann could help me out of here. But I'd have to handle this delicately. After all, I couldn't exactly tell her about my mother's detective work. I'd have to act as if it were all my doing. *Sorry, Ma, I'll make it up to you. Maybe a trip to Atlantic City, God help me.*

"It's been all over the papers," Toniann was saying. "But it wasn't Otis's fault. The goddamn DA held a press conference to announce they'd caught the double murderer. God. Uh, there's more," she said. "That boss of yours called. Geez Louise, what a mouth on that woman."

I wondered if Donna was still on drugs. Maybe that's

what she was really doing at the twelve-step program all this time, dealing with her own stuff instead of her parents' problems. "What did she say?"

"Minus the foul language, she said to tell you that if, and when, they let you out, you were fired. Unless they proved you were not guilty. I thought in this country, you were innocent until proven otherwise."

I sighed. "Not according to Donna."

"She sounds like a royal bitch."

"Her one virtue is that she's not a letch. Toniann," I said slowly, "I need your help."

"Anything I can do, I'll do. Except something…uh… illegal. You know, like a file or a knife or something." She was looking uncomfortable.

"No, no, nothing like that. Don't worry. This is just a phone call, that's all. Nothing involving sharp instruments."

"Oh," she said, obviously relieved. "That's great. Tell me what I can bring you. You want to write letters? They say journaling is great therapy. I've got a couple of blank books I bought. You know, with those decorated covers that say 'Your Days,' that I never—"

I stopped her in mid-explanation. "Thanks, but no thanks. Listen up. Ever since Dr. Ditstein died, I've been trying to solve this thing."

"You?"

"Why not? Would it be better to just let them decide I'm the killer and rot in jail?"

She shook her head. "But what can you do? Other than wait for the trial, I mean. Believe you me, Otis is doing all he can," she said, a bit defensively.

"I know, I know, and I thank you for that. Anyway, I've been digging around." *Sorry again, Ma.* "And I got some dirt on the other members of my group. Plus that weird Dr. Shokum down the hall. Plus Dr. Ditstein's boyfriend. Not to mention the good doctor herself."

She was all ears. "Okay, whaddaya got?"

I regaled her with Chris's sex change, Ron's pedophilia, Maxine's hate-on for Ditstein and Beth, Zoltan's womanizing, Dr. Shokum's fakery, and Ditstein's blackmail career.

"Whew! That's some wild and crazy group. How did you manage to get all that info?"

"It wasn't easy." I smiled modestly, figuring she'd forget about it in a minute, which she did.

"So, from what you're saying, they're all fakes or nuts in one way or another," she said.

I told her about Henry Nusbitt, the biggest faker of all.

"He'd better watch his behind," she said. "With all that snooping, he's gonna get his. Just like Dr. Ditstein and that Beth." She clapped her hand over her mouth.

"S'all right," I said. But she had a point. The thought that Henry could also be in danger had never even occurred to me. Of course, I had been a bit occupied with nearly being killed and landing in jail. But right now, I had other fish to catch. And Toniann was just the person to help me land the big one.

"Here's what I want you to do…" I told her.

Chapter 46

In her next flying visit, my mother gave me news about Lucy and Sam, both of whom I'd been worrying about. Lucy was back on her corner, looking a little thinner but rested. She'd been in the hospital with pneumonia. Sam was nearly crazy with worry about me, my mother said. He'd learned about my whereabouts from the papers and was frantically calling every lawyer he knew, trying to get someone else to take my case. Paid for by him, of course.

"That sweet, sweet man," I murmured to my mother.

"If we'd only had a little more time," she said, with a sigh.

Meanwhile, a week went by in an unpleasant blur. Every day it was the guard barking at us for breakfast, a stroll around the exercise yard, lunch, exercise again, dinner. The only variations came with the weather. If it was bad, we walked around our cell block. Whenever I could, I opted out and stayed in my cell. I much preferred my own company to that of my fellow cons, who continued to torment me whenever the opportunity arose.

To break up the routine and my bad hair days, I

made an appointment with April, the prison hairdresser. April was tall and skinny with spiked blonde hair. She wasn't bad, except that she talked nonstop with a speech impediment because of a tongue ring. Her conversation was mostly about her boyfriend, who was locked up in the men's prison. Two-to-five, GTA. That's Grand Theft Auto to the uninitiated. He was innocent, of course, according to April.

"Framed by hith thonovabitch brudda-in-law. Ya know what I'd like ta do to that thonavabitch?" April said, demonstrating with her scissors.

I got the idea.

In addition to April's salon, the prison library was a breath of fresh air. Although it was scantily stocked, at least it was a place to sit quietly, other than my cell. The selections seemed to be either law books, textbooks for GED qualification, or romances, including the collected works of Danielle Steele and Barbara Taylor Bradford. I would have loved a juicy murder mystery. But it seemed that stories involving stabbings, shootings, and blunt force trauma weren't considered proper reading material by the warden. The magazines were pretty tame, too—mostly outdated copies of *Time* and *Newsweek*, the *Ladies Home Journal*, *Redbook*, *House Beautiful*. I could just imagine some of these women—like Ivy, the boobs lady, or Gerry, the body piercings queen—relating to *House Beautiful*.

Who knows, maybe in their cells at night they dreamed about decorating a house, planning the kitchen, picking out wallpaper, choosing curtains? Poor things. I was actually beginning to feel sorry for some of them. Even the really nasty ones.

I wrote a letter to John. He wrote me a lovely note, saying he missed me terribly, that he was talking to lawyers—even though I'd told him not to—and that he was going to get me the hell out of here, no matter what it took. He even enclosed an eight-by-ten-inch glossy of Harpo to cheer me up. Harpo was drooling with delight. Probably because he'd just eaten someone.

I asked the guard for some scotch tape and taped Harpo to the metal dresser. It made me smile whenever I looked at that grinning, drooling face. But it didn't help the fact that I was here. With not much hope of getting out.

They hadn't even set a trial date yet. I shuddered, thinking of a trial and a jury of my peers, whoever they may be. Maybe Otis could plead me out on temporary insanity. But then I could be locked up in an asylum, rather than prison. What a wonderful choice.

Chapter 47

That afternoon, Henry Nusbitt showed up in the visitor's room. Good old Toniann had come through again.

Henry scratched his ear and leered at me insanely.

"Cut the act," I said. "I know."

He shrugged. "Okay. Whazzup, dude?" Now he sounded like an overage teenager, though he'd never see thirty again. Maybe he was so used to affecting another persona that he had a compulsion to keep doing it. Or maybe that was the real Henry, who knew? "So, your friend tells me you've been sniffing around the members of the group. Well, what've you got?"

I hated the sly tone of his voice. Hated the way he was practically salivating about the salacious possibilities for the filthy fish-wrapper he worked for. Hated the fact that he'd been lying to us and spying on us. Hated everything about him, in fact. But what could I do? I needed his help. I gave him what I had.

He looked impressed at my sleuthing, but only for a minute. Unlike me, Henry wasn't a bit shocked about Ditstein being a blackmailer. As a student of human nature—the worst aspects, I'd say, considering the rag he shilled for—nothing surprised him. Not to be outdone in the snoop department, he said, "I was…uh…hanging around—"

Translation: spying.

"—Dr. Ditstein's that day, and I just happened to see Maxine leaving the building."

"She always works late on Thursdays," I said slowly. "She never has an appointment that day."

"Right! But Beth does." He was looking very pleased with himself.

"So maybe Maxine killed Dr. Ditstein—" I said.

"And Beth saw her," he finished.

"And Maxine must have killed Beth, too," I said.

Even though Maxine was a difficult person, to put it mildly, I couldn't quite see her as a double murderer. I wiped that thought from my mind. What did a double killer look like, anyway? After all, the cops had no trouble picturing *me* as a two-time killer. As for Maxine, we had no proof. Just Henry's and my educated guesses. So I still had to put my plan into motion.

I could see the guard getting ready to break up our tete-a-tete, so I spoke quietly and rapidly across the table. Given that Henry was hot to trot after a new story—now that our group of poor, trusting neurotics was no longer available to spy on—he liked my plan. Catching a murderer would be his next thrill.

Henry nodded a few times. "Cool!"

He actually looked excited about the whole thing. A little too excited, I thought.

"Let's be careful out there, okay?" I said.

He waved my fears away. "Hey, I'm a black belt, and I can really kick ass. Not to worry."

"Watch out for sidewalk sideswipes," I said, as the guard pointed to the clock.

I was worried plenty. Henry was headed straight for the murderer's lair, armed with only a few swift kicks. I fervently hoped that, when the time came, his right foot knew what his left foot was doing.

Chapter 48

My plan called for Henry to phone every suspect, saying that I could blackmail them with information that could prove they were murderers. And that they should each come to see me in prison to find out what I knew. I told Henry I had someone undercover who'd keep an eye on him, because they were bound to think that he had the goods on them, too, even though he insisted he didn't need looking after. My mother, being invisible, certainly qualified.

As soon as I thought about her, she appeared.

"Sometimes it works that way. When the signals are signaling, I guess," she said.

Fortunately, I was back in my cell after Henry left, since she'd landed fairly noisily.

"You called, sweetheart?" Wearing the beatific smile of a mother who was needed by her only child, she sat down on my cot with a groan.

I told her why I wanted her to watch over Henry. "To be a kind of hovering presence—an angel on his shoulder, so to speak. Can you do that?"

"But of course, sweetheart," she said, with a grin. "I

didn't get these powers for nothing. Anything else, while I'm at it?"

"Yeah. Report back to me about his activities. Number one, I'm worried about him. Number two, I don't trust him." *Then again*, I said to myself, *who else is there to trust?*

"Me, of course," my mother answered. "And your friend Toniann. Such a nice young woman and so attractive. So tell me, why isn't she married already?"

"Ma."

"Okay, okay," she said. "I know when to keep my mouth shut. I'm off." She kissed me goodbye and disappeared into the ceiling.

The queen of self-awareness my mother was not.

Chapter 49

Hopefully, I'd be able to smoke out the killer by pretending to blackmail all of them. I tried not to think too much about using myself as bait.

Then I thought about the fact that I was doing this for myself. Was I really doing this, taking charge of things, my life?

Wow. Scary thought.

I gave Henry a day to contact everyone with the bad news. Then I sat back like the proverbial spider, waiting for my flies.

The first of my visitors, Chris, arrived in the visitors' room, wearing a very sad expression. Almost as if I'd betrayed her.

"Hi, Marabella," she said in her whispery voice, wiping her eyes. "I'm doing a little better now." Sniff. "I hope you are, too."

Oh, yes. And how. "I've been lucky enough to discover an…item…that belonged to Dr. Ditstein. That leads me to suspect that you murdered her. And Beth."

A gasp. "What item?"

"A copy of a birth certificate belonging to Christopher Ragamoni." I told her that I knew all about her previous gender.

She moaned and sniffled into a hanky. "What are you going to do?"

"Exactly what Dr. Ditstein did, Chris," I said. "I plan to follow in our dear doctor's footsteps, since she set such a shining example."

Silence again. "You have no right, no right, to that information." The voice had a definite edge to it now.

"Possession is nine-tenths of the law," I said. "Now, let's get down to business, shall we?"

"What do you want?"

"Hmm…about a thousand dollars a month will do…for now," I said.

"A thousand dollars!" she shrieked. "Ditstein only got seven hundred and fifty dollars."

"Inflation, dear."

"I can't afford a thousand dollars a month," she whined.

"Well—" I paused, acting as if I were thinking it over. "I tell you what. Since you've always been so nice to me, I'll let you off with eight hundred and fifty dollars. For now."

A sigh. "All right, I guess. What choice do I have?"

"Absolutely none," I said. We made arrangements for her to deposit the money into my savings account.

After she left, I realized that there was something off about her tears. The handkerchief she'd used looked totally dry.

Very interesting.

When Zoltan, the gigolo, arrived, I told him I knew that Dr. Ditstein had stopped supporting him because he was cheating on her. And that I knew about his problems with the immigration authorities regarding his status of an illegal alien. He practically foamed at the mouth about

American fascists, secret police plots. And that he and his family had had a lot of experience in "taking care of" such people in the old country so that they never bothered his family again. I wondered if his family had already "taken care of" Ditstein and Beth.

As for Maxine, the embezzling comptroller, after using language that I certainly wouldn't lower myself to repeat, she finally agreed to my terms. Being that she had no choice. But she told me what she'd like to do to my body parts. Sweet Maxine had a killer temper, all right. Not to mention what Henry told me about seeing her in Ditstein's building the day of the murder.

And Ron-the-pedophile made some very uncomplimentary remarks about my femininity. He said that "real women" didn't sneak and slime their way into other people's private business. Unlike the "real men" who molested their teenage sisters. And that people who did that kind of "dirty work" ended up getting what was coming to them.

I'd decided to skip dealing with Donna. Since she hadn't given in to Ditstein's blackmail—and more importantly, since she was the source of my less-than-living wage, I thought blackmail wouldn't be a good idea.

So far we had three people who were openly threatening me and one who was hiding her feelings. I had no more clue as to who the killer was than before. Meanwhile, my mother informed me that Henry was getting threatening phone calls. Though she promised to keep an eye on him, I worried about how much protection a seventy-year-old woman with congestive heart failure could provide—even with her special powers.

"Don't you worry, sweetheart. Just trust in Mother," she said in her next fly-by.

The next day, Shokum-the-Voice arrived, dressed entirely in black. The better to hide from the world in?

Mourning the loss of a new long-term phone client?

He gave me an oily smile. When I told him what I'd found out about his non-existent credentials, the smile evaporated.

I told him my price for keeping my information and suspicions quiet.

He sat back in the chair and laughed. "My dear, you are sadly mistaken," he said, shaking his head. "I'm not the fake. Your Dr. Ditstein was the nut case and the fake. She was utterly delusional. Pretending to be a therapist gave her a sick sense of power."

I was stunned. *But wait, why should I believe him?*

"You should believe me, my dear, because why should you believe someone who used her therapy sessions to conduct blackmail?"

Was he a mind reader like my mother? But he had a point. Why should I believe that Ditstein was for real, considering the scumbag she'd turned out to be? Not only that, I had to admit being just a little bit pissed that she thought my private life was too boring for blackmail.

Which would I rather believe? That she was a rotten vicious blackmailer who didn't deserve the title of therapist? Or that she was a fake, a criminally insane person, who didn't deserve the title of therapist?

But Shokum was acting a little too nonchalant, if you asked me. What did I expect? Would I be less suspicious if he were begging for my mercy? So why not believe him?

"I understand your eagerness to find out who did this terrible thing," he said smoothly. "Maybe we can work together. After all, it must be hard for you to get information while you're here. Why not tell me what you know, and I'll try and follow up? That way, we might be able to figure it all out."

Why did I have the feeling that he was trying to

pump me to see how close I was? Maybe he wanted to know what I knew because he was the killer.

What I was going to do if the killer tried to kill me again at some point, I hadn't figured out yet. After all, he or she had only tried and failed once. So far.

Well, at least our meetings were taking place in a place that couldn't be more public. Though that wouldn't rule out someone following me, if and when I ever got out of here.

Chapter 50

My mother arrived to give me the first install-ment of her report as I was re-reading John's comforting note. I whisked it away before she could read the whole thing.

"Hmmm, sounds serious," she said, looking over my shoulder.

"Reading other people's mail is not nice. Especially if it's your daughter's." I gave her a dirty look. "It's bad enough the guards open it first."

Instead of looking guilty, she actually seemed pleased with herself. "You should appreciate my interest in your welfare. Anyway, your mail is the least of our problems."

"Now what?"

"It's that Henry. I think maybe he really is crazy, even though he writes for a newspaper."

"What did he do?"

She sank down on the cot. "Well, for starters, when he called these people, he used a very scary voice. He threatened them on the phone, saying: 'I know what you did. You can run, but you can't hide.' I think maybe he's been watching too much TV."

"Go on."

"Then he told them that you and he figured out who the killer is. And that you were going to tell the police."

I groaned. Henry was trying to play cowboy. Probably thought it would make a better story. Unfortunately, it could also end up being a posthumous one. There was nothing that could be done. I just prayed that his karate kick was as good as he said.

An uneasy feeling swept over me. Henry's luck couldn't hold out forever. Even with my mother hovering over him, he could still be in serious danger.

Chapter 51

To take my mind off Henry and not, incidentally, to be kind to my hair, I went to April's salon again. She was in fine form. Seemed that her boyfriend was up for parole.

"I can't hardly wait," she said, after clucking over the state of my hair. "Even though he'th got hith faulths, he'th got a thertain thomethin', ya know what I mean?"

It was hard not to figure it out, since she was pointing to her crotch.

She attacked my frizzies with a vengeance. "Ya got a guy waitin' for you on the outthide?"

I closed my eyes and conjured up John. "Mmm," I said.

"Be careful," she warned. "Juth make thure no other broad trieth ta warm up ya bed while you're on the inthide. No offenthe."

"None taken," I said. I certainly didn't want some other broad jumping John's bones in the meantime.

"It'th different with a guy," she said. "My Leo knowth I won't give no other guy da time a day. And if I ever did, he'd—" She made a slashing motion across her neck with her scissors, which made me a bit nervous.

"What does Leo do on the outside?" I said, hoping to calm her down. When he's not stealing cars, that was.

"He'th a en-tree-pree-newer," she said, drawing herself up proudly. "He'th got some fan-tathic dealth goin'. He sayth when he geths out, we're gonna be rich. We're gonna move ta Vegath."

"That's great," I said, hoping whatever his deals were, they didn't involve other people's vehicles.

As usual, she finished up with a ton of hair spray. My hair felt like a hardhat helmet. But I had to admit, it was an improvement over the frizzies.

"Thanks, April," I said. "I hope things go well at Leo's parole hearing."

She gave me a hug. "Youthe a helluva lot nither than mosth of da broadths I get in here. An' youthe got clath, too. What're ya in for, anywayth? Couldn't be no big deal."

I hated to break it to her. But I didn't want to be rude. She was eagerly waiting for my answer.

I sighed. "Double murder."

Chapter 52

Back in the cozy comfort of my cell, I started thinking about Henry again. It occurred to me that one reason he could be so eager to be my partner-in-crime-solving was that it would be a great cover-up if he were the killer.

What if he really was an ex-mental patient? Just because he worked on that poor excuse for a newspaper didn't mean he couldn't have been institutionalized in the past. The newspaper wouldn't have to know. He could have faked his credentials to account for any time lapse.

By pretending to be my partner, he could weasel information out of me, find out how much I really knew. With the ultimate aim of doing me in, of course. Even if he wasn't the murderer, his playing cowboy was pissing me off. And scaring me, to boot.

The more I thought about Henry, the more I realized I had to do something. I tapped on my cell door to get the attention of the guard. A few minutes later, the door opened.

"Yeah?"

What did I expect, "May I help you?" I gave Ms.

Surly an ingratiating smile and lied. "I need to speak with my lawyer."

She led me out to the phones. "Five minutes, that's it, unnerstand?"

I nodded. I quickly dialed Toniann's work number, waiting for her to accept the collect call. Thank the gods, she answered.

"Marabella? What's wrong?" she asked.

"Nothing. Everything. I need your help. A life may be in danger."

She shrieked.

"Calm down. It's Henry Nusbitt. Tell him to get his behind over here, 'toot sweet,' as Donna would say."

Toniann's voice got a tad less shrill. "And speaking of Donna, I've got some news about her."

I hadn't given Donna a thought in weeks. One of the few nice things about being here.

"The temp she hired to do your job has been screwing up real bad."

"How bad?"

"Bad enough so the administration has been threatening to fire Donna," Toniann said. "She even called me at the office and begged me to do some free-lance writing. I told her, in no uncertain terms, no way in hell would I do anything for Chelsea College ever again."

Of course, they all thought that Donna had been the one doing the writing, since she always claimed credit for everyone else's work.

"I guess the good news is that if—when—you get out of there, she'll be happy to have you back again."

Whoopie. Now that was something to live for.

Chapter 53

I was ready to kill Henry, whether or not he was a crazed killer. If he was the killer, it wouldn't make any difference. If he wasn't, it might knock some sense into him. At any rate, it couldn't hurt. And it might even make me feel a little better.

He turned up in a grimy tee shirt and worn jeans, wearing a cocky grin that I wanted to wipe off his freckled face.

"You idiot," I hissed across the table. "What's going on in that so-called mind of yours, anyway?"

He had the nerve to try and look innocent. "What's the problem?"

"Calling people up and doing a scary number on them, like on a second-rate TV show, is the problem," I snarled.

He actually laughed. I noticed he had a chipped front tooth.

"Sure shook the shit out of them, didn't it?" he said.

"Keep it up, and it'll get you a lot worse than a broken tooth."

He pointed to the tooth in question. "Oh, that happened during karate practice. I banged into a wall. Guess I got carried away."

I groaned. "And you're the one who was going to kick his way out of a jam? The person who can't even see a wall coming?"

"Hey, that's nothing. You should have seen the wall."

"A wise-ass partner I can live without," I spat.

His voice was cold. "You don't exactly have much choice in here, do you?"

Unfortunately, he was right. "But how do I know you're really what you say you are?"

"What do you want, my blood type and a DNA test?"

"I really don't know much about you—nothing, as a matter of fact, "I said. "Except that you had the nerve to pretend you were a mental patient so you could spy on our group for that wretched fish-wrapper you work for."

"We have the biggest circulation in the world," he said, with an air of defiance.

"Stop bragging about the stupidity of the general public. So, you appeal to the lowest common denominator, so what? That makes you legitimate? Anyway, you're avoiding the question."

"Which one?" he drawled. "I can't keep track."

What a piece of work. "Number one, I don't know anything about you. So talk."

"Born in Brooklyn, parents journalists, graduate of NYU, one girlfriend—mine, that is—apartment in the Village, brilliant writer, charming, witty, literate..." he rattled on.

I could see the guard pointing to the clock.

"So you're just going to have to trust me." He folded his arms across his chest. "I'm your only hope."

"Lucky me," I muttered. "But you can't keep threatening people. That's not going to help us, and it could get you seriously dead."

"Got any better suggestions?" He was beginning to sound like that young snot-nosed cousin of mine who'd come to a bad end.

"Yes. Investigate, *si*, intimidate, *no*. Be circumspect. Be discreet. And be careful, for godsakes, okay?"

"Yes, Mother." He flashed me another of those wise-ass grins. For some strange reason, I was beginning to find it oddly appealing.

"And get your damned tooth fixed."

He grinned again, flashing his chipped tooth.

Chapter 54

I was sure the prison food was going to kill me way before anything else did in here. I didn't know how much more my delicate palate, not to mention stomach, could take of the crap. The only good thing was that the food was so terrible, I was actually losing weight.

Luckily, Mei Lee Yung had sent a note saying she was baking a special batch of brownies for me. I was salivating mightily in anticipation.

My letch for brownies went way back. It was one of the few things my mother had never attempted to make and foist on my tender digestive system. So their taste wasn't ruined for me at a young age. They remained pure, delicious—and of course, terribly fattening. And therefore sinful. I'd even heard they had a certain aphrodisiac quality. If I ever got out of here, I'd have to test that theory on John. Especially since, wonder of wonders, he actually seemed to appreciate my generous hips.

While I was gently musing on John's…everything… the guard opened my cell door and said there was a package waiting for me.

It had already been opened, of course, according to

prison rules. Since it evidently contained no sharp instruments, it passed muster.

When I brought it back to my cell, the guard stood there, her eyes glued to the box. One sniff told me why. Joy of joys, Mei Lee's brownies had arrived. But the exquisite pleasure of eating them would have to be postponed until after I got rid of the guard. I wasn't in any mood to share. I shoved the box into my locker and lay down on the cot.

"Time for a nice nap," I said, pretending to yawn.

She finally got the point. "Humph," she said, shaking her head. "Some people just don't know who their friends are."

I pretended to snore. Glaring at me, she left, slamming the door.

I jumped off the cot and retrieved the brownies. They didn't look like Mei Lee's usual batch. Then I remembered she'd said they were special. Even better.

Closing my eyes to shut out the world and be alone with the experience, I selected my first one and inhaling deeply, slowly raised it to my lips.

It never reached them. Before I could sink my teeth into the delicious chocolate, it was snatched out of my hand. My eyes snapped open. My mother was biting into my brownie.

Of all the gall. I was furious. "Did you have to eat mine? You couldn't take your own? There's plenty for both of us," I snarled, reaching into the box for another. Few things made me lose control like someone preempting my brownies.

She smacked the brownie out of my hand again, spitting out the remains of the one she'd been eating.

Was she losing her marbles? "What are you doing?"

"Saving you from an untimely death, sweetheart."

I knew she was jealous of women who were good

cooks, but this was just too much. I'd have to be tactful. Her sensitivities seemed to be more easily bruised these days.

"Ma," I began, "Mei Lee Yung was trying to cheer me up, that's all. She makes very nice brownies." An understatement if there ever was one.

I stared at her. Her face had a greenish pallor. Jealousy alone shouldn't have made her look that bad.

"What's wrong, Ma?"

She sank down on the cot, breathing heavily and clutching her chest, her face screwed up in pain. "What makes you think these were Mei Lee's brownies? Did you look for a name and a return address?"

"Oh my God!" I'd been in such a hurry, first to get them away from the guard and then to dive in, that I hadn't even bothered to look. I'd just assumed of course, since Mei Lee had sent the note, that they were hers.

And now my mother was—

I knelt down beside the cot and threw my arms around her. "Ma!" God, she was so pale, I could almost see right through her.

She smiled weakly. "I'll be okay, sweetheart. Poison doesn't affect us that way."

"What *does* it do?" What was going to happen to her? Was she going to disintegrate before my eyes?

She sat up and let out a loud belch. "Just really bad heartburn, that's all."

Chapter 55

My mother and I decided that I would pretend to be the one who had eaten the brownies. That way, hopefully, they'd be taken to a police lab and analyzed. Unfortunately for me, I didn't realize that I'd be taken to the prison infirmary and analyzed, too. There were many things I'd prefer to do rather than have my stomach pumped. Root canal, for instance.

The good news was that, according to the prison doctor, I was either extraordinarily lucky or had an intestinal system that could take anything. Obviously, he hadn't sampled my mother's cooking. At any rate, I was pronounced free of the heavy dose of pure cyanide that had been added to the brownies to speed me on my way out of this life.

But the ordeal of the stomach pumping had left me pretty wiped out. After I recovered in the infirmary, I had my first visitor. Henry gave me his latest report. When he'd heard what had happened, his face turned white. For a yellow journalist, maybe he wasn't such a sleaze.

"This is getting serious, Marabella," he said.

"And it wasn't before? Count the bodies, Henry—one, two."

"And you almost made three." He actually sounded like he cared. He ran his fingers through his hair, which looked as if it hadn't been combed for days. Other than that, he didn't look much worse than usual. I noticed he'd even had his tooth capped.

"So, what's been happening on the investigative front, Henry?"

"The suspects have all been anteing up. Except Maxine. So what do we do to convince her? Wait a minute." He frowned.

"What?"

"Well, now that this..." he said, motioning toward me. "...happened to you, it jogged my memory about something. While I've been investigating—" He grinned. "—okay, following our suspects—I trailed Maxine to a pastry shop."

I snorted, thinking of Maxine's heft. "Big deal. That's probably her idea of recreation."

He folded his arms across his chest and smirked. I wanted to smack him. "To buy an extra-deluxe assortment of brownies?"

"How do you know that?" I grilled him.

"Well..." He smirked again.

"Cut it out, Henry," I snapped. "This isn't a joke, remember?"

"Sorry. I'm pretty good, very good, actually, at trailing people without being seen. The newspaper business, you know." He had the chutzpah to look proud of his work. "So I just blended in with the crowd outside the shop. There was a huge line at this place, must have good stuff. Anyway, I listened to her order and then split. She never even saw me."

"Are you sure?" This was making me very nervous. What if Maxine decided to kill him, too?

He grinned again. "Sure. Would I lie to you?"

"I sincerely hope not," I said slowly.

Chapter 56

Come to think of it, Maxine-as-killer made a certain amount of sense. She was one angry woman. Angry at her gorgeous slim, shrink sister; angry at Ditstein as a slim, shrink substitute; angry at Beth for her looks, figure, and career; angry at the world, as a matter of fact. But most of all, angry at herself.

I could even forgive Maxine, feel sorry for her. Wasn't that the ploy behind any killer's gain for sympathy? Poor self-image, unresolved childhood traumas, yadda, yadda, yadda.

But any fleeting thoughts of sympathy for her unhappy state vanished when I thought about her allegedly repeated attempts to kill *me*. Especially the poisoned brownies, which I took particular umbrage to as a betrayal from a fellow chocolate-lover. I wondered if brownies would ever taste good to me again. Even Mei Lee's. I sighed.

While I was pondering how to get the police to listen to me about Maxine, a guard popped her head in to tell me a visitor was waiting for me in the lawyer/client room. *Must be Otis Pinckney*, I thought. *Big help he's been. Well, after I tell him about Maxine, maybe he'll get off his behind and do something.* After all, a murdered client wouldn't be able to pay him his legal fees.

But when the guard took me inside the tiny room, I found myself staring at Dr. Shokum seated at the table.

I sat down across from him. "How did you get in here?"

He smiled. "I used an old pass I had from seeing a patient who'd been here."

"That doesn't explain how you got them to let you see me."

"Oh, I just told them I was your new therapist. After all," he purred, "hadn't we already discussed such an arrangement? Wasn't that the reason that you did me the honor—" The purr became a sneer."—of paying me a visit in the first place?"

Uh, oh, I thought. *This is not turning out to be a friendly visit, after all. He sounds really pissed. He must have figured out that besides my new role as a blackmailer, I've been investigating the murders. But wait. Maybe he can help Henry collar Maxine. After all, whether or not he really is an imposter, as far as the police know, he's a respected psychotherapist. If they don't believe me, maybe they'll believe him.*

Or maybe he was the killer. Why not him? First of all, he was nuts. Nuts enough to be locked up in the funny farm. Nuts enough to pretend to be a therapist. And certainly not happy about being blackmailed by a real therapist?

I remembered that Shokum knew about my love affair with brownies. I'd been chomping on one the day my mother and I paid him a visit.

And he knew where I worked, too. So it would have been no big deal for him to catch up with me on the way to the campus and push me into traffic. And present me with a box of poisoned goodies. Now that I was looking him in the eye, what was looking back at me was very scary. *Think, Marabella. Think. Very. Fast.*

Okay. I'd have to make nice until I could get away from him and tell Rivera about my suspicions. And I had to stop my leg from shaking. Or at least, shake quietly. *Deep breaths, Marabella.* I leaned forward in my chair. Unfortunately, my voice came out in a squeak. "You're right, Dr. Shokum. I really apologize for not being honest with you. I've been trying to find out who killed Dr. Ditstein and Beth Hronska. And—"

"And you have discovered who it was," he interrupted, in a cold voice, leaning across the table. He stared at me, his eyes glittering.

I shivered. If looks could kill. His mouth was twisted into a snarl. Now he looked really crazy. Well, he was crazy, right? And a killer. A crazy killer. Criminally insane. *Oh, God.* I jumped up from my chair and started for the door.

Shokum removed something from his jacket pocket that glinted in the sunlight from the window. It was a syringe.

Oh, God, I thought again. *He's really going to kill me. Right now.*

He bounded across the floor and grabbed for my arm.

Chapter 57

I tried to jerk away, but he was too strong. I kicked at his leg, but he just laughed. "It's no use, my dear," he said, aiming the syringe.

Just as he was about to jab me, my mother knocked the syringe out of his hand.

"Thanks, Ma," I mouthed. Then I yelled, "Help!"

The door flew open, and Detective Rivera and another cop came barreling in. They slapped cuffs on Shokum, who was flailing away and yelling obscenities.

My breath was coming in gasps. My first thought was that my mother wouldn't want me to hear such language. *Priorities, Marabella.* Then I wondered why I was being rescued by Rivera, whom I thought was out to hang me.

Turned out, Rivera had been clued into the poisoned-brownie affair by the prison. Which made him think that someone else might have committed the murders. He'd put an officer on to each member of the group, Ditstein's boyfriend, and Shokum.

"We tailed Shokum to a nearby pharmacy where he purchased a syringe, saying he was diabetic," Rivera said.

"He also bought a bottle of heavy tranquilizers with a phony prescription that said he was a psychiatrist."

"Just being a phony psychotherapist wasn't good enough anymore," I whispered, still shaken.

Rivera frowned. "Still with the bad jokes, right? As I was saying, then we put a couple of policewomen on duty here, pretending to be guards in your section. Shokum came in, handing in a pass and flashing credentials. He said he was your new psychotherapist and was very concerned because you'd called him and said you were very depressed. And he was worried about what you might do to yourself."

"So he decided to do it for me," I said slowly, trying to take it all in.

He nodded. "We're taking the syringe to the lab. It's probably got enough tranquilizers in it to kill a horse."

The word horse had the effect of conjuring up lovely, sexy thoughts of John. Then I realized I'd better listen to the rest of what Rivera had to say.

"I'm betting that it was timed so that you'd start by being a little groggy, and by a half-hour or so, stop breathing. I figure he was going to shove an empty bottle of pills into your hand so that people would think it was an OD because you were depressed. God knows where you might have gotten the drugs. Maybe stolen them from the infirmary, I guess." He shook his head.

"Diabolical."

"As soon as we get the paperwork cleared up, you're free to go. And if I'm lucky, that's the last I'll see of you," he muttered, yawning.

"Likewise, I'm sure," I said, with a grin. "Hey, get yourself some sleep."

He shot me a look. Then he cleared his throat. "I have a question: how did you manage to knock that syringe out of Shokum's hand? You must have superfast reflexes."

I just smiled. And felt pretty damn proud of my mother. And myself, too, after everything I'd been through. With no help from my former go-to person.

Chapter 58

Believe it or not, while I was waiting for the paperwork to be processed, the guard told me I had another visitor.

Henry Nusbitt was pacing up and down in the visitors' room, tearing at his hair. When he saw me, his face got so pale, his freckles popped out like chocolate M&Ms.

"I thought you were—I'm so glad you're not—You look—" He was stammering, almost like the old crazy Henry.

"Sorry if I seem a little under the weather, Henry, but I just narrowly escaped an early demise."

He groaned. "It's all my fault."

"What?"

"Shokum called me, asking about your health. I should have realized he thought you were dead from the poisoned brownies. I meant to get here earlier today, but I got hung up on a story." He was practically blubbering.

That'll teach me to trust a reporter. After gnashing my teeth. I took a couple of deep breaths. *Inhale. Exhale.* Thoughts of Ditstein went through my head. I sighed. I guess she had a few good qualities, after all. In a few minutes, I was calmer.

"It's okay, Henry," I said, with a smile. "I'm alive and well and getting out of here."

He smiled back. Then he fished a notebook and pen from his pocket. "Can you give me an exclusive on all the details?"

Chapter 59

My mother was waiting for me on the outside with a huge grin on her face.

"After they grabbed Dr. Shokum, he started ranting and raving." She clucked her tongue. "And to think he was a professional man, too. A psychologist."

"He wasn't. He was an imposter, remember?"

"Even so," she said. "Anyway, he admitted he killed Dr. Ditstein. Another one who pretended to be such a nice, professional person."

I sighed. "Ma."

"And that, he killed that actress, that Beth, too. She saw him leave Dr. Ditstein's apartment right after he committed the first murder."

"And she made the mistake of trying to blackmail him," I said slowly.

"How did you know, sweetheart?" my mother marveled. "You're absolutely right." She made a disgusted face. "Of course, if she had just behaved herself in the first place."

"You're right, Ma," I said. "She never should have threatened a murderer."

"Sweetheart, I meant that she never should have made those perverted movies. Then she wouldn't have gotten herself into such trouble, being blackmailed and then ending up getting murdered. And for what? Making those movies that her mother, God forbid, would be so ashamed to see?"

I thanked the gods that this terrible ordeal hadn't hurt my mother's sense of priorities. More important, she wasn't hurt. In fact, she seemed to be thriving, even though her body was so thin, I could practically see through her. Guess playing Miss Marple gave her a reason for coming back.

"No, sweetheart," my mother said. "What was important is that I was able to help you. That's why—" She looked up, smiled, and kissed me. "—I'll keep in touch. Ten-four."

And she took off.

Believe it or not, I was going to miss her.

About the Author

Sandra Gardner is a former contributor and columnist for The New York Times. She is the author of four non-fiction books: *Six Who Dared* (Simon & Schuster), *Street Gangs* (Franklin Watts), *Teenage Suicide* (Simon & Schuster), and *Street Gangs in America* (Franklin Watts). Gardner's first three books in her mother-and-me mystery series are scheduled to be published by Black Opal Books.

Street Gangs in America received a book award from the National Association of Press Women. *Dead Shrinks Don't Talk*, previously titled *Mother, Murder and Me*, her first mystery novel, was the winner of Swyers Publishing's 2011 First New Author (fiction) Contest. Her novella, *Halley and Me*, won the 2012 Grassic Short Novel Prize from Evening Street Press.